"Stop looking at me like that." Charli chopped yet another carrot. "Talk to me. About anything."

"Okay. How about what I heard from the Georgia Bureau of Investigation today about Secret Santa?" Neil asked.

The knife in Charli's hand came down at an awkward angle, and Neil could see she'd almost cut herself. He sprang up to check on her, but she waved him off.

"Sorry! I'm all thumbs tonight," she joked.

"More cutting like that, and you won't have thumbs at all," he said. But his comeback was reflexive. What he'd said had surprised her. That was clear.

"So…" Three more whacks and the carrot was history. "What did they tell you? Chief Hawkins didn't seem to think it would be a high-priority case."

How was it he could still want to kiss her when he was convinced she knew more than she was telling him? Or telling the police?

Dear Reader,

As a kid, I never could understand my mom's deep loathing of any Christmas lights that weren't "white and twinkling." After all, to my six-year-old eyes, our neighbor's outlandish display of Christmas décor, complete with a Santa, a sleigh and reindeer on his roof, was perfect. My mother? Bless her heart, she'd grind her teeth when she drove by.

Eventually, my mom succeeded in converting me to the "white and twinkling" school of Christmas décor. When I married, though, my husband turned out to be a lot like Neil in Secret Santa—Christmas is his time to shine! Every year it's a loving fuss over whether we keep my white lights or break out a new set of "real" (his words) Christmas lights. Still, as Neil and Charli discover, the true meaning of Christmas isn't decorations, but the spirit of giving.

I loved writing Secret Santa… I loved discovering Neil's wonderful, playful personality and seeing Charli learn to enjoy Christmas, despite some formidable obstacles. As you read their story, I hope you root for Neil and Charli as much as I did.

I'd love to hear from you. If you're on Twitter, you can follow me at @cynthiarreese, and why not check out all the Harlequin Heartwarming authors as we blog? You can find us at www.heartwarmingauthors.blogspot.com.

Merry Christmas!

Cynthia

HARLEQUIN HEARTWARMING

Cynthia Reese

Secret Santa

Recycling programs
for this product may
not exist in your area.

ISBN-13: 978-0-373-36650-7

SECRET SANTA

Copyright © 2013 by Cynthia R. Reese

All rights reserved. Except for use in any review, the reproduction or
utilization of this work in whole or in part in any form by any electronic,
mechanical or other means, now known or hereafter invented, including
xerography, photocopying and recording, or in any information storage
or retrieval system, is forbidden without the written permission of the
publisher, Harlequin Enterprises Limited, 225 Duncan Mill Road,
Don Mills, Ontario, Canada M3B 3K9.

This is a work of fiction. Names, characters, places and incidents are
either the product of the author's imagination or are used fictitiously,
and any resemblance to actual persons, living or dead, business
establishments, events or locales is entirely coincidental.

This edition published by arrangement with Harlequin Books S.A.

For questions and comments about the quality of this book,
please contact us at CustomerService@Harlequin.com.

® and TM are trademarks of Harlequin Enterprises Limited or its
corporate affiliates. Trademarks indicated with ® are registered in the
United States Patent and Trademark Office, the Canadian Trade Marks
Office and in other countries.

Printed in U.S.A.

CYNTHIA REESE

Cynthia Reese lives with her husband and their daughter in south Georgia, along with their two dogs, three cats and however many strays show up for morning muster. She has been scribbling since she was knee-high to a grasshopper and reading even before that. A former journalist, teacher and college English instructor, she also enjoys cooking, traveling and photography when she gets the chance.

Books by Cynthia Reese

HARLEQUIN HEARTWARMING

SEEDS OF TRUST
A PLACE TO CALL HOME

HARLEQUIN SUPERROMANCE

1415–THE BABY WAIT
1533–FOR THE SAKE OF THE CHILDREN

In memory of William,
one of my biggest cheerleaders ever.
April is surely the cruelest month.

Acknowledgments

This book was a miracle in the making, impossible without my awesome editors Victoria Curran and Laura Barth—thank you, Laura, for all your cheering!

Many doctors helped me with technical and personal insight into the life of a young doctor, including Dr. Lawton Davis, Dr. Misty Poole, Dr. Gary Branch and Dr. Jean Sumner. More technical advice came from Terrance Shulman of The Shulman Center for Compulsive Theft, Spending & Hoarding, as well as Investigator Ron Bivens, who is not at all like the police chief in this story! All errors are mine, and I apologize profusely for any that may be there.

A huge thanks goes to my critique partner Tawna Fenske, to my sister Donna, and to my Twitter cheer squad—Jessica Lemmon, Linda Grimes, Jeannie Moon, Jamie DeBree, Susan Adrian, Deb Salonen, and Patty Blount—as well as to my wonderful Heartwarming blog sisters.

Most of all, big hugs to my wonderful, long-suffering husband and The Kiddo. I couldn't have done it without you!

CHAPTER ONE

"You're not asleep, are you?"

Dr. Charli Prescott snapped to attention from the doorjamb she'd been propped against. "'Course not," she muttered to her amused-looking nurse, Lainey Edge. "Why on earth would I want to sleep? I've had the luxurious amount of two hours of sleep for three straight nights. If those new E.R. guys don't get in here soon, though, I will be sleeping standing up."

Lainey laughed and slapped a stack of charts in Charli's hand. "Good to know, because there's a broken arm from a ladder fall in Bay 2, and you've still got to sign off on discharge for Food Poisoning in Bay 1. Oh, and your dad says Knife Guy in the trauma room can go home."

Charli had just caught the name of Broken Arm—Neil Bailey—on his chart when Lainey's last words caught her. "Hey!" she hollered after the departing Lainey. "Knife Guy—" She stopped herself from breaking about a thousand privacy violations and closed the gap between her and Lainey. "I wanted Knife Guy—I mean, Mr. Anderson—admitted," she told her. "I signed the admission paperwork. At least overnight. He could have sepsis."

"Yeah, but your dad—"

"Is an old coot who likes to fly by the seat of his pants, and I don't care if he is my new boss and the hospital's chief of staff. Both of us are sleep deprived because *somebody* ran off all the E.R. docs and thought we could handle the E.R. until the staffing service cried uncle. We may miss something, and a twenty-three-hour admit is a good way to be sure we haven't."

Lainey looked about as excited at the prospect of getting in the middle of the brewing battle between Charli and Dr. Chuck Prescott as she would about going on a fast. "Look, he's my boss—and yours, too. So before we put Knife Guy on the floor, can you talk to your dad?"

From behind them, the sounds of Food Poisoning's retching came through the striped curtains dividing the hospital bays. Broken Arm, next door, called out, "Hey, I think my neighbor might need some help here! If you're not going to get around to seeing me, could you help him? Please?"

Charli and Lainey exchanged a long weary

glance. "I'll call custodial," Lainey said. "You sure Food Poisoning's able to go home?"

"Yeah, not dehydrated yet—just be sure he gets some Phenergan before he leaves. He says he wants to go—that he can throw up at home as well as here. Got some sort of phobia about throwing up in public. I guess he should have thought of that when he ate week-old potato salad." Charli shook her head to clear the cobwebs and skimmed Broken Arm's chart. She hadn't felt this tired since her first few weeks of med school.

"Okay, then, Food Poisoning's chart's on the bottom."

Charli riffled through the charts and scrawled her signature in the requisite places. "Make sure he knows he can come back," she told Lainey. She headed toward Broken Arm—Neil Bailey.

"Oh, you might want to do something with your hair," Lainey told her in that understated tone a woman used that meant there was either broccoli in your teeth or toilet tissue hanging out of your skirt.

Charli reached up and assessed the damage. Half the ponytail she'd snatched her hair into that morning—just that morning? It felt like a million years ago—was tumbling out of its rubber band. She used the glass of the trauma bay door as a mirror, and yanked the mess into some semblance of order. Ordinarily her straight hair was tidy and presentable, but now it looked as if she'd been dragged through a bush backward. Giving up, she turned from the door, where she could still hear Knife Guy singing a drunken version of "Walking After Midnight" by Patsy Cline, and didn't bother to suppress her yawn.

Snatching back the striped curtain, Charli pasted a smile on her face. "Well, Mr. Bailey, I'm sorry for the wait, but as you can see, we've been a bit busy this evening. I understand you fell off a ladder? How high were you? Did you hit your head?"

Neil Bailey was a lanky fellow about her age with rumpled brownish-blond hair who would have looked quite attractive if he hadn't been grimacing in pain and wearing a paint-spattered hoodie and jeans that looked as though they had been gnawed on by a rat. Charli didn't wait for him to start his story before checking his pupils for signs of concussion.

"No luck on the negotiations between the E.R. staffing firm and the hospital?" Bailey asked over a quick intake of breath as she began examining his arm.

Charli paused, surprised. "What do you know about any negotiations?"

"Should have introduced myself…" He awkwardly extended his good hand, which was his right one. "Hi, I'm Neil Bailey, editor of the *Brevis Bugle.* I know Dr. Prescott—that would be your dad, right? He got into another tiff with the staffing firm. Anyway, I covered the emergency meeting of the hospital authority board that authorized the hospital to pay you and your dad to handle the E.R. until the hospital could negotiate with the firm or get someone else in."

She gave the proffered hand a quick shake, while she checked that arm to be sure it was injury-free, as well. It was a very nicely constructed arm, with just the right amount of biceps and defined muscles. Charli yanked her thoughts away from their unprofessional admiration of his physique and continued with her assessment.

"Well, Neil Bailey, editor of the *Brevis Bugle,* it's obvious you don't have any signs of memory loss or head trauma."

"You didn't answer my question about the negotiations."

"No comment. That's my answer. You can ask my dad—Dr. Prescott. Or the hospital authority board." She went back to looking at his injured arm, then stepped over to the computer and called up his X-rays. The ulna had a nice clean break, with an additional textbook Colles fracture to the distal radial. She came back to the gurney and poked and prodded, checking his fingers and evaluating the swelling. She raised his arm to check his shoulder movement. "You're not a diabetic, are you? How did you fall off a ladder?"

"Ow! Sorry, sorry, don't mean to be a wimp. Not a diabetic. The fall sounds more dramatic than it really was. I was almost to the ground and stepped wrong. I tried to catch myself. So it's broken, huh?"

Charli couldn't help smiling back at his rueful grin. She'd always been a sucker for dimples. And he had very nice dimples.

"Yep, 'fraid so," she said. "I'll put a temporary splint on it tonight and get you a referral to an orthopedic surgeon—"

The curtains behind her snapped open. "No need for a referral," Dr. Chuck Prescott boomed. "He can come by the office and I'll take care of it. Go ahead and put a permanent cast on it tonight, though."

The easy moment between Charli and Neil evaporated. Charli closed her eyes and rubbed her forehead, her headache surging forward again. "Excuse me, Dr. Prescott," she ground out. "This is my patient."

"Neil? You trust me, don't you? If I tell you that you don't need a bone-and-joint doc, you're okay, right?" her father said, winking. At the wink, Charli thought she'd self-combust with anger. For two weeks, her father had been waltzing into her treatment areas and second-guessing her. This time, though, she was too tired and too frustrated to let it go.

"He's a *writer,*" she said. "He needs full use of his hand, which will require physical therapy, and the break needs to be evaluated by someone who can give him optimum care—"

"Do you hear her?" Her father shook his head. "New doctors. They're all alike, even my own flesh and blood. They sound like they're reading out of a med school textbook. What she means is she doesn't want you to sue her if you can't bend your elbow the full extension once it heals."

"Have you even looked at—" Before any other hot words of defense could leap out of Charli's mouth, she jabbed a finger. "Outside."

"Oooh, don't write about this, Neil, but I think she's taking me to the woodshed." Her father waggled his eyebrows, bushy and gray, over eyes that sparkled.

Beyond the curtain, Charli marched down to the staff lounge. Anna, one of the nurses, quickly cleared out once she saw who Charli had with her. "Uh, I'll let you two talk," she muttered as she swept by with her half-eaten sandwich.

The lounge, like the rest of the hospital, was tiny, worn and had last seen a decorator somewhere around 1980. Her father pulled out one of the folding metal chairs and sat down.

As he did, his phone buzzed. He fished it out of his pocket, glanced at it, frowned and stabbed at the touch screen. His face cleared. "It's Lige Whitaker. Well, he can wait." His tone was entirely more cavalier than Charli would have treated their chairman of the hospital authority—their boss's boss.

Her father pocketed the phone again. He leaned back against the chair. "This is where you tell me that I'm an old fogey, and that medicine has completely changed since I got out of med school myself a hundred years ago, and that specialists are specialists for a reason." His lips twitched at the corner with barely concealed amusement. "I agree. Guilty on all counts." With his foot, he shoved the chair beside him away from the table. "Have a seat. Now that you're a doctor, you'll need to learn to sit when you can."

She crossed her arms. The chair was tempting to her aching feet, but she ignored it and her father's good-old-boy charm, which he always pulled out as his weapon of choice. "No," she said firmly. "This is where I tell you that the next time you undermine me with a patient is when I walk out. What you did—what you have been doing—is disrespectful and not professional. Emory University—along with Georgia Health Sciences, not to mention Memorial in Savannah—are convinced that I am a physician. So is the state board. You may have got away with treating other doctors like this—and the way you treat your nurses is like something you'd see on a 1980s soap opera, by the way—but you will not treat me with professional discourtesy."

Her father wrinkled his nose. "Thank God some of those shows are off the air. All those subdural hematomas and amnesias and people waking up perfectly fine out of months-long comas bugged the stew out of me. Fake doctors."

"I'm referring to the way those fake doctors treated their fake nurses, Dad."

The older Dr. Prescott opened his mouth, shut it, fiddled with his stethoscope. "I'm that bad? I can't be. I haven't pinched a gal on the backside in a decade."

Charli sent her eyes heavenward. Leave it to her father to think that simply avoiding overt sexual harassment was enough to prevent him from being gender-biased. "You're lucky you're the chief of staff at this hospital, Dad. Otherwise, you'd have been a frequent flyer in sensitivity training—and only if you'd had an understanding chief of staff."

He ran a hand over his rumpled silver hair. Suddenly, Charli could see all of her father's sixty-seven years in the lines of his face. "Dad…"

"Nope, give it to me straight. Cut me no quarter just because I'm your old man." He held up his hands to forestall any softening in her stance. "I admit, I could probably do with a few of those sensitivity training sessions. I am an old fogey, but I can learn. And that in there—I was trying to save the poor guy money. He has high-deductible insurance that pays practically nothing. That's what you young punks can't get in your head—you think just because you have all this medical technology available you need to use it." He must have seen her anger as it rekindled and realized his apology was going off the rails. "But you're right. I'd have had your head if you'd pulled the same stunt on me."

Her father stood up, back straight, lab coat

amazingly still showing the creases her mother had lovingly pressed into it that morning. "Apology accepted?"

"Yes," she said. "And by the way…Knife Guy? He's staying."

"You're going to break this hospital, you know that? Knife Guy's got no insurance."

But her father didn't wait for her to answer, just headed past her with a slap on the shoulder. "I'm proud of you, kiddo. You might make a good doctor one day."

The door slammed behind him, and for a long minute she stood there. Would this ever work out? She'd either kill herself or kill her dad. But this was the one thing she'd wanted, right? To work by her father's side, prove to him that she knew what she was doing, prove to him that she could be a doctor—not a nurse as he'd suggested so many times.

Don't forget that by working here, a good chunk of your student loans will be forgiven, she told herself. *It's a win-win. I'm home with Dad and Mom, and I can work off some of my debt. So suck it up, Prescott.*

She went back to see Neil Bailey on her own. "Let me tell you what could happen if you don't see a specialist," she said. "Your wrist has what's called a Colles fracture, and the ulna has a clean break. Either one alone, I wouldn't be too worried about. But since you broke both bones, and since you're a writer, they worry me. I want you to have full range of motion with the wrist. It's your choice. You can do it the—" She bit back "the old-fogey way." Using that expression, even if that's what she thought of her dad's method, would break her own dictates about professionalism. "You can take my dad's suggestion and follow up with him, since I'm assuming he's your primary care doctor. Or…"

"I'll take the referral. No offense to your dad. But I am a writer. Like you say. I'll figure out how to pay for the specialist some way. How long do you think I'll be typing one-handed?"

"Hard to say. But probably, if you don't need any surgery or pins—which I don't think you will—at least six to eight weeks, depending on if you drink your milk and eat your green veggies."

Neil nodded. "I will double my intake of both."

"Now, let's give you some pain medicine and see if we can get the swelling reduced."

"That would be ibuprofen or Tylenol—don't like anything stronger."

"Okay, tough guy. We'll see about that." Charli had seen biker dudes beg for morphine when a bone was being set, but she knew from hard experience you had to let a man figure things out on his own. She headed for the curtain and the other patients who waited for her. "Give us a few minutes while we get you a shot of Toradol—it's pretty much souped-up ibuprofen. That okay with you?"

"Does the Toradol do a better job? It's not a narcotic, is it?" he asked her. "Because I don't want to be zonked out."

"Nope, it's not a narcotic, and, yes, Toradol by injection works faster than oral meds like ibuprofen. Did you drive yourself?"

"Nah. I had my buddy drive me."

Charli paused at the curtain and looked back over her shoulder. "So where was this buddy when you were climbing a ladder all by yourself?"

"Oh, Brinson was there. But he was busy texting Jill—his wife—to get out of the doghouse about being late for supper."

"Wait…" Charli's brain turned over the uncommon first name in combination with a wife named Jill. "Brinson Hughes? He's my neighbor."

"Yeah? Well, what do you know? It's a small world."

"What were you doing on a ladder, anyway?"

"Finishing up my Christmas lights."

She frowned again. "It's the first of November."

"Ya know, that's what Jill said."

Just then, Knife Guy started in on a particularly loud rendition of Elvis's "Suspicious Minds." It served as a reminder to her that no matter how interesting Neil Bailey was, no matter how she enjoyed chatting with him, she had other patients who needed her.

"I'll be back," Charli told him.

"I'll be here," he replied. His dimples jumped and she found herself liking the fact that he didn't whine when in pain.

Outside, she crossed to the trauma bay and checked first on the malodorous Knife Guy, who seemed content enough. She left him warbling on and headed for the nurses' station. Lainey handed her a phone and a stack of charts, Knife Guy's on top.

"So do we kick him loose or put him on the floor? We've got to do something." Lainey wrinkled her forehead. "He's driving us nuts."

Charli scrawled a signature on the admissions order. "Send him to serenade the floor nurses." She put the phone to her ear. "Dr. Charlotte Prescott speaking."

"Charli!" Her mother's greeting was a mix

of relief and irritation. "Neither you nor your father have been answering your cell phones. You have to send your father home! He's sixty-seven years old, and he's not in any shape to be staying at that hospital all night long."

"Mom." Charli sagged against the counter and let her forehead sink into her palm.

"He's an old man, Charli. He needs to be home."

Charli cast a sideways glance down the hall, where her father was doing some shadowboxing with a tree trunk of a man in a camouflage coverall. Her father's fists were light and fast, and his face glowed with merriment. He was in his element.

"I think he's okay, Mom."

"What do you know?"

"Oh, I dunno. Maybe a few years of medical school and residency? Mom. Trust me, if he looked really tired, I'd send him home—I'd have to bind and gag him first, but I'd do it. You don't need to worry, okay?"

"But you and he *need* to come home. I've got a surprise for him! And for you, too, of course."

Her mother's words caught Charli off balance. She straightened up and pressed the phone closer to her ear. "Mom, a surprise? Did you, uh, buy it?"

"No. No, Charli, I made it. I didn't buy it." Her mom's words sounded resigned and hollow. "You know how your father is—he worries so much about my shopping. I'm very careful now. Why everybody always has to obsess about me and my shopping... The surprise is a coconut cake. He's been working so hard this week, so I thought a coconut cake would be a nice treat. So today I bought a fresh coconut, because you know your Mama Grace's coconut cake recipe calls for fresh grated coconut."

"You're not serious." Charli knew that her mother was indeed drop-dead serious. If there was anything Violet Prescott was serious about, it was pleasing her man.

To get the most perfect coconut, her mother wouldn't have thought twice about jumping a plane to Hawaii to pluck it off the tree herself.

That is, if her dad had trusted his wife with a credit card.

Her mother had most likely spent hours on that cake—it was a nightmare of a recipe. Charli looked down the hall at her dad, his face still lit up, and her heart softened. Maybe she could handle the shift until the new E.R. guys showed up—it would only be an hour or so more. "I will tell him what you've said."

"Not the bit about the cake. Let something

be a surprise, okay? Just tell him I'm worried about him."

"How about this?" Her father had left the shadowboxing behind and was grinning as he headed toward the nurses' station. "You tell him yourself." Charli jabbed the phone in her dad's direction. "For you, Dad."

"Sugarplum!" her dad warbled into the phone once he realized who was on the other end. "Are you worrying your little head about me? Do you miss me, sweetums? Are you lonely?"

He sounded pleased as punch that a woman needed him so much she was miserable without him. Honestly, he'd created a monster. Charli shook her head and gave Lainey instructions about Neil Bailey.

Lainey grinned. "Isn't it sweet?" she asked, nodding toward the phone. "Your dad is so in love with her. Still, after all these years."

A sour feeling followed by a chaser of guilt swept over Charli. She'd always felt overshadowed by her parents' mutual admiration for each other—mutual except when they'd battled over her mother's shopping. It wasn't that she was jealous of her mother's ability to wrap her father around her finger. It was that she knew she could never be the sort of sweet little woman her mother pretzeled herself into being for her father. If that was the kind of woman Charli needed to be for her father—or any man—to love her, she was doomed.

But Lainey was waiting expectantly for Charli's reply. "I'm glad they've got each other," she said. "Let me know when the Toradol has had time to work its magic, okay? I'm off to see— who am I off to see?"

"This one. A dad got his, er, backside stuck in a trash can that he was using for an impromptu toilet."

"Huh?" Charli flipped open the chart and started reading. "Eww. Scout camping trip. Got a bottle opener?"

"What?" Lainey fished around in her desk drawer and came up with one.

"He's created a vacuum, and I need to release it."

"No. Not with my bottle opener." Lainey held the gadget out of Charli's reach.

"Come on. I'll buy you another. We need the bed. The waiting room's overflowing, right?"

Lainey hesitated. "A brand-spanking-new one. Tomorrow. In the package. So I know beyond a shadow of a doubt you didn't wash this one."

"And the receipt. That clinch the deal?"

Charli yawned again, tired to the marrow of her bones.

"That'll do it."

Bottle opener in hand, Charli sailed off to uncork the scout leader.

A STARRY SKY. A beautiful, clear November night. Charli soaked in the silence of her car. No more hearing her name paged on the overhead. No more screaming patients. No more Knife Guy singing "These Boots Are Made for Walking." No more telephone calls from her mother, begging her to send her father home.

No more father telling her she didn't know anything because she didn't know the "real world of rural medicine."

I want to sleep forever. I don't care if it's just 8:00 p.m. I don't care if I have office hours tomorrow morning. I'm going to bed and sleeping until next week. Thank goodness they finally sent in those wonderful, wonderful E.R. docs.

Charli turned on her street and saw a line of cars almost to the intersection. What? Traffic? On a side street in Brevis? Red taillights glowed in a long series, looking like Morse code as people tapped brakes and inched forward.

Charli rolled down her window and heard… Christmas carols? Yes, it was a way too cheerful "Winter Wonderland" being belted out of speakers.

She wasn't the only one who had her window down. The car ahead of her had kids hanging out the back window, faces aglow with excitement. What on earth?

Behind her a horn blew. The driver was impatient, a trio of kids bouncing in the backseat. Well, he was no more impatient than she was. What were they looking at up ahead?

She inched around the curve, with her house in sight, and she saw what all the fuss was about. Her neighbor—whom she hadn't met yet, but it was clearly high time to introduce herself—had enough Christmas lights to outshine an airstrip. And music. Loud music. "Winter Wonderland" had given way to "Frosty the Snowman."

Good grief! Her bedroom window was on her neighbor's end of the house. *So much for sleep. It's only the first of November. Why the Christmas lights?*

Finally the car in front of her inched up enough that she could squeeze into her driveway. Just as she did, something tumbled off the roof next door—a reindeer whose nose went black as he dived into a somersault and headed straight toward her car. Charli hit the brakes and prepared for the thing to smash into a million pieces.

But instead, it bounced. She blinked. Yes. It bounced. It was an inflatable. A big huge hulking inflatable Rudolph that had landed between her car and her carport.

Charli got out. Rounded the front of the car. Tried to drag the deer, but found that it was way heavier than it appeared. She stood there, nonplussed, as Jimmy Durante sang about a button nose and two eyes made of coal.

"We're gonna have to deflate it," a voice came from behind her on the sidewalk, barely audible over Frosty. "With this arm, I'm never gonna be able to move Rudolph without letting the air out first."

Charli turned around. There, in the glow of his Christmas lights, a sheepish grin on his face, his arm in the sling she'd carefully adjusted for him in the E.R., stood Neil Bailey.

CHAPTER TWO

THE GOOD DOCTOR looked mighty ticked, Neil decided. In fact, he could almost see a few choice words forming on Dr. Charlotte Prescott's lips.

Gone was the tolerant, somewhat amused professional expression on her face from earlier in the evening. Now her mouth turned sharply down at the corners, her forehead furrowed, and her hands were at her hips.

He could tell the moment she recognized him from the hospital. Her lips parted, but no words came out. Her head, with that silky honey-colored hair that had mostly fallen from a straggly ponytail, shook a little, like a boxer dazed from one too many rounds.

She said something that Neil couldn't understand over the strains of "Rudolph the Red-Nosed Reindeer," which he thought was apropos to the situation at hand. Maybe he did have the music turned up a little too loud. He stepped closer to her.

"What?" he asked.

"I said, you're my neighbor? *These* were the Christmas lights you were talking about?" She swept a hand over the boxwood hedge, in the direction of his lights.

He couldn't help but take in his efforts with pride. Even with the now-blank spot on his roof from Rudolph's untimely high dive, the display looked good—still some tinkering to be done for the final polish, but he was proud of himself. "Yeah. Pretty cool, huh?"

Her expression shifted rapidly from bemusement to ire again. His response hadn't been the right one, obviously. He held up his good hand and rushed to forestall whatever blistering comment she was about to deliver. "Look, the music goes off at eighty-thirty. I keep it on for the kids. And before you think this is all about me, I use the display to take up donations for Toys for Tots."

On the street, a horn blasted, cutting through the cool night air. It encouraged a volley of horns to join in.

Charli's frown deepened, maybe because of the added sound effects. She was visibly shivering now, as she stood without a coat, her arms wrapping around herself to keep her warm. "Let me get this straight. Every night, from now to Christmas, I can expect an electric dawn outside my bedroom window?" she asked. "And canned Christmas Muzak until eight-thirty? Not to mention a traffic jam? *Every night?* Tell me, am I your only neighbor who has a problem with this?"

He thought for moment, considering. Nah, Jill didn't count, really. She was mainly ticked because Neil had monopolized Brinson's available "honey-do" time the past few nights. "Pretty much, yeah. You're the only one. I did this last year, and the guy who lived in your house, well, he tried to outdo me. That's where I got Rudolph, by the way." Neil jabbed a thumb toward the inflatable. "He had it on his—I mean, your—roof. When he moved to a condo on Tybee Island, he didn't have a roost for Rudolph anymore."

"Oh. Awesome." She put her hand to her forehead as though she had the world's worst headache. In the glow of the Christmas lights and the streetlights, Neil was surprised to see that the doctor's nails were polished a nice melon color. He hadn't noticed that in the E.R.

Another volley of horn blowing interrupted the music, and she winced again.

The move prompted a sudden thought. "Dr. Prescott. You didn't hit your head or anything when you slammed on your brakes, did you?"

"No. Why do you ask? And you might as well call me Charli. When anybody in Brevis says Dr. Prescott, I think they're talking to my dad."

"Well, Charli, then. You look like your head's hurting."

"Gee. With all this music and all these lights and all those horns, not to mention no sleep for two weeks, I wonder why." Her words dripped with sarcasm. She must have reconsidered her tone because she made a visible effort to soften her scowl. "I'm sorry. I'm really tired. Exhausted. I'm beyond exhausted. And all that's been keeping me going today—tonight—is the idea that I could park my car, stumble inside and go to bed."

"Sure, sure." He nodded. "I guess you're pretty wiped out—those E.R. hours must be killing you. I'm really sorry that Rudolph took a dive. It's gonna take about an hour to deflate him...."

Charli's face crumpled. She looked a lot like Neil's four-year-old niece did when she'd gone without a nap and was late for bed.

"Tell you what," Neil started. "Why don't you leave me your keys, and go on inside? I'll get Brinson over here. We'll deflate ol' Rudolph a little and move him at least out of your driveway. Maybe over closer to the hedge?" He pointed to the small stretch of lawn between the concrete drive and the boxwoods. "We'll pull your car in, and tomorrow when it's daylight, I'll retrieve Rudolph."

Charli appeared to be ready to argue for a moment. Maybe she was debating whether he had an honest face and could be trusted not to abscond with her car.

But then she shrugged her shoulders, went back to the idling car, switched it off, slammed the door and handed him the keys. "Sold. You wouldn't sweeten the deal with a pair of room-darkening blinds, would you?"

From her weak smile, he saw it was an attempt at humor. "Sure, anything to keep a neighbor happy."

But Charli wasn't lingering. She skirted around Rudolph, who was swaying back and forth in the night's cool breeze, and stumbled up the steps to her back door. In the blink of an eye, the doctor was out of sight.

With a sigh, Neil looked from the keys in his hand to Rudolph. Time was a-wasting, and Jill was only going to get madder the later he called Brinson to help him out of this jam. With that, Neil fumbled for the phone in his pocket to call in the cavalry.

CHARLI KEPT RUNNING out of wrap, and Neil Bailey wouldn't hold still. Every time she'd get his arm splinted, he'd move or the spool of bandage would be inexplicably empty. Finally, she snapped at him, "Just what is your problem?"

And he grinned at her. "I'm taking up money for Toys for Tots, and I'll ride Rudolph to deliver the cash."

And there was Rudolph, nosing in behind her, his red nose blinking and buzzing—

No. She shook herself awake. It wasn't Rudolph. It was her cell phone. What now? She pushed herself up out of her warm snuggly covers and saw—very clearly in the bright-as-daylight glow of her neighbor's Christmas extravaganza— her phone buzzing away on her nightstand.

Caller ID registered the hospital's number as she hit the answer button. "This better be good," she griped into the speaker. The bedside clock told her she'd been asleep only a couple of hours.

"Charli."

Lainey's voice sounded all wrong. Somber.

"What is it?" Charli asked, already reaching for the slacks she'd dumped on the bench at the end of the bed. "I'm on my way, whatever it is. Knife Guy?"

"No…Charli, your dad…"

An icy chill shot through her. She froze on the bed. "What's wrong?" She was surprised she could even verbalize the question, as scared as she was.

"He's had an MI. At home. Your mom called 9-1-1, and the EMTs responded. They're inbound. She's with them and, well, Charli—from the way it sounds from the EMTs, you'd better come right away."

NEIL WAS BUSILY rigging up a plastic bread bag over his bad arm in order to take a shower when first his front doorbell rang, long and loud, followed by someone doing a good impression of the Gestapo on the heavy oak.

He dropped the bread bag on the kitchen counter and made his way through the living room to the foyer. When he threw open the door, Charli Prescott nearly beaned him on the head, apparently ready to pound on the door again.

He caught her fist in his good hand. "Whoa! I'm here." He released the pink-tipped fingers. For a long moment, all she could do was gulp in air. Maybe she was still ticked about his Christmas lights? He tried a smile to defuse the situation. "Can't sleep?"

"My keys... I gave you my keys!" she got out.

"Yeah. I put them under the flower pot by your back door."

"Oh! Sorry! I didn't look there!" She whirled around, purse flying, no coat on despite temps hovering around a chilly forty degrees, and her hair even worse for wear than it had been earlier.

"Wait! What's wrong?" Neil followed her as she stumbled down his steps and down the walkway.

"My dad! He's had an MI—I've got to get to the hospital." She wobbled unsteadily as she shouted this over her shoulder and backed past his Christmas lights.

"A what?"

"An MI… A heart attack." As she turned to head for her own driveway, her purse got caught in Neil's trio of wired angels by the front walk. She snatched at the strap, making the whole chorus of angels rock back and forth.

"Let me drive you. I have my keys, right here in my pocket." Neil held them up and was gratified to see her extricate the strap from the offending angel's halo without doing any damage and without falling herself. "My car's here."

Charli stopped again. Her expression revealed indecision. Neil could literally see her body jerking first one way and then the other.

So he didn't wait for her reply. Instead, he dipped back into the little foyer, grabbed two jackets and shut the door behind him. He loped over the short distance between him and Charli and took her arm gently in his.

"Come on. Let's get you to the hospital." He steered her to his car and assisted her in with a fumbling one-handed approach, though she didn't seem to notice. He wrapped the spare coat around her slim frame. She didn't protest, just folded her long legs into his little Corolla and seemed to withdraw into herself.

Once he'd negotiated closing the door with his right hand, he started the car and backed carefully out of his drive. It seemed to trigger something in her. "I'm never like this," she said. "I'm always cool in a crisis."

"Hey. It's your dad. You're thinking like a daughter, not a doctor." Gravel that had collected in the dip between the street and the drive crunched under his tires as he backed out onto the street and started for the hospital. "What happened? Do you know?"

She jerked her head in the negative. "Lainey— a nurse—"

"I know Lainey. She called?"

"After they got a call in from the EMTs. It's bad."

She would know. She'd probably handled lots of these in her work, Neil figured. At the stop sign, he hung a left and made the subsequent turns to the main road in town.

"Do you want to call your mother?" Neil asked her as they stopped for the last red light between their neighborhood and the hospital. "I didn't think to ask if your mom needed a lift."

In the crimson glow of the light, he could see Charli's swallow. "Should I go back?" he asked.

"No. Lainey—Lainey said Mom was riding with the ambulance."

The light turned green and he took his foot off the brake, trying not to gun it, but still going a little faster than the speed limit.

Charli seemed calmer now, but he could tell from her drawn face in the glow of the streetlights she was anxious.

"You said it was bad. How bad?"

"I don't— What if he dies?" She put her hand to her face. "Listen to me. I don't have any information. I'm just freaking out, and I tell my patients' families to wait, to see, that we're doing all we can. They're doing all they can. They are. I know."

Neil understood why she'd blurted out her what-if. Did he ever know that desperate thought. He'd never forget the night they'd taken his mother to the hospital. A terrified six-year-old, all he could think was, *What if she dies?* And she *had* died.

Now wasn't the time to tell Charli that life was survivable, if far poorer, after the death of a parent. Honestly, there was never a time when anybody should say that, but Neil knew it for the truth it was. Instead, he reached over, squeezed her hand and said gently, "You *are* a doctor. You know way too much about, well, about everything medical. But I think you've just given yourself some excellent advice."

The reminder of who she was seemed to fortify her. She straightened up and leaned against the gray fabric of the car seat. "Well, we *don't* have enough information. We have to wait and see."

"And we will. We will wait and see." Now they were in the parking lot of the emergency room. The small, low 1960s building seemed perfectly preserved in the lights of the vapor lamps, but Neil knew that the morning sun would not be kind to it. It would reveal the overdue paint job, the scraggly bushes that the understaffed and overtaxed maintenance guys never got around to hedging. But for a town this size and this poor, simply keeping the doors open on a twenty-five-bed county-run hospital was an achievement. Across the street lay the town's doctors' offices—the offices where Dr. Chuck Prescott had spent much of his professional career.

Beyond Neil's car, bathed in vapor lights and the Corolla's headlight beams, lay the big circle with the *H* in it, ready for the helicopter that would certainly come for Chuck Prescott, to take him to a larger trauma hospital. If, that is, the E.R. could stabilize him.

Charli didn't budge. For a moment, Neil let her sit there, collect herself. He saw the last vestiges of her earlier emotion hidden behind a mask that covered all the pain and fear and confusion.

"Okay. Let's do this." She flung herself out of the car and strode toward the hospital, back straight, head high. Even without the lab coat and the stethoscope, Charli looked every inch the doctor he'd seen earlier that evening.

Neil shook off his amazement. Scrambling to follow her, he caught up with her halfway to the entry. The doors whisked open in front of them, a belch of hospital air their greeting.

Lainey dashed toward them and wrapped Charli in a quick, tight embrace. "Charli, I am so sorry. He's here, they're working on him…."

For a moment, Neil saw Charli's mask slip. "Who's working on him?"

"Shafer—well, everybody, except me. They're running the full code. Your dad…he didn't have a DNR in place."

Neil noticed Charli's face blanch. "Where's Mom?" she asked.

"Around here.… Come on." Lainey guided her around the corner toward a private family room.

As soon as she saw the door, Charli balked. "Why…why there? That's where we do notifications."

"I had to. She needed some…space. You've got to be strong, Charli. She's in a complete meltdown."

Those pink-tipped fingers were by her sides, and Neil saw her try to stuff her fists into labcoat pockets that weren't there. She looked long and hard at Lainey and brushed past the nurse.

The door shut behind her with a soft thud. Neil stood there, unsure what to do.

"You didn't want to go with her?" Lainey asked.

"Uh, no." How could Neil explain that their acquaintance, such as it was, had existed for only a few hours.

"She might—"

Neil shook his head. "I'm her neighbor. I don't really know her that well—and, see, she needs the time with her mom."

"Oh. I thought you two knew each other." Lainey shook her head. "It's hard to remember that you haven't always been here. I've known Charli all my life—we went to school together. We were best friends. I guess I thought you'd already talked to her. You know, to do an article on her for the paper."

"I'd called, but her dad said to give her a bit—"

He shook his head. Any minute now, he expected Dr. Chuck Prescott to come blasting out of the double doors and tell them the patient was fine.

But the patient *was* Dr. Prescott. Who would fight to save the town's hospital now? Who would keep the doors open on the little community clinic?

Lainey cast an anxious glance at the closed door. "Violet wouldn't let go of him when they brought him in. We had to peel her off him. She kept saying that if he'd come home, he wouldn't have gotten sick."

Neil fiddled with the coat in his hands. "Maybe I should have gone in with her," he murmured. "But I figured they needed their space."

"You could peek in, see if Charli needs some help? You know how high-strung her mother is." A noise behind them attracted Lainey's attention to some people coming in the E.R.'s main doors. "I've got to—"

Neil waved her away. "Don't worry. I'll wait for her." And as Lainey shot him a grateful look, for the second time that night, he dropped down into one of the E.R.'s uncomfortable chairs to wait. Despite Lainey's suggestion, he didn't think Charli would appreciate him intruding on her private moment.

CHARLI MARVELED AT the fragile quality her mom exuded. A petite woman who'd never come to more than midchest to Charli's dad, Violet felt tiny and almost birdlike in Charli's embrace.

There was nothing petite about Violet's outflow of emotion, though. Sobs racked her mother's slender shoulders, and Violet seemed mindless about the stained carpet as she knelt against an equally stained love seat. Charli understood all too well why Lainey had tucked her mom in the notification room.

"Mom, Mom..." Charli stroked her mother's golden hair, the only thing she'd inherited from Violet. She was tall and gangly where her mother was petite. She had her father's big hands, where her mother's hands were barely big enough to wrap around a liter of soft drink. She was pragmatic and strived for a cool facade…and her mother?

"You have to save him, Charli! You have to!"

"They're doing everything—" She halted before she tried that path again. "Tell me," she said, trying her best to distract her mother and get her to focus on something besides her own emotions. "What happened?"

Her mother hiccupped, ignored the tissue Charli had extended her and wiped her eyes on the sleeve of her turquoise blue cashmere cardigan. "He was tired…." Here her mother shot her an accusatory glare. Charli chose to overlook it.

"So he came home tired?"

"Yes, and I asked him what he wanted to eat. I'd made him some supper, but of course he was late. And…he didn't touch the coconut cake." Violet drew her brows together. A spasm of guilt coursed through her features. "I don't care if he's late every night if he'll just be okay!"

I'll send him home early every day if he'll just be okay. Charli's mental bargain echoed not only her mother's but every patient's distraught family member she'd ever talked with. *This is what they feel like. I thought I knew what they felt like, but I didn't. I didn't have a clue.*

"He didn't eat a thing...said his stomach felt iffy, some indigestion." Violet blinked. "Oh, no. Indigestion. It was his heart all the time. Why didn't I—" But she got nothing more out beyond a torrent of tears.

Charli gave up on soothing her mother. She dropped down on the floor and twisted to lean against the love seat. Beside her, her mother shook with grief and recrimination.

Thankfully, though, her mother ran out of steam a few moments later. She sniffled loudly. "They're not telling us anything!"

"I could go and find out...." Charli hesitated. Should she leave her mother alone in the state she was in? "Why don't we see if Lainey—"

Her mother was on her feet in an instant and headed for the door. "You go! They said I couldn't see him, but they have to let you because you're a doctor!"

Inexplicably Charli's feet felt nailed to the ground. Did she want to see her father as sick and weak as she'd seen other patients?

Violet threw open the door to reveal Neil Bailey still in the waiting room. He'd sat down in a chair in front of the door. Now he and Charli stared at each other.

She was embarrassed that he'd caught sight of her on the floor, as though she'd collapsed from emotion. Scrambling to her feet, she joined her mother. "You'll wait here?"

"I can't take that room a minute longer," Violet insisted. "The walls are closing in on me."

Charli agreed, but still was uncertain what to do with her wreck of a mother. She craned her neck to find Lainey, but didn't see her.

"Hey, if you like, Mrs. Prescott, you can wait here with me," Neil offered.

Violet swooped through the door and dropped into the chair beside Neil. A flicker of irritation poked through the welter of Charli's emotions. Why did her mother insist on latching on to men for support? She'd done it all her life with Charli's father, and here she was now, already gripping Neil Bailey's arm with her neat little hands and gazing up into the man's face as though he were her knight in shining armor.

Honestly, her mother might as well have been a character off *Madmen* or a 1960s sitcom. Women's Lib had completely passed her by.

No need to look a gift horse in the mouth, though. At least her mother was calmer with Neil than she had been with either Charli or

Lainey. Charli shook off the irritation and murmured a thanks to Neil. Gathering her courage, she walked toward the doors to the E.R. treatment areas.

She heard it before she even got to the nurses' station. It was a full code, expertly run, and she could predict the orders of the attending as he got feedback from each of his desperate attempts to restart her father's heart.

"Clear—shock him again!" came the latest order.

"Rhythm still in v-fib!" a nurse called out.

"Come on! Come on, old man!" the doctor shouted. "Don't you give up on me now! Another push of epi!"

"We've lost rhythm!"

Again with the defibrillator. Again with more meds. Again with more compressions. Again with no sustainable rhythm.

And over and over again, until the doctor choked out, "How long without a rhythm?"

Charli couldn't hear the nurse's answer.

The attending swore. In a quieter, more resigned voice, he said, "I'm calling it."

Silence descended in the tiny E.R. Not even an errant beep from a monitor seemed to penetrate the quiet.

In the middle of that quiet came the doctor's next words. "Time of death, uh, 11:31 p.m."

Charli put her hand to her mouth and felt her knees give way as she crumpled to the cold tile floor.

CHAPTER THREE

CHARLI DRANK IN the silence of her car's interior with guilty relief as she sat in her driveway. Nothing but the ticking of the cooling engine disturbed her. No chatter of helpful women, no well-meant condolences of her father's friends, no bustle of people preparing food, or asking for the hundredth time if they could "fix you some little something, Charli? For heaven's sake, you've got to eat!"

Charli had spent the horrible, horrible week following her father's death at her mother's—who'd had a houseful of her friends hovering over her the entire time.

Violet's entourage had buzzed around Charli like a hive of bees, busy and industrious and trying to take care of her and her mother's every need and whim. The incessant chatter had been just what her mother needed—but it was torture for Charli.

She'd escaped out the back door at a near-dead run, accepting the stack of Tupperware containers filled with goodies from one of her mother's friends just so she wouldn't be delayed by an argument. Charli hadn't even had the courage to say goodbye to her mother. She'd go back. Later. She'd call. Later. But for now, she simply needed some quiet.

At that exact moment, Gene Autry started belting out "Rudolph the Red-Nosed Reindeer." Charli banged her head against knuckles that gripped the steering wheel. Neil and his blasted Christmas lights. All they did was remind her that this Christmas was going to be the absolute worst Christmas ever, in a long, long line of horrible Christmases in the Prescott family history.

That wasn't entirely true. Neil's Christmas lights reminded her of that. But Neil himself... He'd been so sweet. He'd hung right in there with her and her mom the night her dad had died. He'd come by her mom's every day, and Charli was so grateful for the way he'd made her mom smile in those early moments.

At the funeral, Neil had waited patiently for the many, many people to greet them at the graveside. There, under the green tent the funeral home had provided, he'd gripped Charli's hand in a tight comforting squeeze and assured her she could ask for anything she needed. The man had a kind heart—she could tell that.

So maybe if she walked through the gap in the hedge and asked him for this one night if he could forego the music…he might.

She hoisted herself out of the car on legs that still felt wobbly. As she approached the hedge, she saw Neil, his back to her, happily tinkering with a snowman's lights, adjusting the display with his good hand.

She cleared her throat, but the music drowned out the sound. Somehow it seemed too intimate to watch him without him knowing of her presence as he fiddled with the lights, completely engrossed in his task. His attention to detail rivaled some of the surgeons she'd trained under, and he could have no greater focus to his task than her favorite chief resident.

"Neil?"

The name got his attention. He turned around. A smile lit up his face and warmed her, despite the raucous rendition of "Rudolph" in the background. "Hey! You're home! How's your mom?"

"She's—she's okay." Charli's throat closed up on her as she thought about her mom and how much she'd loved her dad. All her mom had ever wanted was to make her dad happy.

And now the main purpose of Violet Prescott's life was gone.

Neil crossed the lawn to where she was. He stood there, smiling, his eyes full of energy and merriment that the music seemed to fuel. Suddenly Charli thought it way too much to ask him to cut off the Christmas carols—would he think she was some sort of Scrooge? And he got so much joy out of the display.... Would she get that amount of joy out of anything ever again?

"I've got some hot cocoa if you'd like," Neil offered. "Or I could scare up an omelet."

She shook her head. "No, no, thank you. My mom's friends have all conspired to make sure I don't starve to death for the next century. I've got a carload of Tupperware filled with food."

"Oh, okay. Yeah, every time I went to visit, it was always packed with people—the funeral home, your mom's house...."

Charli felt tears burn her eyes. She turned her head, embarrassed that a week after that awful night, she still had to be on guard against her emotions. She was a doctor. She couldn't be falling apart every minute of every day.

Neil touched her sleeve. "I—I'm sorry."

For a horrifying moment, she thought she wasn't going to be able to keep back the tears. His voice was so kind, so gentle, as if he understood exactly the depth of the pain she was going through. She was certain that if she looked Neil straight in the face, she'd surely lose it.

But the will that had gotten her through medical school and the grueling years of residency saved her. She swallowed it all down and promised herself a good cry later when she was alone.

"I—I have a silly favor to ask," she said when she was able to face him again.

"Sure, anything," Neil told her.

"Could—just for tonight—could you go without the music? I—I can't explain it…."

Neil didn't hesitate. He walked over to a weatherproof box she hadn't seen before and killed the music. He turned around, palms ups, and said, "That better?"

Charli had been prepared to argue and debate and prove her point—something she had many years of experience doing first with her dad and then with every single one of the professors and doctors who'd trained her. To have a guy not question her, but just give her the thing she asked for, was almost too much. She felt her composure begin to falter.

Neil must have seen something on her face, because he closed the gap between them and steered her to the front porch steps. She sat there, staring at his awful decorations, unsure what she might say that would end the silence but not reveal what was on her mind.

Before she could figure that out, her phone buzzed.

She fished it out of her pocket and glanced at the screen. "My mom," she said apologetically, and answered it.

"Charli!" her mom exclaimed in greeting. "Honey, where did you go?"

"I—I had to have some air, Mom. I just needed to be alone. I'm sorry. I'll come back." The thought of being in that hive of activity nearly undid Charli.

"No, no, don't come back for me…but, honey, you don't need to be alone. You need people, people who care about you. Right now, the thing that will do you the most good is— Oh, thank you, Ellen, thank you for the tea. Charli, the thing that will help is to be around people."

Charli knew her mom meant well, but this was a meeting of the minds that would never happen. It was the same vast chasm of difference that had made her mom think ruffles and lace would suit Charli, when in reality, all Charli had wanted to do was pull on a T-shirt and jeans and tag along with her dad. How could Charli explain to her mother that being among people was the thing she could stand least right now?

It wouldn't happen. Charli knew that. "I am around people, Mom," Charli told her. She glanced at the man who sat quietly beside her, looking off into the distance and pretending not to listen. He actually made a move to get up and give her privacy—score more points for him—but she laid a hand on his arm. "I'm with my neighbor, Neil Bailey."

"Oh!" Her mother's tone slid from its prior worry straight to relief and delight. "Oh, Charli! That's good. That's very good. I should have known you'd need some companionship your own age. And Neil is so nice and so handsome, too."

Charli couldn't help but blush at her mother's words. She knew where this was heading. She tried to cut her off, afraid Neil might overhear her mother's effusiveness.

"Mom, it's not like that—"

"He was just too kind! And did you see that beautiful write-up in the paper about your father? Neil did a fine job. Will you tell him that? And tell him to come by and visit me, so I can thank him properly. Oh, Charli! You couldn't have found a finer gentleman."

"Mom, I don't need that sort of—"

"Oh, nonsense! Every woman needs a good man. That's what we are made for. I had your father." Here, her mother's voice sounded choked. "For all these years, he stood by me, when I was so— He could have left me. And he didn't. All the misery I caused him."

"Mom…" Charli didn't need to hear her mother's regret play out again. She didn't need to be reminded of her mother's battles with her shopping addictions.

Her mother, though, pulled out of her sharp dive into moroseness. "You stay. Charli, stay right there. And get to know that young man. Your father would approve."

And with that, her mother hung up, leaving Charli feeling churlishly contrary, not wanting to do anything that lined up with fitting her parents' cookie-cutter plans for her. But that, she knew, was childish. Besides, Neil wasn't anything more than a neighbor, a good guy who'd helped her out in a really rough patch—and one who had extremely tacky taste when it came to Christmas decorations.

Charli dropped the phone into her pocket and rolled her shoulders to ease the tension in them. Beside her, Neil still waited with a patient quiet that seemed restful after her mother's energy.

"Everything okay?" he asked.

"Yeah. I ducked out without saying bye to my mother—my mom has a whole entourage attending her, and I just needed a breather."

"She has friends from everywhere, doesn't she?" Neil mused. "Even some ladies from Macon came down. Old college roommates, I guess, right?"

Charli bit her lip. She knew the ladies Neil had referred to. They were members of her mother's compulsive-shopper support group. She'd been glad they'd made the trip down for her mom, but it did lead to questions Charli wasn't quite sure how to answer.

"Something like that. They've been friends for a long time," Charli told him, hating that she was lying. To change the subject, she asked, "So how did you get started with all these Christmas decorations?"

Neil seemed taken aback by the lightning-quick subject change. "Oh, well. That polar bear over there was my first one. Saw it at a big-box hardware store and I swear the rascal was so cute I couldn't leave him there. Got him on sale, too."

"One little polar bear? Led to all this? Remind me not to put up so much as a Christmas light. I might catch your Christmas spirit."

"I don't think it's contagious, not so much,

anyway, without years of exposure. My family has always made a big deal out of Christmas, so I had a lot of encouragement. My mom loved Christmas." Here, Neil's words were husky and she noticed his jaw worked a little.

"Your mom…"

"I lost her a long time ago. When I was six. But she always decorated for Christmas—all the lights, all the mistletoe and the popcorn garland. I still smell popcorn and think of her stringing together garland for the tree."

"Oh, that's sweet." Charli swallowed past the lump in her throat. He'd lost his mom so young and still his grief was almost palpable. Whoever said time healed all things was just full of it. She'd never be able to think of the holidays without remembering how she'd lost her dad so close to them.

Neil cleared his throat. "Yeah, well, that's why I love Christmas. And when I moved here, people just seemed to urge me on."

"Well, you're decorating enough for the two of us, so forgive me if I skip Christmas," she said.

Neil cocked his head and pinned her with a look. "You mean to tell me you don't plan to put up a single Christmas decoration this year?"

"Nope. Not even a wreath." It wasn't really a

big stretch, actually. Christmas in the past for Charli had meant huge blow-up fights between her mom and dad over her mom's secret shopping sprees. Her mom had just wanted to get the perfect gifts for her family, while her dad had simply wanted to stay in the black and out of debt. And then college and medical school and residency had meant Charli had spent the holidays apart from her parents the past few years.

"Come on! Your dad loved Christmas! You can't skip it!"

She whipped her head around to look at Neil. She wasn't one to lay out dirty laundry for people. She tried to speak to the truth of her memories without putting in all the details. "My dad? Christmas was just another day for him. I mean, we opened presents, sure, went to the Christmas cantata most years, but Christmas Eve and Christmas morning he spent at the hospital mostly, with patients. I know. I was with him a lot of the time."

Neil's eyebrows went up in surprise. "That's not the guy I got to know. He's one of the main people who suggested I use my display to raise money for charity. And he was the Christmas parade grand marshal for two years running, plus he served on the Christmas downtown celebration committee. Are you sure we're talking about the same guy?"

Charli wasn't. But it irked her that Neil had known a different side of the man she'd thought she'd known inside out. "He always—well, he always said he could take it or leave it," she said.

Neil shook his head and reached over to tweak an errant light into place from where he sat on the steps. "That's amazing. Your mom and dad were a force to be reckoned with around the holidays—your mom was a fixture on the Christmas tour of homes. Yeah, maybe their decorations weren't as—shall we say— dime-store tacky as mine, but they went all out. Your dad even beat me out on the Christmas lights competition last year."

Charli couldn't reconcile what she was hearing with the dad she'd known and loved, despite his flaws. She couldn't help but mutter, "I've been gone so long…maybe I didn't know him at all."

Neil sprang up and stretched out his arm. "Then let me introduce you to him, the man your father became."

She hesitated, then placed her hand in his. It was a nice hand, with just the right grip—warm and comforting and sure of itself. Part of her wanted to yank free and run for her house, because she didn't want to contemplate how she could have missed knowing one thing about her dad. But his hand in hers seemed to reassure her. That, and her curiosity, got the better of her.

"Okay."

Five minutes later, Neil had parked on the downtown square. "Ready to commence the walking tour?"

On the sidewalk, a brisk wind tugged at Charli's hair, but her jacket kept her warm in the darkening evening. Neil strolled beside her, in no hurry. As they went, he pointed out various buildings and causes and people that her father had championed. It was a revelation to Charli—she'd known of his fight to keep the hospital, but she'd had no idea he'd worked to revitalize the downtown area or to assist the Boys and Girls Club, or that he'd served on the permanent homes for foster children board.

"No wonder he had a heart attack," she said as she and Neil came to a stop on a street corner. "He worked himself to death."

"Oh, no, you don't think that, do you?" Neil peered at her. "Nah, I didn't think so. It seemed to energize him, actually. And he'd recently taken on a new project."

"Yeah? When did he have time?"

"Come on. You'll like this." He started off down the sidewalk toward the rougher side of town.

She hesitated. "Neil...things may have changed a lot, but the direction you're heading in used to be a hotbed of drug sales."

"It's okay. It's cleaned up now—at least a little. Thanks to Dr. Prescott."

A five-minute walk brought them in front of a new metal building with big glass windows, the lights on and the paved parking lot still dark with crisp yellow lines. The parking lot was overflowing with cars of every shape and size, none of them any newer than a decade. On the building's metal exterior were simple block letters: Brevis Community Clinic, and underneath, in Spanish, Clínica de la Comunidad.

"Huh?" Charli gawked at the building. "What is this? Why isn't it near the hospital and the rest of the doctors' offices?"

"Let's just say the hospital authority didn't welcome this addition to the Brevis medical community," Neil said. "But your dad saw the need for a community clinic. He said that a lot of people were uninsured and couldn't afford or wouldn't go to a regular doctor. But they'd come here. He really fought for this place."

A group of people came out of the building, walking down the painted concrete block steps, talking excitedly in Spanish. Another car door opened and more Hispanic people headed for the clinic door.

"It's an indigent care clinic? For migrant workers?" she asked. She couldn't wrap her head around the idea that her father, who'd been so opposed to the migrant workers flocking here when she was a girl, would fight for a community clinic.

Neil smiled. "Yeah—well, of course it's open to anybody, and a lot of the community's uninsured use it. But mainly it's used by the migrant workers. Your dad volunteered as the medical director, but a doctor who comes in a couple of days a week and a couple of nurse practitioners provide most of the care. At least, I think so."

"Wow. I—I—" She turned to Neil, grabbed his good hand and squeezed it. "Thank you. Thank you. I have to admit, the man you've described isn't one I would have recognized… but he sounds like a great guy."

"He was. And he must have been with you, too, because…well, you turned out pretty terrific. I'm just sorry that he didn't get the chance to show you all this. I'll bet he would have—if he hadn't been battling the E.R. staffing problem," Neil told her.

Charli wasn't so sure. Granted, she hadn't

been home much in the past seven years, but she and her dad had spent time together. Never once had he mentioned any of these things that Neil had shown her. Of course, a lot of that time her dad had spent trying to talk her out of pursuing an M.D., and talk her into getting married—to have some babies and be happy—all the things that she didn't want to do.

Maybe they'd just spent too much time arguing without ever truly understanding each other.

"So...now you see," Neil said, interrupting her thoughts. "Your dad loved Christmas—you've got to at least let me help you put up a tree and hang a wreath."

Perhaps it was because she was flat-out jealous that Neil had seen a side of her father she hadn't known, or maybe Charli simply wasn't ready to be rushed into anything. Whatever the reason, Neil's emphatic "got to" grated on her nerves.

"No," Charli retorted, "I don't. And I don't appreciate you trying to guilt me into it. Why can't you just live and let live?"

Neil put up his hands. "You're absolutely right. I just thought it might make you feel better."

"Everybody from my mother on down seems to think they know what's best for me, including you. I can't turn around without someone suggesting another way to move on with my life. Well, maybe I don't want to move on just yet! And maybe seeing a tree in my living room would just make me miss my father even more!" Charli knew the words weren't fair, but they came tumbling out, anyway.

"Whoa." A muscle in Neil's jaw worked. She could see he was angry—or at least trying to bite his tongue. Very carefully, he said, "I lost my mom right before Christmas. So I understand what you're going through. I know how afraid you are about forgetting your dad, about how guilty you feel—"

"I don't have anything to feel guilty about," she snapped. "Not a thing." It was a lie, a big one. She did feel guilty, horribly, horribly guilty, especially now that Neil had shown her the father she'd never get the chance to know. Still, she wasn't about to let Neil Bailey know it. "And I think I want you to take me home now."

CHAPTER FOUR

CHARLI SAW LIGE WHITAKER, the bank president who also served as the hospital authority board chair, come out of his office when she approached the bank's customer service desk. Today he was in banker's garb, but usually, even to the hospital authority board meetings, he wore jeans and a flannel shirt.

"Charli, how's your mama? Neil called me, wanted a quote for the paper. I hope I did all right."

Charli couldn't help but frown at the mention of her neighbor. The night before was still bothering her. She was angry at herself for the way she'd acted, but she still felt a little resentful toward Neil. She pushed down her emotions and smiled at her father's old friend.

Lige was thin to the point of boniness, about the same age as her father. Where her father had put on a little weight—all those coconut cakes, after all—Lige had kept the rangy build he'd had as a young man. "Thank you," she said to him. "You said just the right thing. My mother was so grateful. You and my dad made a great team."

Lige waved away the comment. His rural twang seemed so out of place for a bank president, but Lige had always prided himself on being just another fellow. "Darlin', last week, you saw me at my worst, tryin' to deal with that staffing situation in the E.R. I hope that didn't contribute to...well, to the heart attack. All the stress, I mean. Your father's a hard man to lose. He helped me keep this hospital here when I didn't think it was possible."

The smile on his lips was matched by his bright blue eyes, but she could see his jaw tense. He changed the subject. "What can we do for you? Do you need another loan against the practice? Your dad had just paid the last one off. I can understand if things are tight. Your father never was, bless his heart, much of a businessman. He was always way too generous with his skills and talents."

"No, no, we're good," Charli assured him. "I think, anyway. He had just enough life insurance to pay off their house and buy an annuity for Mom. To tell you the truth, I haven't really dug into the practice's books yet. But I'm sure we'll be fine. I'm not looking to add any debt to my student loans. No, what I came in here for was to access the safe deposit box. Jed Cannady—he's the lawyer who's helping us with probate—suggested I come and check it out."

"Well! That's all? My gracious. Such a little thing." He didn't take his eyes off her, but snapped his fingers. "Nora! Charli here needs to get into her safe deposit box. Why don't you help her with that, all right?"

Nora Evers, who'd been at the bank since Charli was a little girl, scurried up to her, obedient as any dog Lige might own. She darted her eyes toward her boss, then at Charli. "Why, sure, why don't you come with me?"

Alone, the woman greeted her with genuine sympathy. Several other bank staffers took a moment to share their condolences. Apparently, like practically everywhere else in town, her dad had them thoroughly charmed. He could do that. He might have been arrogant and peremptory at times with his family and with many of his patients, but he always won them back with his charm.

"Jed brought over a letter of testamentary this morning since you weren't a signatory on the box," Nora told her. "As the executor of estate, he authorized you as the signatory, but of course he'll have access, too. You inherited the practice, so he figured the box had to do with it. It was part of your dad's business account. You have the keys?"

"Yes, Jed had a spare one, just in case."

She guided Charli to the safe deposit area, negotiated the whole business of the keys and manhandling the box to a carrel and said, "Now, just let me know if I can help you."

With that, she left Charli alone with the closed box.

For a long while, Charli wasn't sure she was going to have the courage to open it. Did it really need to be opened right now? The only sound in the little room was the insistent buzzing of the fluorescent light fixture above her. Everything else seemed muted by the thick carpeting and the rows and rows of safe deposit boxes behind her. A portrait of one of the bank's founding fathers—one of Lige's kin, she knew—glowered down at her.

Looking at the box, Charli couldn't think what it might contain. The will had been with Jed, as were all her dad's important papers. If her dad had felt the need to give a key to Jed for safekeeping, maybe the box contained something important.

Jed said the box might have computer back-

ups or something else I need for the practice, she told herself. *Or maybe it's empty.*

Her hand felt heavy as she flipped back the lid to reveal the interior jammed tight with a creased manila envelope.

It was mustard yellow, worn at the corners, having long ago lost its crispness. Charli had to tug at it to pull it free from the confines of the box. The envelope itself had some heft to it. On the back, she could see that her father had several times taped the envelope with his initials scrawled across the tape.

Her heart twisted at the sight of his familiar handwriting. She'd seen those initials many times, and seeing them again made her realize afresh she'd never stand beside him again while he scratched out patient notes.

What could be so important that her dad would want to be sure no one else had opened this envelope? Charli worked a finger under an edge of the tape and pulled it free.

When she turned the manila envelope upside down, thick packets of cash tumbled out.

Ten bundles of hundreds, with bands saying ten thousand dollars on them, landed in a heap on the highly polished wood of the bank table, along with another couple of bundles of fifties and three bundles of twenties, one of them simply rubber-banded.

A hundred grand, easy. In cash.

Charli's mind did the calculations but couldn't process the answer to the bigger question.

Where on earth had her father got a hundred thousand dollars in cash? And why was it stuck in a safe deposit box?

ON HIS DAILY WALK to the bank, Neil spied Charli huddled on a downtown bench and did a double take. Though the day was deceptively warm for the season, Charli hunched over as though a stiff north wind was cutting through her.

She looks plain miserable.

Maybe she'd rebuff his attempts to help her like she had the night before, but he couldn't stand to see someone in the depths of so much grief.

Neil eased down beside her on the bench. For a moment, Charli didn't even notice him. Then she did. He could see emotions swamp her face and felt like a foolish optimist that he could detect the flash of pleasure that disappeared in the wake of irritation and grief.

"Is this an attempt to be alone again? Am I horning in?" he asked.

She shrugged her shoulders. "I don't think I

can be alone in this town. But it's a free country."

It wasn't the enthusiastic welcome he might have hoped for, but at least she didn't tell him to beat it. He pressed his luck and remained beside her.

"Want to talk about it?"

He'd tried to keep his voice neutral, like he'd remembered his aunt and his father had done with him in the days following his mother's death. It had been hard for him to open up. He'd blamed himself because she'd been killed in a car wreck while on a run for Christmas goodie bags for his first-grade class.

It had taken weeks for his aunt to dig that little tidbit out of him, but when she'd folded him in her arms and assured him that it wasn't his fault, his healing had really begun.

Now he saw Charli's lower lip quiver. Tears welled up in her eyes. She lifted her chin and managed to school her face into submission. He didn't dare reach for her hand, though that seemed to be the thing that would have helped him the most. He just waited.

His wait paid off. In a halting voice, she said, "I don't think I really knew my dad at all."

"Because of what…what I showed you last night?"

She started to shake her head, but stopped. "I guess."

Neil didn't believe her—not totally. Charli had been angry with him last night, but only after she thought he'd been bossing her around. Maybe he had—or at least he could see how she could take it that way. Before that, she had been awestruck, not sad, about her father.

No, Neil was certain her confession had to do with something else.

He wasn't quite sure what to say. "I guess it is kind of confusing to have one idea of who your father is while other people knew a different side. If it makes a difference, he was really proud of you," Neil said. "He was excited that you were joining his practice."

Her face lit up. "Was he? Really? I mean, I know he *told* me, but I figured it was—" Charli broke off.

"Yeah. Really. He'd already had me promise to do a big feature on you. That sort of got derailed with your upside-down schedule when you first got here. I wish you could have heard the way he talked about you. I was kind of intimidated—figured you'd be a spoiled-brat arrogant doctor with her nose up in the air after all that advance billing."

"Hopefully—aside from last night—I haven't lived up to that, huh?" she said, not looking at him.

"No. I like you. I like the way you stood up for me that night in the E.R. Your dad could be, well, hard to sway once he got his mind fixed about something."

Charli's laugh was rueful. "I had a lot of practice standing up to him. He didn't want me to be a doctor. Did you know that?"

"He told me that. He said he'd tried to talk you out of the medical field altogether—said you got so mad with him you refused to let him pay for medical school."

"Ah, yes. And I have a huge mountain of student loans to show for my stubbornness. He offered to help me out, but he really wasn't in a position—" Her openness came to an abrupt stop, with her mouth clamping shut to bite off her words.

Neil took the hint and didn't press her. "I just paid off my last student loan. I can't imagine what yours must be like."

"A nightmare. But it's doable. After all, I had something handed to me that few family practice newbies get—Dad left me his practice." Her shoulders slumped at her last words, and Neil speculated the reality of such a bittersweet gift was hard to accept.

"But you'd rather have your dad."

"Yeah. Yeah, I would."

"Well, his patients will love you, just like they loved him—and he loved them."

Charli nodded, doubt furrowing her brow. "Maybe. It's all changed. I've been gone too long. I can't remember everybody."

"Well, it just so happens I have the cure for that," he told her. "Your mom called me earlier today to thank me for my article about your dad, and we were talking about everything your dad was involved in. She reminded me about how he always participated in the community Christmas cantata, and she suggested I invite you to fill his place. I know, I know, she said you're an alto and certainly not the tenor he was, but you know what I mean. They'd be thrilled to have you. We start rehearsals tonight."

Charli put a hand to her face. "Oh," she said, the word a groan. "My mother."

"What? Did I make a hash of things? Did I get it wrong?" Neil asked. "She said you'd participated when you were in high school and really enjoyed it."

Charli groaned again. "Neil, let's face it. I'm just so not ready for anything to do with Christmas. I know you're the holiday's biggest cheerleader, but...I just...I just can't." Her voice broke. "My mother is trying to get you to baby-sit me, and I don't need babysitting. Honestly. I need to be working." She sprang up from the seat. "Thanks, but no thanks. I've got a lot on my plate now. Okay?"

With that, Charli took off down the side-walk, her businesslike stride full of purpose and showing none of the vulnerability he'd witnessed just a few moments before.

CHAPTER FIVE

FOR ALL HER craving of silence and solitude, even after that first tough day back at the office, Charli found herself dreading going home.

The night was quickly darkening as she left her father's practice. Hers, now, she reminded herself. Instead of turning toward home, she drove back to the downtown area and found herself cruising by shabby storefronts that told of a dying town.

Now that Charli'd had time to think, all the cash in that safe deposit box weighed on her mind. And she didn't like where her thoughts were headed.

She knew of her dad's financial struggles over the years. Not only was he a small-town family-practice guy—that in itself was not the road to fabulous riches—but he'd been saddled with debts from her mother's shopping sprees and counseling over the years. Apparently, from what Lige had said, her dad had continued the practice of borrowing money to bail the practice out of the red.

But if he'd had a hundred grand in a safe deposit box, why had he needed to borrow money at all? Why hadn't he used it? And where had the money come from if he'd been paying off the second mortgage on her parents' home and a mortgage against the practice?

These same questions had robbed her of sleep the night before. She'd called her mother and hinted around about whether her dad had kept a secret slush fund, but her mom had seemed absolutely clueless. No, the only thing to do was to ask either Jed Cannady, the family's lawyer, or Floyd Lewis, the CPA who'd done their taxes and helped with the practice's books.

She'd get the truth then.

At the community center, cars filled the parking lot and crowded along the grass shoulders of the driveway. Lights blazed in the big front windows. At first Charli couldn't figure what could be going on. It was a weeknight and the Brevis supper hour.

Then it occurred to her—the community cantata. Neil had told her about it, invited her. She couldn't imagine her dad actually singing in the choir, though he was a good singer. He just wasn't one to take direction from anyone, except maybe her mother.

On a whim, she parked the car and made the hike across the grass to the front steps of the center. The lobby was filled with people crowding around a long table laden with sandwiches and snacks. She hadn't expected this—she'd hoped to slip in the back to hear them rehearse. Charli turned to leave.

"Charli Prescott!"

She stopped. Flora Smith, the bubbly choir director Charli recalled from cantatas past, strode up to her. "Oh, Charli! I'm definitely in need of another good alto! Neil was telling me—"

Now Neil slid in beside the woman and smoothly interjected, "How interested you were about your father's participation. I did tell you Charli had said no."

"Oh, yes, he was so wonderful!" Flora trilled. "And of course we have room for you this year! Even if you did miss last night's first rehearsal. If you're worried about being rusty, don't— we'll have you shaped up in no time!"

Charli's feet itched to take her out of the crowded room. She opened her mouth to make excuses, but didn't know what to say. The last thing she wanted to do was join the community choir and sing Christmas music. She opened her mouth to politely and firmly say no, knowing that would invite a flood of protests from Flora.

Neil interjected. "Maybe Charli should watch a bit of the rehearsal before committing herself—you know, Flora, it is a big commitment."

Flora didn't look happy about it, but at that moment, someone called her attention away. She nodded and hurried off.

"Did I get you off the hook?" Neil asked.

Charli looked past Neil in search of Flora. "Where'd she go? I need to tell her definitely no, or otherwise it will be like water torture."

"Stay. Watch us. You might change your mind."

She glared at him. "I won't."

"So…what are you doing here, then?" he asked.

Good question, she thought. His pointed question served to cool her irritation. *What am I doing here?*

"Just curious." After all her protests that she wanted to be alone, Charli didn't want to admit that an empty house wasn't something she was looking forward to.

Behind her came a clatter of noise, and Neil put a hand on her arm to steer her away from someone loaded down with more trays of food.

He pulled her into a quiet alcove that served as a coat-check area.

A tug against her throat halted her. She turned and realized that the end of her scarf had snagged on a nail at the doorjamb. "Wait— my scarf, it's caught…."

Neil bent down and freed the fluffy pink knitted ruffles from the head of the nail. "There you go," he said, lightly dropping it back in place over her shoulder. "That's some kind of scarf. I don't think I've seen one like it before."

Charli picked up the end of the scarf and stroked the kitten-soft yarn. "It's something, isn't it? My mom knitted it for me—she's on a knitting frenzy since my dad…passed away. I hated not to wear it after she worked so hard to finish it. Even after all these years, she's still trying to force me into pink ruffles."

"You're not the pink-ruffle type?" he asked. Now he reached over and stroked the soft knit. "Well, I think it looks nice on you. She obviously put a lot of effort into it, and I like the fact you wear it even when it's not to your taste. Your mom—she stays busy, doesn't she? I can't think of a single important committee in this town that she's not a part of."

"So strange." Charli closed her eyes. Her fingers continued to stroke the yarn. "I never knew either of them to be involved in much of anything, community-wise. It's like I'm Rip van Winkle, and I've woken from a long sleep and come home to find everything's different."

She opened her eyes again and found that she'd uttered her words so softly Neil had been forced to lean in to understand them. He was close enough for her to see the stubble on his cheek, to breathe in his scent. Close enough to kiss.

He must have heard her quick intake of breath at his nearness, because he moved away a half step.

"Sorry—the noise in the background. Better?" Neil asked.

Oh, no. It wasn't better at all. Had her mother's matchmaking put ideas in her head? She realized with startling clarity that she'd wanted to see Neil tonight—maybe not talk to him, but just see him, hear him sing. She'd wanted to know what he sounded like, whether he was a clear-voiced tenor or a strong bass.

But how to say that without coming across like a blithering idiot? "You asked me why I'd come tonight. I guess you made it sound interesting," she finally said.

"Good. I'm really glad to see you. It seems like I keep ticking you off, and I don't mean to do that." He leaned against the doorjamb, giving off that I've-got-all-the-time-in-the-world vibe Charli found refreshing. The men she'd known—in college, in med school, her fellow residents—had never been so patient.

"If you'll give me a pass on all things Christmas, I expect we'll get along swimmingly," she said. "I'm not usually a Scrooge...."

"I know." He nodded and grinned. "It's the timing. I get it. I guess I'm like Flora—I try to convert the world to my own obsessions."

She liked his self-deprecation. Again, this was like none of the guys she'd been around for a while. They seemed to take every opportunity to remind her that while she was planning on going into the lowly family-practice field, they would be elbow-deep in neurosurgery or cardiothoracic surgery or trauma or oncology.

Here, Neil had no such pretensions, and she liked the way he seemed at ease with himself.

It soothed her—and her anxiety about her father's money, and what that amount of cash could mean. She felt certain, all in a moment, that she could tell the man in front of her anything and he'd understand it, help her through it.

It was on the tip of her tongue to blurt out about the money and ask Neil for his opinion. But then the lights dimmed twice, and she recalled it was Flora's signal to get back to the grindstone.

"Gotta go," he told Charli. "Why not stay and watch?"

She did. As she slid into one of the old wooden seats in the back of the auditorium, she discovered Neil's voice to be a strong, clear tenor that nailed a solo in an old English Christmas carol.

He probably had sung right beside her dad the Christmas before. She hadn't come home for Christmas last year. She would have if she'd known that Christmas was to be her father's last one. It was a regret she knew she'd have for the rest of her life.

Still, as Charli watched Neil sing with the rest of the choir, she was glad of the interruption that had prevented her from spilling the beans about the money. What on earth had made her think telling Neil about the money was a good idea? What could he do about it? And he owned and edited the newspaper. Would he feel compelled to report her discovery before she had a chance to figure things out?

The more she thought about it, the more convinced she became. That amount of money couldn't mean anything good.

THE NEXT MORNING, Charli awoke gritty-eyed and groggy. Thoughts of the money and Neil had chased themselves around in her head until the small hours of the morning. When she faced herself in the mirror, seeing the bags under her eyes, she knew something had to give.

She called Marvela at the office and told her she'd be a half hour late coming in. "I've got a stop I need to make first," she told her.

That stop was at Floyd Lewis's house. Floyd had been her dad's CPA for years. Charli hadn't seen a professional listing in the yellow pages for his office, so she'd rung his house and he'd told her he'd retired three years before, but to drop in at home.

When she pulled up to Floyd's house, she saw a Corolla parked at the curb—a Corolla that looked suspiciously like Neil Bailey's. Her heart went into overdrive as two emotions battled for primacy—a little jolt of joy at seeing Neil again, and frustration that she wouldn't have a chance to talk to Floyd alone.

Maybe it's not Neil. There have got to be a dozen cars in Brevis that look like his. She soldiered on, up the steep little hill of grass between the curb and the sidewalk. Good thing she'd ditched her heels in favor of flats today.

But, no, it was Neil. There he was, struggling

to get out of his car one-handed, diving back in for a camera he slung around his neck and the skinny reporter's notebook he jammed into his back pocket.

"Fancy running into you. I figured you'd be neck-deep in office hours, or at the hospital," Neil said by way of greeting. "I see you're sporting another one of those scarves. Your mom's handiwork?"

Charli's hand went to her scarf du jour, a frilly confection of aqua and black. "Yeah. Should I put in an order for you? She's about to bury me in yarn."

"I'm kind of a hot-natured guy—hardly ever wear a coat if I can get out of it. Maybe you should ask her to knit you a throw or something—that would take longer, right?"

She chuckled. "You might have an idea there." Twining the scarf's end around her fingers, she said, "You visiting Floyd?"

"Yeah. So…you here to see the chicks, too?"

"What?" Did he mean chicken chicks, or…

"The baby chickens. Floyd is raising chickens in his backyard, and he wanted me to do a story on it. He called me and said he had about a dozen hatchlings."

"Oh." Charli groaned. "What a lovely way to raise a good case of salmonella."

Neil came to full alert. "Really? That'd be a good counterpoint to balance the article. Can I quote you on that?"

"No!" she said firmly. "It's just that I treated a whole family who had an outbreak of salmonella after the mom had decided eggs from the supermarket were nasty."

"Wow. How do you get it?"

"The salmonella? From the chickens. Wait. This is not on the record. I don't want to come across as the new-in-town know-it-all doctor who's out to be a spoilsport. So before I say anything, I repeat—this is off—"

"Got it. Background only, so I'll know what to look up on Google."

"Chickens can carry salmonella, and people can get it from handling the birds or their… poop. And there's the whole bird-flu worry. In China, it was domestic flocks, not commercial, that really started that scare. But—" Charli could see him struggling to one-hand his reporter's notebook out of his pocket. "I'll send you a link, okay? If you're careful when you raise chickens, you're not likely to get sick. I just don't want people to think growing your own chickens is as easy as simply throwing some chickens and scratch into your backyard."

"Thanks. Now let's go back and see if ol' Floyd is a Typhoid Mary."

At least I distracted him from wanting to know why I'm here, she thought.

In the garage, empty of a car, and full of chicken brooders, Floyd was leaning over one waist-high pen. "Hey, Neil! You made it! And Charli, too! I mean *Dr. Prescott.*"

"Hi, Floyd. Thanks for the flowers you sent—and the egg salad." Suddenly her stomach churned. Had she eaten salmonella-laden homegrown eggs?

"Hatched those eggs right here! My very own flock of chickens! Can't beat the taste, can you? Made the mayo myself, too. My mama's recipe."

Honestly, Charli couldn't remember whether she'd partaken in any of the egg salad. She usually steered clear of any buffet-served dish that had mayo—homemade or otherwise—in it, for precautionary reasons.

But she was pleased to see Floyd was wearing coveralls and elbow-length gloves. At least he was taking his care seriously.

Floyd brought out a few chicks to show off, fluffy little balls of feathers he had raised in an incubator. "Got 'em in the garage because the weather's cold. See my heat lights? Got two of 'em over each brooder in case one of 'em fails. Redundancy. That's the way to go."

Neil dived into the interview, bracing the notebook on the top of the brooder and scrawling notes with his good hand. Charli looked on with dismay. She wasn't going to have time to wait out the interview for a chance to speak to Floyd alone.

As she was about to go, Floyd said, "Neil, why don't you go on and get a picture of my big girls in the backyard? I can't leave these little guys just now—I'm sexing 'em, and I need to do it now."

"Sexing?" Neil's eyebrows shot up, and Charli burst out laughing.

"He means he's trying to detect the gender of the chicks. He's not doing anything to them."

"Oh. Okay. I'll go get those pictures." Neil left them, albeit looking a little confused.

Now Floyd asked, "What's on your mind, Charli? I guess I didn't think you'd have anything private to say, or I would have told you Neil was coming."

"I can come back—"

"Nope. Me and the missus are heading down to Savannah for some Christmas shopping, and we'll probably crash at Lila's to see the grandkids. I won't be back for a week. Got a buddy of mine to check on the chickens for me. So? What's on your mind? Make it quick, because Neil will be back any second."

"Um, did you know if my dad had a lot of cash?" The tentative way she asked certainly didn't fit in with his suggestion to "make it quick."

"No. He didn't. I told him years ago not to take cash. Makes the IRS look at you harder when you run a cash business. Sure, people will write bad checks, but it's a lot less of a headache than going through an audit. Why?"

She craned her neck to see where Neil was. Through the garage door, she could see him in the backyard, clicking away with the camera at the chicken coop. "Well, what if he did? I mean, do you know how he might have accumulated a chunk of—"

"Whoa!" Floyd dropped the chick he was holding back into the brooder and stopped her with one gloved hand. "I don't need to hear this. But hypothetically, if someone found some cash, if they declare it now, it would mean amended tax returns for all the years the cash could have been accumulated. And it doesn't stop there. The IRS would probably assume there was more cash, so you'd have penalties. Lots of penalties. And anybody—say, like a *wife*—who signed a joint return… Well, it wouldn't be pretty."

"So what do I do?"

"You?" Floyd raised his eyebrows suggestively. "Why, Charli, you know you didn't find any cash. Chuck didn't have any." This was delivered with pointed suggestion of the answer she should be giving if someone quizzed her on the subject. "I was his accountant. I should know. By the time he bailed your mama out of debt from all her shopping sprees, he'd just about got to the point where he was turning couch cushions over, looking for spare change. But hypothetically?" Again with the suggestive lift of his eyebrows. "If you ever did find some money, I'd leave it lay. Spend it in small amounts."

Charli saw Neil turn and head back toward them. "But if you say he couldn't have gotten it legally, what if I can't bear to keep it?" She saw him fix her with one stern eye at her question. "Hypothetically, I mean."

Floyd eyed her. "It can't be much. So don't screw up everybody's life to make nice with the IRS."

She swallowed. Neil was almost back within hearing distance. To cover up the conversation, she said, "I'm glad you're being so safe with your chickens, Floyd. Be sure to tell Neil all about it so that people will understand the risk."

Floyd had once again assumed that "aw shucks" air he'd had before he'd sent Neil to photograph the chickens. "You bet, Doc! Good to see you. Tell your mama I said hey."

With a wave to Neil, who looked rather suspicious at her departure, she headed for the car and the patients waiting at her dad's office— no, *her* office.

CHAPTER SIX

THE DOOR TO HER father's private office squeaked as it opened, giving Charli a moment's notice to jam the pocket-size notebook into her pocket. Marvela's head popped around the door.

"Hey, there you are! I know you're dead on your feet," Marvela began, then broke off. "You looking for something?"

"No, I...wanted to sit here. It's like being with him," Charli told her. It was true enough. After her last patient of the day, she'd come in here for that very reason. Then it had occurred to her to do some digging, to find out anything that could explain where all that money had come from. Her father had not been a rich man, wouldn't have been even without her mother's shopping compulsion.

Charli had found more than she'd bargained for. A stack of notebooks in her father's bottom drawer.

They were journals of sorts—a combination of medical notes about patients and personal reflections. She'd pulled a notebook off the bottom of the stack, seeing a set of dates from the early 1980s in her father's favored blue fountain pen ink.

Now, with Marvela's eyes alight with curiosity on her, Charli toed her father's drawer closed. "Did you need something?" Charli asked her office manager.

"Louredes Garcia over at the community clinic is on line one. In a jam. Your dad...he'd help them out sometimes."

"Okay. Give me a minute."

Marvela hesitated. "You okay? You look a little peaked."

"Sure. Fine." Charli flashed her a smile that she hoped would reassure her.

Marvela pulled the door closed. Charli knew she should pick up the phone, but she couldn't resist the words she'd just read in the notebook.

Hernandez, Miguel: TB seems progressed, and patient's lungs show textbook lesions. Not responding to antibiotics.

A few pages over, he'd noted in clinical, detached language that one Miguel Hernandez had died of complications from the TB, and that other family members showed similar symptoms.

No. What she was reading couldn't be right. Her father hadn't let a man die of TB. There hadn't been a reported case of TB in Broad County in decades, much less a fatality—

Unless…maybe he hadn't reported it. But why not? It was state law to report all cases of tuberculosis. Her father had been a meticulous man…in his notes, in his charting, in his dictation.

With a shaking hand, she set the notebook aside to read it more carefully later. There had to be an explanation.

The red light on the phone blinked insistently. Charli marshaled her strength and punched the button.

"Yes?" she asked, her eyes straying to the notebook.

"Dr. Prescott, I am so sorry to bother you, this is Louredes Garcia, over at the community clinic." The woman rushed the intro as though she was afraid Charli would hang up. "Your receptionist said you were about to leave for the day, and I really hate—"

"What's the problem?"

"Our nurse practitioner is out with the flu, and our backup doctor is out on medical leave. We have a waiting room stacked. Is there…? There's no way—I'm sorry. I mean, your father has just passed away and all. I shouldn't have asked you...."

Charli recalled the Hispanic names in the notebook. Could the money in the safe deposit box have something to do with the clinic? "Didn't my father help you?"

"Yes, yes, he did. He was very generous with his time. And we couldn't have had this clinic without him."

"Then I can help for a while this evening. It's the least I can do."

"*¡Es increíble!* Thank you, thank you! You are a miracle!"

INSIDE THE CLINIC, the slightly dingy waiting room was packed. A roomful of people turned their faces to take her in like sunflowers in a field. A cluster of dark-haired tots played under the clinic's white plastic Christmas tree, shaking what Charli hoped were fake presents. *¡Feliz Navidad!* banners and Santa cutouts were liberally sprinkled around the walls, and despite the Spanish lyrics, Charli could recognize the tune of "Jingle Bells" over the speakers.

A murmur swept through the room and she could see elbows jabbing into neighbors' ribs. Clearly, they were excited to see her.

Not as excited as Louredes Garcia. "*¡No me*

lo puedo creer! You really came! I can't believe it! Thank you!" The short, plump woman's dark eyes snapped with joy.

Charli's conscience nagged at her. If she hadn't hoped to find some clue about the money and her father's notes, would she have said yes so quickly? "It's my pleasure," she said simply. "Show me where I'm supposed to be."

Four hours later, well past eight, Charli was numb with exhaustion. She'd treated six ear infections, two cases of the flu, four sprains, two pulled backs and a host of stomach ailments, and now, her last patient had sky-high glucose readings.

Louredes hovered near her shoulder, waiting for her recommendation so she could translate.

Charli reviewed the thick file. The man's A1C readings had stayed high, his kidney functions had been abominable the last time he'd had them checked and now he had the beginnings of an ulcer on his foot.

He sat on the exam table, his hands folded, his mouth a straight line.

"Louredes, he needs to be in the hospital. We've got to get these readings stabilized, and that foot is only going to get worse. Plus, I'm afraid he's heading for renal failure. Can you tell him all this?"

But Louredes didn't immediately start translating. She shook her head. "Dr. Prescott, he's got no insurance, and his permit is a work permit, so if he goes in the hospital, he'll lose his job, and then he'll be illegal."

Charli sighed and pinched the bridge of her nose. "How'd he get in this situation? Has he been educated on diet? And is he compliant? Does he check his blood sugar at all?"

Louredes burst into the Spanish Charli wished she'd become fluent in. Spanish 101 and 102 seemed a distant memory and a completely foreign language to what she'd been hearing that afternoon.

The man rumbled back a response that was accompanied by an accusing look of scorn in Charli's direction. He folded his arms across his chest and lifted his chin.

"He does check his blood sugar, but he can't afford any more test strips. He ran out of the ones we gave him. And it doesn't do any good, he says, because he can't afford the insulin, either."

Shame coursed through Charli. Of course the man couldn't afford test strips. Most likely, just like all the other patients she'd seen that evening, he worked for less than minimum wage and had a houseful of children to feed.

"Does the clinic have any more test strips and insulin? He's got to have a shot now. But he'll need some to take home—after the hospital."

"You're still going to send him to the hospital?" Louredes made it sound as though Charli was getting ready to deport him.

"One night. He can leave in the morning. Tell him to go to the emergency room, that they can't turn him down there. No, wait. Let me call."

She used her cell phone to call the hospital administrator, Walter Campbell, and explained the situation. "He needs help. One night won't break us, and we'll discharge him back to the clinic, and they can—"

Louredes's alarmed face stopped her from making too many promises, but Walter grabbed hold of the implied assurance. "One night. And don't make this a habit!" he told her.

"I'll donate my care, so the hospital won't have to bill the E.R. docs. And I'm faxing over a copy of the labs so the hospital won't have to duplicate. Deal?"

"Deal. What are you doing there, anyway?"

She was taken aback by the question. "They were in a jam."

"Ha! They're always in a jam. If you want to donate your time, you can start right here. We're open to any volunteer hours you can give. You know how Lige is always going on about how tight our budget is."

It was delivered in a "just joking" way, but Charli heard the bite in his words.

"I'll keep that in mind," she told him.

"Oh, and, Dr. Prescott? I wouldn't advertise the fact you're donating care to the community clinic. Your paying patients wouldn't cotton to subsidizing other people's medical care. Folks are real sensitive about that around here these days," he told her.

"My goodness. Thanks for the warning." She hung up before the odious little man could give her any more words of wisdom—or her sarcasm could get her in hotter water.

Once Louredes had translated the deal Charli had worked out, and that she was personally treating him at no charge while he was in the hospital, the man's face lit up.

"*¡Madre mia!*" he burst out, and he followed it with several sentences of Spanish she couldn't understand, along with much gripping of hands and many, many repetitions of *"¡Gracias!"*

The day done and the patient packed off to the hospital, Charli sagged in her squeaky chair. Louredes beamed at her, as though Charli had sprouted a halo or an *S* on her chest.

"You are incredible!" the woman said. "I can't believe you stayed so long! And you're such a good doctor!"

"You buttering me up for another run?" Charli's stomach rumbled. It surprised her, because, really, she wasn't in the mood to eat. Maybe she should stop for a pizza on the way home.

Louredes dipped her head a little. "No. I hate to say it, but this is really like rearranging deck chairs on the *Titanic*. A big donation fell through. Unless we get a miracle, we'll have to close the doors on January 1."

"What?" Charli thought about the huge number of people she'd seen that evening, patients who'd had no money, no insurance and nowhere else to go for care. "Closed? What happened to your grant?"

"It wasn't a grant, exactly…. The donor who'd said he'd help… He can't now." Louredes busied herself with cleaning up the exam room.

"Who was the donor? Maybe I can talk to him. Or maybe there's someone else?"

Louredes closed the cabinet door and stared at the painted wood as if trying to decide what to say. "I don't think so. I mean, who's got a cool hundred thousand dollars lying around at this time of the year? We tried to apply for some grants, but most of the application windows are closed and all the funds are exhausted."

A tingle went up Charli's spine. Was it pure coincidence that the clinic needed the amount of money in that safe deposit box? And that suddenly the clinic's main patron was no longer available?

"Who was the donor?" she asked again.

Louredes turned to sag against the counter, then shook her head and shoved her hands in the too-tight pockets of her scrubs. "It doesn't matter. He can't help now. A lot of the community will be happy to see us go. Neil Bailey says he could paper his bathroom with all the letters to the editor complaining about what a source of trouble we are to this town. I'm glad he doesn't publish them all. He publishes enough, that's for sure. It's not your problem—and could you please not advertise that we're closing?"

Charli nodded. "I won't breathe a word. If I can help you, I will. You've made me a true believer—*today* has made me a true believer."

"You sound like your father. Dr. Prescott was a good man." Louredes's voice was husky.

This new revelation surprised Charli yet again. Who was this man? When she was younger, all she'd ever heard from her dad about migrant workers were complaints.

"He volunteered here?" she asked.

Louredes's gaze slid sideways and her knuckles whitened as she gripped her hands together so tightly the joints made that awful cracking sound that never failed to unnerve Charli. "Some. He was our medical director. And…he saw a lot of the local Hispanic community at his office. After hours."

Charli recalled the notebooks with their inked patient notes. Before she'd left the office, she'd flipped through some of the other notebooks and bundled them up to take with her.

The later notebooks had been filled with entries detailing simple illnesses, cold and flu patients, not TB deaths. What she'd seen today had mirrored her father's notes. She needed to read them. Tonight.

Charli was even more convinced that she didn't know her father at all. Which was sad. Because if this had been the man he was, well, she really would have liked to have been his partner.

And the hundred thousand dollars? Maybe he'd intended for it to go to save this clinic.

CHAPTER SEVEN

NEIL RAISED HIS FIST to knock on Charli's door and hesitated. She'd just come in. Maybe she'd been held up at work, and if that were the case, she probably wouldn't want company.

He'd looked for her at the cantata rehearsal and hadn't seen her. Maybe he owed her an apology for siccing Flora on her—even if it had been in the best of intentions.

If we're honest here, Bailey, you just want to see her again.

He banished thoughts of silky blond hair and china-blue eyes that shone with fierce determination. *To make sure she's okay,* he amended, and swore he would believe the lie he told himself.

That bit of housekeeping attended to, he knocked on the door.

It took Charli a moment to answer. When she did, she opened it a scant two inches, enough to see who it was.

"Oh! Neil!" The door opened wider, then she

closed it back a little. Still, that was definitely a smile—a small one, but still a smile.

Wow. Not the reaction I was expecting—I figured she'd be all "Beat it, Bailey."

But she wasn't. At least part of her seemed pleased to see him. However, he could detect some hesitation in her face.

"Is this a good time?" Neil asked. "Because I can always, you know, come back another time."

"Oh, no, no, come in. Just…give me a minute. I have to…"

She shut the door before she told him what it was she had to do. Had he caught her in her jammies? It was only eight, but doctors had weird hours, after all.

He heard a series of bumps and chair squeaks. Didn't sound as though she was yanking on anything over Hello Kitty pj's—or whatever she wore to bed.

Stop that. Right now. She's your doctor. She sees your naked butt, you don't see hers.

Neil's chiding had rendered his face awash with heat at precisely the moment she flung open the door to let him in.

"Sorry! I had patient files out."

He saw no sign of the files or even a laptop, but he did see a pile of notebooks on a pine dresser beside the kitchen's eat-in dining table. Otherwise, the kitchen looked Spartan—no personal knickknacks, cabinets bare and empty. He was used to seeing it with his old buddy Owen as an inhabitant. *Well, she's a big improvement over Owen on the slob scale.*

He realized she was waiting for an answer. "Oh, wow. You take patients' privacy very seriously, don't you?"

"Got to." Charli had clasped her hands behind her back, and her face glowed with an innocence that would make his niece's efforts after eating the last cookie pale in comparison. The good doctor was definitely up to something, and if he had a reporter's bone in his body, he'd bet it didn't have a thing to do with patient files.

Was it just curiosity, then, that made him want to stay?

And don't forget the other possibility, Bailey, his conscience nagged at him. *The one where you hang around just because you're starting to really like her?*

"Are you hungry?" Charli asked him. "I just ordered a pizza, but they said it would take a good thirty minutes." She leaped to the fridge and flung open the door. The light shone down on a bare refrigerator, save for a few stacks of Tupperware, some tubs of yogurt and a carton of half-and-half. "Oh, wow. I've really got to go grocery shopping. How about some Greek yogurt? It's got blueberries. And lots of protein." She peered back around the door of the fridge, looking slightly bemused. "Oh, right. You don't look like a yogurt kind of guy."

Neil couldn't help but chuckle. "And what exactly does a yogurt kind of guy look like?" he asked.

She blushed and smoothed a hand over her hair. Shutting the door with a shrug, Charli said, "Not somebody like you—you look like you're a straight-up meat-and-potatoes kind of guy."

"I think I'll wait for the pizza, if you're offering," he said. "Because, truth be told, I've never been much of a fan of yogurt."

"See? My instincts were right." She tried to push her hands into pockets that weren't there, then swept one toward the kitchen table. "How about a seat? Are you a seat kind of guy?"

"I am." He crossed to the kitchen table and pulled out a captain's chair. "I—not to press my luck here, but I didn't see you at the rehearsal. Was my singing that bad?"

Charli sat down across from him. "No. You're very good. I didn't go by for a couple of reasons—one, I called Flora earlier today and told her definitely no."

Neil couldn't help feeling disappointed. He'd hoped from the expression on her face the night before that she'd change her mind. Maybe he was wrong, but what had helped him when he was a kid was the way his dad and his aunt had coaxed him into joining in with activities that involved a lot of people.

Still, everyone was different, and people worked through their grief in different ways. He'd found himself talking to his dad earlier in the day about Charli, and his dad had advised him not to rush her—to give her space.

"No chance you'll change your mind?" It was the wrong thing to ask her. He could tell that from the way her face closed down a little, lost that openness it had.

"No. I'm really busy, Neil." Charli said this gently but firmly. "Like tonight—I just got home. I had to admit a patient to the hospital. And before that, I wound up helping out the community clinic."

He smiled, reassured by what she'd told him. "Wow, that's great! How'd that happen?"

"Louredes was in a jam—they didn't have a doctor. Hey, have you heard anything about the clinic…?" Charli seemed to change her mind midsentence.

Neil could bet he knew what she was talking about. "About it closing, you mean?"

"You know? Louredes asked me to keep it under my hat, and here I go, blabbing about it, and to a reporter, no less." Charli sprang up from her chair and walked over to the sink. "You thirsty? I can offer you tap water...or tap water."

Neil laughed. "Hmm...I think I'll take the tap water."

Charli reached for a couple of glasses and asked in a way-too-casual voice, "So what happened to the clinic? Did they have a grant fall through or something?"

Again, Neil tried to ignore the red flags that Charli's tone sent through him. "Or something. They'd been funded with a federal grant, but then budget cuts really hacked into their bottom line, and I don't think they were funded again—at least at the same level. Louredes had told me some time ago—maybe a couple of months ago—someone had volunteered to donate a sizable sum on the condition of anonymity. But...she came in a week or so ago and asked me what I thought of trying to do a 'save the clinic' fund drive leading up to Christmas. Apparently, their Mr. Moneybags had a change of heart or a change of circumstance, and the money wasn't coming, after all."

Charli added ice to two glasses and filled them with water, then set one down in front of Neil. "So it was a man, then? The donor?"

Neil paused, the glass halfway to his lips. "Huh? Oh, I don't know."

"But you said 'Mr. Moneybags.' Like he was a guy."

Neil took a sip and considered her comment. "Sorry. I guess it could have been Mrs. Moneybags. To tell you the truth, Louredes was pretty closemouthed about the whole thing."

Across from him, Charli ran the tip of her finger around the rim of her glass. Her eyes were unfocused, as though she were concentrating on some memory or imagining being somewhere else. "I hate to see the clinic close," she said.

"Me, too. It does a lot of good here. Your dad really worked hard on it. You know, for a while, I thought maybe Mr. Moneybags *was* your dad, because he was such a strong supporter of the clinic, but Louredes told me no when I tried to guess his identity."

"Really?" Charli chewed on her bottom lip. "And you asked her? Straight out?"

"Yep. She was pretty adamant about it. Why?

Are you or your mom in a position to help out the clinic?"

"Me?" Her eyebrows shot up and she shook her head. "I'm buried in student loans. One reason I came back here—besides the fact that I wanted to practice with my dad—was that it's a medically underserved area. They'll forgive part of my loans if I work here for three years. As long as Lige and the hospital staff don't mind filling out a gajillion papers."

She finally took a drink of her water. Putting the glass down, she added, "And my mom... Well, there's no huge lump sum there. My dad's life insurance went to pay off their house and buy her a small annuity—he wanted to be sure she had an income stream she could count on."

"Funny. People always think doctors are rolling in the dough," Neil commented.

A sad smile played across Charli's lips. "Not small-town docs. And not my father. Keeping his practice going was always an exercise in creativity. He never wanted to increase his fees, and he tried to keep a lid on expenses—you know, just hiring one nurse and Marvela to run his office and do his billing."

"So no slush fund, huh?"

Charli jumped—or at least Neil thought she did. She looked positively guilty. Then a loud knock came on the door and she did jump. She was so keyed up that she covered the distance to the kitchen door in two bounds.

It was the pizza guy. Neil got up, dug for his wallet, crossed the kitchen. Reaching over Charli's shoulder, he handed the delivery guy the cash. "Least I can do," he told her as she tried to protest. "I did invite myself to supper."

The delivery guy gone and pizza slices on their plates, Charli asked, "There's nothing that can be done about the clinic, then? All those people... I can't imagine what they'll do for care. And some of them are pretty sick. What about Louredes's idea about a fund drive?"

"Oh, I've been putting that in the paper along with my Empty Stocking Fund Drive. But if Louredes told you they were still slated to close, I suppose no white knight's come to save the clinic. I guess it's just...gone."

Charli slowly chewed on a bite of pizza, then pushed away her plate, the slice almost untouched. "There's got to be *something*."

"I have to warn you, the clinic's not a very popular cause around here. A lot of people don't care very much for immigrants."

Charli jutted out her chin. "It wasn't just Hispanics that I treated there today. But even if it had been, they deserve care, too."

"I know, I know." Neil lifted his hand to ward off her anger. "You're preaching to the choir. The clinic serves as a lightning rod, that's all." He was impressed with the fierce indignation he saw lining her face. "I have to say, you remind me a lot of your dad—he was just as passionate about that clinic. I don't think he would have let it close—at least not without a fight."

He heard Charli's quick intake of breath and saw her jerk her head, but not before he detected a tear streak down her cheek.

Stupid jerk! he swore inwardly. "Oh, jeez, I'm sorry...."

His apology seemed to have the opposite of its desired effect, for now she completely lost it, burying her face in her hands, her shoulders shaking with deep wrenching sobs.

Neil pushed back his chair and stood by her, not sure what to do. Gingerly he touched her shoulder, feeling some comfort in how she didn't immediately slap his hand away. He hadn't meant to make things worse.

Neil's touch seemed to rally her. She straightened up, scrubbed her face with her hands and tamped down her tears with one final, single shuddering sob. "Sorry," she whispered. "I don't know where that came from."

"Me being an unfeeling clod," Neil told her.

She shook her head, but he noticed it lacked conviction. "People tell me it gets better. Easier."

"They say a lot of things," he agreed. He would have stepped back, given her space, but she gripped his hand.

"You—you said you were six…when your mom died. And you got through it. How?" The naked pain in her eyes made Neil's heart ache with the grief he knew she was feeling. Instantly he was six years old again, wrestling with the fact that his mother was never, ever coming home.

He squatted beside her, wanting to be honest with her. "Don't make me out to be a hero," he told her. "What happened to you is no different than me. One minute you have a parent, the next you don't. Doesn't matter how old you are, it's tough. And the only ones who can understand are people who have lost their parents."

For a moment, Neil thought maybe he'd forged a connection with her—something beyond an acquaintance or a neighbor. He'd seen a flicker of trust—real trust that he knew what he was talking about—in her eyes."What you need is a cup of cocoa. Or tea. Or coffee. Want me to fix you some?" He twisted around to check the counter.

"Cocoa?"

Her tone was flat with disbelief. He didn't need her to say the rest of what she was thinking—that a cup of cocoa could fill the hole left by her dad's death.

"Yeah. A nice warm cup of cocoa," he said. "I can run over to—"

"Thank you. But I'm fine."

Her eyes didn't agree. They were cool, and that warmth of trust was gone now. He was trying to be helpful, but still, he'd said the wrong thing.

Whatever chance he had at making a recovery was blown to smithereens by the sound of a long blast of a car horn and joyous shrieks of children penetrating the walls of Charli's kitchen. She shoved back her chair.

"Let me box up the pizza for you," she said. "Your adoring fans apparently await their Santa Claus."

He could tell she'd meant it as an attempt at humor, but her voice had cracked on Santa Claus.

"I can stay—" he offered.

"No. Really. I'm fine." Charli pushed the box into his good hand. "Perfectly fine."

CHAPTER EIGHT

CHARLI STRETCHED OUT on her father's lumpy couch in his office, feeling the hills and valleys created from years of catnaps. *I'll wait ten minutes more, and if Neil doesn't show, I'm going home.*

She'd not slept well again last night—she could blame it on Neil and his Christmas lights, but the truth lay closer to the money still lurking in that safe deposit box. And a day's busy schedule with patients had left her exhausted.

Marvela had told her that she'd squeezed Neil into the schedule after Charli's last patient, saying he needed to have his arm checked on.

Charli had to admit mixed feelings about Neil. On the one hand, his blithe recipe for curing grief with hot chocolate and Christmas had just about got on her last nerve.

But on the other hand, she was disappointed that he hadn't shown up for his appointment. The prospect of seeing Neil again had kept her energy up through the back-to-back patients—

and her thoughts away from that money. Maybe what she needed to do was convince Marvela to extend their office hours and keep her too busy to think.

But Marvela had other ideas. "Honey, I mean, Dr. Prescott, you got to take care of yourself. You got to pace yourself. Your daddy just died. People will understand if you ease into things around here," Marvela had offered.

Charli wasn't so sure. Everyone she'd seen today and yesterday and all the days since she'd been home had complained that she didn't examine them like her father had.

Down the hall, she heard Marvela thumping and bumping around the front office, closing out the day and getting prepped for tomorrow. In truth, she was glad Marvela was running interference for her, watching over her. Marvela had been proud of Charli—"my little chic-a-dee," she'd said, wrapping her into a voluminous hug her first morning on the job. "All grown up and a doctor!"

So it was easier to bear since Marvela's helpfulness had been that way from the beginning, not since she'd lost her father.

She drew in a lungful of air still tinged with a trace of her father's cologne. The couch smelled like him. It felt like him. It was the closest thing she could get to a hug from him after a long and tiring day.

Why did you do it, Dad? Why did you put that money in that safe deposit box? Why didn't you report the outbreak?

She had thought of little else in the scant moments she'd had between patients, that and Floyd's advice to spend the money. Charli had a dozen good uses for that money—student loans to pay off, for one.

But the idea of spending money earned in any sort of cover-up—if that was what had happened—stuck in her craw.

Apparently, it had for her father, too. Unless he'd been intending to spend it on that clinic.

The front door opened. That squeak—she'd told Marvela to get someone to see about it, but Marvela said it was cheaper than a door sensor, with no batteries to change. Straightening up to a sitting position, Charli loosened her hair from its ponytail and began the business of tying it back.

"Don't do that on my behalf," Neil Bailey said from the doorway. The unexpected quietness of his arrival made her jerk in surprise.

"Marvela said she was busy, and that I was late, so I could just show myself back here and throw myself at the mercy of the doctor."

"She didn't."

Neil's dimples jumped again. "She didn't. She wasn't up front, so I just came back here. I'm really sorry for being late."

"Well, let's have a look at that arm, shall we?" Charli stood up and brushed off the couch fuzz. Her slacks still had deep creases from sitting all day, and the minicatnap had not been kind to them.

You're not out to impress him.

Was she?

"It's not really hurting anymore. Not badly, anyway. Do you have to look at it now?" he asked.

"I thought that was why you were here. Why you got the appointment." Charli yawned before she could cover it with her hand.

"Okaaay." Neil said, sounding as if he were going along with whatever she said simply because she'd said it.

Trying to inject a measure of professionalism—he had caught her more than once in a less than stellar condition—she walked briskly to the first exam room and opened the door, grabbing his chart out of the holder. "Here you go, and here's your chart."

"What? No nurse to take my blood pressure

and tell me to wait a bit for the doctor to see me?" Neil hesitated at the door.

"Since you were late, I told our nurse to head on home. You're our last patient."

"Oh. I really am sorry I kept you waiting when I'm sure you'd rather have gone home. I got tangled up with a phone call about an out-of-town subscription complaint. Lady is paying for her paper but only getting it every other week. Not a happy customer. I should have called."

"It's okay. It's not like I've got anything to run home to. I can't sleep, not with your lights next door. On second thought, maybe I should take a few minutes and run to the nearest Wal-Mart for a room-darkening shade."

"The lights really bug you that much? Yikes. I'll spring for the shade. How about it?"

"First, let's have you on the scales. Remember, I have nothing in my house to eat save blueberry yogurt, so I've got to do something about that, too."

"Blueberry yogurt is not food." Neil nodded his head a couple of times. "Yes. By all means. Let's go do something about this right now."

Charli laughed in spite of herself. "I'm beginning to think you have a phobia about doctors."

"I wouldn't say phobia. Phobia is too strong

a word. I don't go to doctors unless I really, really need them. Kind of like lawyers."

"Oooh, you didn't go there. Come on. I promise. I won't hurt you."

Maybe her dad was right when he'd bemoaned the fact that insurance companies and Medicare reimbursement fees mandated doctors have such a high volume of patients they couldn't do this simple start to an exam. It did seem very personal, to stand beside Neil as she adjusted the scale to his weight—a nice one hundred and seventy pounds that was distributed well over his six-foot-two-inch frame. Even more personal? Wrapping the blood pressure cuff around his muscled biceps. She hoped he didn't notice how her fingers fumbled. Who knew newspaper editors could be so buff?

But his systolic and diastolic pressures surprised her when the machine beeped its answer. "Wow. It's a little higher than I expected, given your weight and overall fitness, and so is your pulse rate," she said. "Does high blood pressure run in your family?"

"Er, no. I just get, ah, white-coat effect." Neil shifted his shoulders and wriggled on the exam table, making the paper covering rustle.

Charli bit back a smile. "Oh. Well, keep a check on it at home."

"It only does this when I'm with you." He gave her a sheepish grin and said, "I mean, with a doctor."

A little thrill stole through her—maybe it was her specifically who had bumped up his pulse rate. And not doctors in general.

He's your patient. And he's the number-one newspaperman in this town. You don't need...

What? What didn't she need? Why was Neil Bailey all the wrong things for her at this moment in time? When he was near her this way, she forgot all about those very good reasons.

Charli retreated from her mental confusion into the sanctuary of her medical training. She asked him to take off his sling, examined his fingers and the way the cast was holding up. It didn't go all the way up to his elbow, so she could check his range of motion in the joint. It seemed more limited than it had in the emergency room days earlier.

"You probably need to ditch the sling and start using that elbow more. You don't want the joint to freeze up," she advised him.

"Huh, the ortho guy, the one who put the cast on, told me to keep it in the sling."

Charli couldn't forestall a roll of the eyes. "Wait. Who's following up on this ɔrm? Is it me? Or the ortho guy?"

"I kinda didn't like him." Now Neil ducked his head and massaged the back of his neck.

"No?"

"No. I didn't. He was bossy. Told me that while I would probably be okay without surgery, he couldn't see me anymore if I didn't elect to follow his advice and have an operation."

"Ouch. He'd get a D in bedside manner and patient care." She considered Neil for a moment, noted the jut of his chin and the firm set to his jaw. "Looks like I'll need to find another orthopedics doctor to refer my patients to, one who will listen better to patient preferences," she muttered as she gave his fingers one more tweak. She froze, realizing what she'd said and to whom she'd said it. "Oh. That was unprofessional of me. I don't know why you bring out my candid side, but I find myself blurting out just about anything to you."

"That's good." The faint lines around Neil's eyes crinkled in amusement. "That's very good. Right?"

"No. It's not." She turned back to the desk and jotted down some notes. "Any pain? Swelling?"

"Some pain, but nothing Tylenol can't handle. And the only thing really irritating me is the itch."

"Be glad that it's not the summer. Take a hair dryer and blow down into the cast on the cool setting. And no coat hangers! You could scratch the skin and create an opening for infection."

"All done?" The rustle of the exam table paper almost rendered his question inaudible.

She looked up from his chart to see him yanking on the sling and already at the door. Neil had grasped the doorknob in his good hand and swung it open. "You going to bolt out of here?" she asked.

"No. I'm going to take you out to eat."

Yes! Her insides quivered in immediate reply. Common sense prevailed. "No…no. You're my patient. I can't."

Neil didn't seem at all convinced. "Come on. You know you want some supper. Company would be nice, too, right?"

Charli straightened up and closed his chart with all the primness she could muster. "Really, I don't—" A rumble from her stomach completely spoiled the effect.

To his credit, Neil didn't laugh. She could see the corners of his mouth quiver, but he managed to keep it to that.

She got up and ripped the table paper off.

Crumpling it up, she tossed it in the large trash bin. Sometimes if you didn't look temptation straight in the eye, it would leave you alone and in peace. And Neil? Well, he definitely tempted her right now.

From behind her as she went about the business of tidying up the exam room—everything her staff would have done for her the next morning—Neil said, "I still need that information about chickens. I'm interviewing you. Off the record. And you need to eat. We can get this done all at the same time."

Charli's stomach rumbled again, louder, like this time it meant business. "I don't know," she heard herself saying, and hated the way her voice lacked conviction.

She should go check on her mother—who didn't really need her as she still had her entourage clucking over her. No, Charli should go home and toss and turn until she figured out what to do with her father's slush fund.

She dispensed with the busywork and turned to face him full-on. He wasn't taking no for an answer. Neither, for that matter, was her appetite. "This is a conspiracy between you and my stomach. You're out to weaken my every resolve," she said, only half joking.

"Come on. You need fun. And I happen to

have two tickets to the county fair, which I, as a very bad member of the fair committee, still have not sold. I need you to go with me and use them."

"I thought you said supper." He had her confused now. To her horror, Charli realized she'd been picturing a more romantic dinner—complete with white tablecloths, a black-jacketed waiter and candlelight. *Oh, boy, Neil Bailey, you have got me in a twist. I shouldn't spend five more minutes with you.*

"I did. There will be corn dogs and hamburgers and cotton candy and funnel cakes—"

"Fair foods?" This was his definition of supper? "But I can't keep eating junk food and pizza. Oh, sorry, the pizza that you very kindly paid for was delicious, thank you, but it's not the most nutritionally dense food out there. I should never have ordered it. And anyway, a doctor shouldn't be seen—"

"Okay." Neil nodded, unfazed. "You could be a very good influence on me. I always figured pizza had the four food groups on it when you got the supreme version, but I can see your point. We'll grab a Subway sandwich on the way. You can't argue with that. I'll even make you drink water. But I tell you, you're gonna love the funnel cakes!"

"I…" Every last vestige of her willpower seemed to be deserting her. Had she used it up pulling too many all-nighters in med school and residency?

Neil tried again. "I'm going to tire you out so much, and distract you so much, my Christmas lights won't even register tonight."

She sighed and began pulling off her lab coat. "I need to grab my purse. I'm going to regret this, aren't I?"

"Not one second of it." And when he grinned, and those dimples jumped, Charli was toast.

CHAPTER NINE

As THEY APPROACHED the fairgrounds, the pulse of the Wurlitzer music lifted Neil's spirits even more than they already were. *I could get used to this,* he thought as he guided Charli through the turnstile line and handed over his tickets. *I could indeed.*

Once they cleared the turnstiles and they stood on the edge of the midway, Neil breathed in deeply; popcorn and the hot sugary smell of funnel cakes permeated the air. High-pitched squeals of excitement rose up from a neon-blinking flying-saucer ride that apparently was the hot ride of the fair. A beribboned clown with a rainbow wig hawking a big bouquet of pastel-colored cotton candy strolled past them. Neil took two quick steps in the clown's direction.

A half beat too late, Neil realized Charli had hung back. He turned, letting the clown make a clean getaway.

Charli's mouth was twisted in anguish, her

jaw clamped shut. When she saw him looking at her, she ducked her head.

"What?" Neil asked. A boisterous pack of middle-school boys had raced by as Charli had said something. Neil put his hand on her shoulder, tipped her face up to meet his. "What's wrong? Did you hurt yourself?"

"I don't think I can do this. I'm sorry." She started to say something else, broke off and tried to turn away from his gaze.

Neil guided her face back to meet his again. "Hey, Charli. What's going on?"

She closed her eyes, shook her head. "You go ahead. This was a mistake."

He took one of her hands in his and gently unfurled it. "You thinking about your dad?"

"Yeah—no, not exactly. The last time I was at a fair, my dad took me. I was maybe eleven."

From the wry expression on her face, that childhood trip to the fair hadn't been a raging success. Neil tried a noncommittal, "Yeah?" to encourage her to keep talking.

Charli shoved her hands into the pockets of the cardigan she wore. "Dad got ticked off with one of the guys running the games and cussed him out and it was—oh, well. Let's just say it wasn't a fun trip to the fair after that." She laughed, the sound broken and rusty. "I hid the panda bear I won—Dad said he really bought it for forty bucks—because every time I saw it, I'd think of that awful…" She shook her head.

Her shoulders slumped. Charli met his eyes, then dropped her gaze down at the straw at their feet. "This is crazy. What am I afraid of?"

He squeezed her shoulder. "I think you're afraid you'll have a good time."

Beside him, Charli sucked in a quick breath, and he realized he'd hit the nail on the head.

"Charli, I've been where you are. I know how bad it hurts to lose a parent. All I'm trying to do is to help you the way my dad and my aunt helped me."

"They took you to a fair when your mom wasn't even good and cold in the ground?"

"Work with me here," he pleaded. He looked around for some sort of inspiration, anything to help him get his next few words right for Charli. If he blew this, like he had with the hot cocoa, whatever door that was cracked open would surely slam shut.

But there was nothing to help him. The cotton-candy guy swapped his last bundle of the fluffy stuff for a token from a guy with three screaming kids. Neil wondered about the wisdom of trying to split one thing of cotton candy among all those mouths. Somebody was going to feel shortchanged.

"No, really." Her body was going rigid as she apparently worked up the willpower to refuse him. "I appreciate this…."

Neil saw how the dad knelt down, patiently dividing the cotton candy in handfuls for the kids, making it a game. It reminded Neil of *his* dad's patience with him in the days after Neil's mom passed away. He remembered the scary feeling that he would forget his mom, forget her by having fun.

The memory helped him keep his voice light and easy and calm. "Give me a half hour to snap some pics for the paper, a couple of rides, some cotton candy…and after that we'll go. You can endure anything for thirty minutes, right?"

Charli looked torn. He was sure she was going to do an about-face and dash out of the fairgrounds. But then one shoulder lifted and she scuffed aside a little hillock of straw with the toe of her shoe. "Okay. You win. I got through med school and residency, and that was a lot longer," she told Neil without much excitement. "Thirty minutes."

"At least." He offered her his arm. "M'lady? Our chariot awaits in the bumper cars!"

She blushed and wrapped her arm around

his. In a lighter voice, she said, "Lead on, my knight in shining armor. The spell ends in—" she glanced at her watch "—about twenty-nine minutes."

Forty-five minutes later, Charli hadn't looked at her watch once. She'd laughed, she'd proven she was no candidate for special-forces school with her bad aim at darts, she'd even consented to share a funnel cake with him.

They were high up on the Ferris wheel, her fingers gripped tight on the safety bar. "This isn't like any Ferris wheel I remember!" she yelled. "What happened to the slow glide?"

The wheel jerked back and forth, more like a mild version of a kid's first roller coaster. Neil actually preferred it. Charli? She looked petrified.

"Eh, we're okay. Open your eyes! You can see the whole midway and we're not even at the top."

She shook her head and left her eyes firmly closed. "I. Can't. I. Am. Praying."

"About what?" He tried to smother his laughter, but she must have felt it shaking his body beside her, because she scowled.

"That all of these nuts and bolts are tight!"

The contraption would pick that exact moment to give a mechanical groan as it winched its way higher still. The chair they were in was set to a violent swaying. "Aww, now," Neil said, feeling chagrined that what would be fun for him was obviously not for her. "It's not so bad, is it? Here, I'll hold your hand. That better?"

She kept her eyes closed. The breeze picked up tendrils of her long blond hair and whipped it across her face. Neil took his fingers, still holding hers, and pushed the strands out of her face. The curve of her cheek and her skin felt so smooth to his touch. But what really got him was how she had stopped freaking out. She had this studious look, as though she were examining sensory input from Ferris wheels for some sort of research project. Smart and brave—a killer combination. Impulsively he leaned in and kissed her.

"Oh," she murmured. She sagged against him, leaning into his kiss. She tasted of sugar from the funnel cake, and he decided at that moment this was the world's absolute best way to sample funnel cake icing.

The chair swayed again, breaking their kiss. Charli put her hand to her mouth. "I— Is—"

"First time for me. Never kissed a girl on a Ferris wheel." He held up his good hand in a palm-out "I swear" move. "But hey, look, it's going down. We could ride it up again and see if it's just as great a second time?"

"Oh, no—I've had enough of this contraption. Once my feet hit the ground, I won't be leaving terra firma again any time soon."

Neil liked the way she was at ease beside him as they stepped off the Ferris wheel. Back in the wash of the crowd, she seemed in no hurry to leave, didn't even check the time on her watch.

And then an unholy wail went up—a woman's anguished cry.

"My baby! My baby's hurt!"

Even over the raucous marching rhythm of the Wurlitzer, the fair suddenly seemed silent. It was as though the fairgoers were frozen in space for a moment.

Frozen except for Charli.

She'd taken off at a run, shoving through the crowd. "I'm a doctor, let me through, I'm a doctor, let me through!"

Neil followed her. She'd reached the merry-go-round, which had come to a stop. A small boy with impossibly curly dark hair was splayed out on the dirty floor of the carousel.

"Aw, just got the breath knocked out of him," shouted a big burly man in a plaid flannel shirt. He was pulling the woman away and had his hand outstretched to yank the boy up. "He'll be fine—"

"Don't touch him," Charli ordered.

Neil recoiled at the ice in her voice. He'd never seen this side of Charli. It didn't matter that the boy's father—for that's who it must be—was twice her size. She threw herself between the man and the boy. "I'm a doctor. Let me look at him. It may be you're right. But if he hasn't moved by now, he's at least got a concussion."

A woman fell on her knees beside Charli. "Oh, please, Doctor, help my baby—is he breathin'?"

"You mean, he could be—" The father broke off, not finishing his question.

Charli had leaned over, started assessing. She looked up. "Somebody call 9-1-1, tell them closed head trauma, possible spinal injury, get a chopper ready. Neil? Do you know CPR?"

His blood ran cold. "No."

She'd immediately started compressions, elbows locked, two hands locked together in the middle of the kid's chest, shoving so hard he was sure she was going to break the boy's ribs. "Anybody? CPR? I could use some help here!"

A guy with long greasy hair and wearing a muscle shirt showing off a sleeve of tattoos on each arm—had to be one of the carnival workers—swooped in beside her. "I do. You want chest compressions?"

"Better let me keep up with the compressions—careful with that neck—I'm at ten, eleven, twelve…"

"Got it," he said, and bent over the boy's mouth to give two breaths. She continued compressions and, despite the mother's wailing, never missed a count of the relentless, measured rhythm of her hands. She hollered out, "Did somebody call 9-1-1?"

Neil could barely work his fingers to get the phone out. By the time he had, someone else had been able to muster the strength to make the call. A pool of nausea formed in his gut. That child could die. Right here. The only thing between him and heaven was Charli and a tattooed carnival worker working in eerie synchronization.

The carnival worker jerked back as the little boy coughed and sputtered and flailed his arms. The crowd gave an audible gasp of relief. The worker swapped high fives with Charli.

Now she was hyperfocused on examining the little boy, murmuring to him to soothe him. He seemed scared and combative, not really making much sense, but Charli seemed elated at his change. The carnival guy leaned in, distracting the kid, cracking jokes that Neil wasn't sure the kid even heard.

He felt envious of the worker, a total stranger who'd known what he was doing, who could somehow understand the short, staccato orders Charli had snapped out.

And standing there, Neil felt less than worthy of Charli. She did something meaningful. She saved lives. She'd saved that kid's life. And him? He wrote articles about people's pet chickens.

The EMTs pushed through with their stretcher and loaded their tiny bundle on a backboard. Charli stayed beside them while they wheeled the kid over the uneven ground as gently as they could.

It was only when they loaded the kid into the ambulance, with the interior backlighting Charli leaning over the boy's stretcher, that Neil remembered his job. He lifted the camera, careful to avoid getting the kid's face due to privacy concerns, and captured the moment. Charli's expression had been filled with compassion—and professionalism. She definitely knew what she was doing.

As Neil dropped the camera back against his chest, she seemed to realize he was there. She looked up. "I really need to go and make sure he's stabilized. Sorry, I had fun—I did."

The ambulance doors closed, and Neil was left alone among the crowd.

CHAPTER TEN

CHARLI SCANNED THE emergency room's waiting area to see the parents of the little boy. The father appeared considerably more contrite now, while the mother's face was pale and drawn. Beside her sat, of all people, Louredes from the community clinic. Neil sat across from the trio.

"Mr. and Mrs. Chatham?"

Everyone scrambled to unsteady feet. "My baby—" Mrs. Chatham got out.

Charli grasped the woman's hands in her own. "Luke is stable enough for transport, Mrs. Chatham. We're flying him to Memorial Health University Hospital in Savannah. From what I can tell, he has a severe concussion. With these little ones, you don't want to take any chances."

"Can I see him? Can I ride with him?" the mother asked.

"Yes, you can see him, but no, you won't be able to ride with him. The chopper is very small, and the crew needs all the available space." Charli took in a deep breath before she plunged ahead as gently as she could. "Before I take you back, I want to get you prepared for what you're about to see. We've had to put Luke on a ventilator—a breathing tube—to help him breathe."

Mrs. Chatham crumpled and would have fallen had Louredes and Mr. Chatham not caught her. Neil stepped closer and helped guide Mrs. Chatham into a chair.

Charli felt the seconds ticking in her head— she couldn't wait much longer. The boy needed transferring. If she'd had her druthers, the helicopter would have met them on the scene, but that hadn't been possible in Brevis.

"Mrs. Chatham, we don't have much time before they fly him out. Why don't you come on back with me, and see Luke, and then afterward I can answer any questions?"

The family struggled up and toward the door, the mother mumbling regrets and prayers under her breath. Louredes and Neil stopped abruptly at the access doors, but Mr. Chatham turned to Neil.

"Could you—do ya mind? I'd appreciate it a whole heap if you'd come back here—you and Louredes. I might… I'm not too steady on my feet."

So Neil and Louredes followed behind them,

Charli wondering if Neil knew the family, and how Louredes figured into all of this.

Charli guided Mrs. Chatham into the trauma room, where blue-suited flight nurses were getting Luke switched over from the hospital's vent to the portable unit they used on the flight.

She stepped back, allowing the woman to keen over her son, the father to grasp his boy's pale hand in his. In her move to give the family privacy, Charli accidentally trod on Neil's toe.

"Oh, sorry," she told him.

He gestured for her to follow him into the hall. Louredes followed, as well. "Look," he told her, "These are just country folks. They don't have insurance. They're worried about the bills—that's why they called Louredes, because they usually go to the community clinic."

"It's okay. Memorial will help them with all that. They're not going to turn down a kid this sick just because he doesn't have insurance." Charli switched her gaze to Louredes. "I hope you told them that."

"I did...but they're worried about driving in Savannah, so Neil's going to take them down there."

"Oh, what a good idea! Louredes, you think of everything."

The woman beamed. "No, Neil was the one

who offered. But keep that good impression of me, because I'm gonna need a reference when the clinic closes."

"So it's still closing?" Charli glanced over her shoulder to be sure that the family didn't have any questions yet, then turned her attention back to Louredes. "There's nothing that can be done?"

"No." Louredes's chin wobbled, but she straightened up and lifted her head. "It's okay. It just wasn't meant to be. But bless your father, Dr. Prescott. Because of him, so many patients got care for a little while."

Charli's heart seemed to twist. To see what her father—this father she had never known—had worked so hard to build...

She didn't have the luxury of asking for more details now. A family waited—and one way to carry on her father's legacy was to be sure, insurance or no insurance, that this child got the absolute best care possible.

Charli returned to the bedside and began the process of guiding Mr. and Mrs. Chatham away so that the flight crew could complete the loading protocols. Charli knew from her own experience with her father how their hearts raced, how their minds couldn't take in her answers to their questions, how terrified they were at the prospect of Luke not making it. It gave her extra patience to answer questions she'd already answered, to give them time to stumble over what they needed to ask, to give them one more chance to squeeze Luke's hand before the flight crew whisked him away. The parents ran after the gurney, and Charli knew they didn't want to let him out of their sight.

She turned to Neil. "Thank you for doing this. It seems like you're always rescuing somebody."

"I'd say it was my pleasure but…is he going to make it?" Neil whispered.

"Kids are resilient—still, cross your fingers and pray. We've given him every chance. And he's stable. That's good."

"If nobody else tells you, I just want you to know…you were amazing," Neil said. With that, he pressed a quick kiss to her lips and dashed off in the wake of Luke's parents, leaving Charli to press her fingers to her mouth in complete and utter shock.

FROM CHARLI'S POSITION across the street in her car, the lights of the community clinic were dark, with only one or two fluorescents on for security purposes.

The day had been overcast, with low clouds

holding the promise of a rare snow flurry, and the temperatures had taken a sharp downturn. Now it was inky black, with rain beginning to drizzle.

All the better for what she was planning to do.

Charli's heart rate spiked as she reached for the envelope of cash.

Was she really going through with this?

The clinic can't close. And Dad wouldn't have let it, not with this much money squirreled away.

Charli had made up her mind only that afternoon, after she'd read Neil's article in the paper about the clinic's doors closing. Most people had thought she was reading Neil's laudatory article about how she'd saved Luke Chatham—who was doing much better but still at Memorial in Savannah.

In reality, she'd read and reread the article beside it—Neil's last-ditch plea for someone to save the community clinic.

People like Luke Chatham's parents and that proud diabetic she'd treated used the clinic. Without it, where would they go?

True, she could absorb some into her practice, but no other doctor in town seemed interested in the slightest about helping to fill the vacuum.

She had the money, even if it wasn't exactly hers. She had the means. Hang her med school loans. She'd pay them off some way. With that decision, she'd made a beeline for the bank, liberated the money and put together a shaky plan to drop off her donation.

With a label gun Charli had used in college, she'd printed out FOR THE CLINIC and ATTN: LOUREDES in the most generic Helvetica ever. She'd even used latex gloves to move the money into a priority mail envelope and put the label on. A bit paranoid, and definitely evoking cheesy TV crime shows about kidnappings, but it was better to be safe than sorry.

She'd toyed with the idea of just giving it to Louredes with strict instructions not to reveal who donated it. But what if Louredes was questioned about who'd given it to her? Maybe the IRS would need to know, even if the public didn't.

Charli wanted to avoid making trouble for her mom—who was already in enough pain—and her father's accountant had been crystal clear; declaring large sums of money could mean years of questions and large penalties from the IRS.

No, she'd thought. Better to do it in an anonymous way. But how?

Charli didn't want to send that much money through the mail, and she couldn't FedEx it—there'd be a record of who sent it. The best option would be to drop it off at the clinic and rely on the staff to do the right thing.

So that was why she sat, surveying the clinic. Casing the joint, so to speak. The rain pelted down harder on the roof of her car.

Now, how to avoid the video camera that was installed over the door? She'd stopped in earlier this afternoon to update Louredes on Luke Chatham's progress, and had noticed that very item. A businesslike camera perched over the door, and another one inside pointed toward the front entrance.

The only thing she could do was make herself as unrecognizable as possible—or give up on the whole enterprise. She'd have to walk through the empty parking lot and try to disguise herself as best she could.

In the car, Charli pulled a knit cap down low on her forehead, wrapped her scarf around her neck and tightened the belt on her raincoat. It was nondescript and black, and between the hat, the coat and her father's big black umbrella, maybe it would be enough to hide her identity.

Man, she felt as if she was preparing to rob the clinic, rather than gifting it with money it desperately needed.

She opened the car door and gasped at the knifelike cold swirling around her—both from the rain and the wind. Pulling her coat tighter around her and grateful for the knit cap she'd donned as part of her disguise, Charli crossed the street.

She almost lost her nerve at the corner of the vacant building beside the clinic.

This money isn't mine. It might not have even been Dad's—at least, not legally. It might have been a payoff. A man died.

She stood on the sidewalk, wind tearing at her, rain driving into her back, despite the umbrella. What she should do was go confess all to her mother, then talk to the police or the medical board or somebody who had jurisdiction over a twenty-year-old crime.

She leaned against the empty storefront, seeking shelter from not only the weather but also her whirling thoughts and doubts.

The same questions that had plagued her for days—weeks, now—kept yanking at her. Charli sighed, then stiffened as a lone car zipped down the deserted street. She ducked her head just in case anyone was looking her way. Yellowed newspapers dated from two years earlier covered the inside of plate-glass windows of the store, and no light gleamed from within.

If I don't do this, the clinic will be just this empty.

The car's engine noise faded as it rushed away, leaving her alone once again.

What Dad did or didn't do, I can't help. And probably nobody else could, either. If I report the money, nobody gets it, and the clinic closes. No matter what mistakes he made, he got this clinic right.

Charli sucked in a breath, squared her shoulders and called up the fortitude that had gotten her through every tough exam, every cranky professor's interrogations, every time her father had questioned her medical school ambitions. She was a few dozen steps from doing something good and lasting—and something she knew would make her father proud.

Across the blacktopped parking lot. Up the concrete steps. In the darkness, she fumbled, one-handed, for the mail slot by the door. For a heart-stopping moment, the thick package wedged itself in the slot and wouldn't go in or come out.

Despite the cover the porch offered, the wind yanked at the umbrella, threatening to turn it inside out and deprive her of part of her disguise. She tightened her grip on the umbrella's handle and pushed even harder on the envelope. She could do this. It would go. It had to.

Her scarf began unwinding, but she dared not let go of the umbrella—what if the video camera above her got a clear glimpse of her face? Finally, the stubborn envelope surrendered to the mail slot and dropped in the bin with a satisfying thud. Done.

The money was gone, the clinic safe and nobody had to know who'd come to its rescue.

CHAPTER ELEVEN

NEIL'S ARM ACHED. As he climbed out of the car and headed toward the doors of the community clinic, he wondered if maybe he should try something for the pain. A little ibuprofen in addition to the Tylenol wouldn't hurt, would it?

It was barely eight in the morning, and cold as a polar bear's toes. All Neil had really wanted to do was to roll over and go back to sleep until this wintry mix moved on and they had more palatable weather.

Still, Louredes had called in with some sort of crazy tale about an anonymous donation. A community newspaperman couldn't turn down a story. Last week's newsstand sales had been through the roof, what with the article about the little boy Charli had saved. Of course, the fair committee had bellyached about how he'd cut into ticket sales with his negative coverage.

Well, Neil had a business loan to pay off. He didn't intend to sensationalize events for the sake of increasing his print run. But that didn't mean he was averse to a genuine good story.

Including this one. The parking lot was empty except for what appeared to be the staff's cars. And...was that Charli's car?

No. It was the same make and model, but this little car had a spoiler on the back, and Charli's didn't.

Buddy, if you can already tell the difference between her car and every other one just like it, you might be in over your head.

Charli had called after last week's paper and given him an effusive thank-you for the article. He could tell she wasn't used to being on the front page of the paper. Neil had wanted to ask her out, but he figured maybe the reason she hadn't called him earlier—or come around the hedge to his house—was that he'd been completely useless in an emergency. Or maybe he shouldn't have kissed her so impulsively in the E.R. before he'd driven the Chathams to Savannah.

The whole thing had fueled a bunch of second-guessing but at least had inspired him to sign up for the next Red Cross CPR training session.

The door to the clinic was locked, though the lights were already on. Teeth chattering, he rapped on the glass. He wasn't usually cold, but the frigid temperatures gnawed at him through his jacket and jeans.

Louredes bounded up, inserted the key and unlocked the door.

"Come in! Come in! A windbreaker? Neil! We'll be treating you for double pneumonia if you don't dress warmer than that."

He stepped through the door to find the waiting room empty. The inside of the clinic felt blissfully warm after the bone-chilling cold outside. "Hey, Louredes. What's this about a donation? Couldn't it have waited until later today?"

The keys jangled as she locked the door behind him. She didn't wait for Neil. She marched to the door to the exam rooms with a quick stride that made her short legs appear as though she were almost jogging. "No! And besides, the police are coming, so you can get a picture of them, too."

"Police? For a donation? Why?" Louredes had him thoroughly confused as he followed her through the door marked Authorized Personnel Only.

"You'll see." Her words, delivered over her shoulder with a cryptic smile, mystified him.

He rounded the corner to find Wanda Headley, the clinic's interim board chair, at Louredes's workstation. She straightened up from inspecting several bundles of cash. *What the...?*

"Look, Neil! A miracle!" Louredes swept her hand over the money as though she were a magician pulling a rabbit out of her hat.

"Wow—who donated this?" It didn't take an expert in banking to see this was quite a haul.

"That's just it. That's the mystery. We don't know. It just appeared. Poof!" Louredes shook her head and sent her eyes skyward. "A miracle."

Neil tended to be a bit more cynical about miracles than Louredes apparently was, especially when the miracle turned out to be several thousand dollars. No—closer scrutiny revealed the heap of cash to be tens of thousands of dollars.

He worked his notepad out of his back pocket. Honestly, the one-handed note taking was the most irritating thing about his broken arm, that and the trouble he had to go to in order to shower. Maybe he should get one of those digital recorders.

But Neil hated the way a recorder made people anxious about what they said—plus, going through the recorded interviews was time-consuming and aggravating. No, it wouldn't be much longer until he would have two good working arms again. He flipped the notebook to a clean page and jotted down the date and the time. Pen poised above the page, he fired off the first question: "How much is it?"

Louredes clasped her hands together and squealed. "Oh, Neil! It's over one hundred thousand dollars! Do you know how much medicine that will buy? How many labs this money will pay for?"

Wanda spoke up in a subdued tone. "Don't count on it yet, Louredes. It may be a joke...or counterfeit...or stolen."

Louredes's shoulders slumped, but only for a moment. "It can't be, Wanda. We need it too much, and who would be so cruel as to do that to us?"

"So you don't have a clue as to where it came from?" Neil asked. Louredes had been right. This was a good story.

"No! It was in a priority mail envelope. Somebody shoved it through the mail slot. We've got them on video!"

"Louredes, I've been thinking." Wanda spoke up, her face pinched. "Maybe Neil shouldn't write the story at all until we get the all-clear from the police."

"But it's news," Neil insisted. "What would you gain from sitting on it for a week? It's going to be common knowledge by day after tomorrow, anyway—you know Brevis. So wouldn't it serve your purposes better if we went with the story and perhaps jogged a witness's memory about seeing someone drop off the money?"

Now Louredes's head bobbed in response to Neil's question. "Wanda, we have to let Neil tell the story. That's the only way we can thank this person."

He surveyed the women's faces. Louredes had her hands clasped in hope he would do the story. Wanda looked ready to collapse first and call her lawyer second.

Wanda ended the suspense. "I can see Louredes's point, Neil. I guess it can't hurt to go ahead and share it. And the public might have information. I guess if the police chief doesn't want you to do the story, you two can work out any embargoed information."

Neil let out a breath he hadn't even realized he was holding. "Okay. So let's hear what all your Secret Santa has been up to."

Louredes giggled, her eyes crinkling. "I like that. He *is* a Secret Santa. He's gonna make lots of our patients' Christmas dreams come true." Before Wanda could get out a word of warning, Louredes hurriedly raised a finger and added, "*If* we get to keep the money, that is."

A PERSON WOULD have to be under a rock to have escaped the buzz the donation had created in Brevis. And between her chatty patients and Marvela—who was plugged into all the gossip networks—Charli couldn't claim to be under a pebble, much less a rock.

Who would have thought it'd make such a big splash? Charli had halfway expected that Louredes would have kept the donation under wraps. But no—everyone and his brother knew about it, with some really weird tales about how and why it had happened. It was a million dollars, it was from a migrant who'd hit the lottery jackpot, it was from a farmer, it was from the hospital to keep the migrants out of the E.R... and on and on the stories went.

As she left the office, Charli was exhausted from having to pretend surprise every time a patient brought up another version—always slightly wrong and even wilder than the one before—of where the money had come from. After that sort of day, the last thing she wanted to do was field more questions about it, but that's exactly what the caller ID on her phone told her to expect.

"Charli!" her mother bubbled into the phone. "I've tried to get you all day! Did you hear about the clinic? Who on earth could have done that?"

No good deed. Charli wanted to bang her head against the steering wheel. Instead, she snapped her seat belt in place and started the car. "Mom…" Her hands-free switched over, and now her mother's excitement was in surround-sound stereo.

"It was a million dollars! A million—"

"Mom," Charli started again. "I heard. But it's not a million. It's only a hundred thousand."

Suddenly her mom's voice sharpened. "Really? How do you know? What have you heard?"

Charli gave herself a mental kick. "That it was closer to a hundred thousand and that someone's blowing smoke about the million. Besides, I don't think a million dollars would have fit in a single envelope." There. That sounded better. "Listen, Mom, I'm tired, I'm sleepy and I may have my facts all screwed up. You're right. What do I know?"

"Oh, honey. Why don't you come by the house and I'll make you some of that tea you like so much? And some supper? I'll bet you haven't eaten a real meal all day. You're a carbon copy of your father."

Charli knew better than to risk being around her mom—who could spot her telling a fib in a nanosecond in person, especially if Charli were this tired. One slip was warning enough. "It's all right, Mom. I'm too tired to even chew."

"Soup, then. I can make you a nice hot cup of soup. You could slurp that down."

For a moment, Charli was tempted. It would be nice to have someone waiting for her at home, with a steaming pot of soup on the stove. But if she went by her mother's, she'd surely screw up. And the one thing she didn't want to do was make her mother a knowing accomplice, even one after the fact, of her crazy, impulsive decision.

Time for distraction. "What did you hear about the donation, Mom? And why does it get you excited?"

The tactic worked like a charm. "Well, Clara Long was the first one who called me...."

And on it went, a convoluted tale of one gossip queen calling another to pass on the latest juicy news. Thankfully, nobody seemed to have a clue about who could have donated the money, and everybody referred to the donor as a man—for once Charli was glad to have gender bias work for her instead of against her.

"And Thelma was telling me that your Neil Bailey was planning on finding out exactly who this fellow is, and why he did it! Seems there's a video and maybe Neil can identify the donor—"

Charli gripped the steering wheel. "What?"

"That is a fine young man, Charli. I think he's a very good match for you. But you didn't join the community cantata—that would have been an excellent way to get to know him better."

"Mom!" Exasperated by the memory of her mother's clumsy matchmaking efforts, Charli still tried to tamp down the irritation so it wouldn't spill out in her voice. "I'm not some nineteenth-century girl who needs to be married off. Neil's just…well…he's—"

Her mother's response was uncharacteristically pragmatic. "He's one of the only single and eligible young men in town, Charli. You have to marry somebody. As to why I'm so excited about the donation…maybe because it was something that reminded me of your dad—something your father wanted to do, but he didn't have the money. Because of me. Because of my mistakes."

Charli turned onto her street. Even over the road noise, she could hear the sudden note of sadness in her mom's voice.

"Mom?"

"I'm going crazy, Charli. What am I supposed to do all day? All night? I never realized how much of my life centered around your father.

And now…" A muffled sob came through the car's surround-sound speakers, twisting Charli's heart. "I feel so useless. Nobody *needs* me anymore."

"Mom—Mom…" Charli tried to interrupt her mother's tears. She could hear her crying in earnest now and recalled those long tear-filled days leading up to the funeral. She should go stay with her. She could, maybe for an hour.…

"Mom," Charli tried again, this time more softly. "Forget about people needing you. How about the people who *want* you? Hmm? Your friends—the garden club ladies, the women in your Sunday school class. They adore you. They want to help you. They told me so."

Her mom made a little "meh" sound that could have either been agreement or despair.

"Well?" Charli prodded. "They've been eager to help out, right?"

"Delores Sanders did invite me to go to Macon with her and another of our girlfriends," her mom allowed in a near-whisper. "And Beattie Trilby suggested I help her teach a floral arranging class at the public library. Oh, and the Christmas bazaar… We have to get that started because that's the main fundraiser for the senior center. And…well, there's the Christmas tour of homes that I always do to help the Cancer

Society. I don't know, though, how I feel about decorating the house. I mean, it's not like your father's here to enjoy it."

Charli still couldn't imagine decorating for Christmas, either. Her mom had always obsessed about finding the perfect gift for her dad.... Charli didn't even want to think about how tough this Christmas would be.

Instead, she fixed on the thing she could feel good about encouraging her mom to pursue. "See? You are one busy lady—Neil told me so. I'll bet they're waiting for you to help them organize that bazaar. Besides, you do a much better job at arranging flowers than Beattie does." *Please don't let Beattie Trilby find out I said that. But anything to get my mama out of the house.*

"You don't think they're feeling sorry for me?"

"No, Mom. You're always the life of the party. You know that. They tell me that all the time—there's no fun until Violet gets here."

"Oh, you." Her mom's smile came through loud and clear. "You're just like your dad. You both always knew what to say to make me feel better."

I'm not like him at all. I love her, but living with my mom all the time would drive me bon-

kers. Instead, she settled on, "Well, I guess I'd better let you go so you can get started on the Christmas bazaar thing."

"Okay. Bye, honey."

Neil's blazing vista of lights welcomed Charli home. It was after eight-thirty so the music had shut off, but the lights would stay on until midnight, then come back on promptly at 5:55 a.m. to greet the morning working stiffs. She sat in the car for a long moment and stared at his Christmas display.

Meticulous. Detailed. There was not a bulb out, and even Rudolf, previously on the roof, had been set up in his new quarters on the last few square feet of real estate on Neil's front lawn.

If he puts half as much effort into investigating the donation at the clinic that he puts into his Christmas lights, I'm in trouble.

Charli had thought her angst would be behind her. She was rid of the money. She hadn't spent it on herself. So why didn't she feel better?

Stupid, stupid, stupid. Maybe if she'd looked harder at figuring out a way to wire the money or mail the money to the bank to be deposited to the clinic—but, no. In this post 9/11 world, large sums of money were suspicious, and cash doubly so. There simply hadn't been any other way.

You could have told the truth.

That boat had sailed. She'd given up that chance when she'd anonymously donated the cash instead of going to the police.

One of her professor's favorite mantras came back to her: "Fix it or forget it, or better yet, do both." Her prof had not been a big fan of self-flagellation. He'd hammered the quote into their heads, trying to get them not to sink into "the seductive swamp of self-loathing," he'd called it.

Right now Charli felt neck-deep in a swamp. A cold one. The chill of the night air had robbed the car's interior of its heat. She grabbed her briefcase and the piles of paperwork she still needed to go through and heaved herself out of the car. She felt like a pack animal, what with all the stuff she carted back and forth to the office.

Slam the door with her foot. Juggle the strap of her briefcase. Feel for her iPhone—yep, it was there. Fish out her house key. Avoid tripping on the steps—

The sound of a car's squealing brakes got her attention right before the headlights bore into her. Squinting into the glare, Charli saw a black-and-white police car turn into her drive.

CHAPTER TWELVE

HER HEART THUDDED in her chest. The car door swung open with a loud squeak, and the car's suspension groaned. Someone in uniform stepped out. She couldn't quite make out his face as the figure was backlit with all of Neil's Christmas lights. He hitched up his gun belt and limped toward Charli. His right foot came down quickly, then his weight shifted to the left, then the quick right, then the left. *Neuropathy from diabetes? Flat feet? He* is *a cop.*

"Dr. Prescott?"

She jerked her gaze above his ankles to his face, still shadowed by his hat. "Yes? Is something wrong?" She dropped her keys. Drat her numb fingers! Bending down, she scrounged around on the concrete for them. As she did, she heard the uneven thud of his footsteps carry through the cold night air.

Her fingers found the chilled metal of her key ring. She snatched it up and rose to a standing position. The cop had swept off his hat in deference—or maybe it was to scratch an itch, because he was rubbing sausagelike fingers across a bald pate that gleamed.

Good gracious. This member of Brevis's finest was a dead ringer for Mr. Clean—well, how Mr. Clean would look with a luxurious, over-the-top handlebar moustache. And he was bigger. And burlier.

"I'm Chief Hawkins with the Brevis P.D. Just needed to follow up."

Charli gulped. Chief? This was not the kind grandfatherly chief she remembered. This fellow must have been hired since she'd been away from Brevis. "Follow up on what, sir? I've been seeing patients all day, and I am dead on my feet. Can we possibly talk about this tomorrow?"

"Well, no can do on that. I prefer to interview witnesses when their memories are fresh."

"Fresh about what? Is this to do with one of my patients?"

"Oh, sorry. Didn't mean to alarm you. No, no. This is about that donation. At the clinic. Louredes said you were one of the last ones to visit yesterday. So I figured…"

Charli started to put the key in the door. She hesitated. Had she put away her dad's notebooks? Or were they locked up? She thought she'd put every one of them back into the desk, except for the one she'd been reading at bedtime the night before. If she let in the chief, then wouldn't he have implicit permission to poke around?

I haven't committed a crime. Not exactly.

Chief Hawkins stood there, as patient as an oak tree, waiting for her response.

"I'm sorry," Charli told him. "I couldn't tell you anything about that donation. I thought it was pushed in the mail slot?" *Okay, if you don't invite the man in out of this freezing cold, he's going to be even more suspicious.* Charli stuck the key in the door and turned it. "Won't you come in?"

"I believe I will. You know, these are some record lows. If you've got any plants out, you'd better get 'em in tonight."

The chief closed the gap to the steps in a couple of uneven strides. Charli let him in and realized she didn't even have so much as a doughnut to offer the man. She dumped her briefcase and the pile of folders onto the pine dresser. She worked her way out of her coat, her gloves and her hat.

"I'm sorry, but I haven't been grocery shopping, so I can't offer you much. I can make some coffee."

"Coffee'd be great," he said. He settled into the chair Neil had sat in a few nights previously. Neil had graced the chair a lot more than Mr. Clean here did.

Charli started in on the coffee preparations. In her anxious haste, she put one too many measures of coffee in the basket.

Oops. Hope he likes it strong enough to wake the dead. She scooped out what she could in as an unobtrusive manner as possible. She was wired as a coat hanger as it was, and drinking this lethal brew would screw up any chance at sleep she had.

"So what do you think I could tell you about that donation, anyway?" she asked as she dumped as much of the extra coffee back into the container as she could.

"I figured you might be able to tell me if you saw anything suspicious. Ya know, anybody hanging around. And I had something particular that I was wanting to ask you."

"Well, I'm honored, then," she said, and realized too late it came out flippant. "I'm sorry. I'm so tired I'm punchy. You'll have to forgive me."

"Punchy myself. One of my guys up and left, and so we've been working killer overtime. Mayor's not happy about it, but what do you do?"

The coffee burbled into the carafe, and its strong aroma swept through the tiny kitchen. Charli plunked the sugar bowl onto the table with a teaspoon from the drawer. The chief sat in the chair, his arms folded across his chest, his eyes narrowed.

He knows it was me. He's going to ask me where I found the money. And I don't have a clue what to tell him. Desperate to escape his penetrating gaze, she jerked open the fridge.

"You'll want cream, right?" The carton of half-and-half sat beside the Greek yogurt in the otherwise bare refrigerator, now that she'd washed and returned the Tupperware. Taking a sniff of the half-and-half, she shuddered. "I'm sorry. That one is a dead soldier," she told him as she closed the carton and tossed it in the garbage. "I think I may have some nondairy creamer...."

Back to her cabinets, where she rooted around, at last coming up with a microscopic jar of the fake stuff.

"Don't hang out here much, do you," he observed.

"Like I said, I'm always busy with patients. Tonight was supposed to be an early night."

What am I supposed to say? To hide her confusion and anxiety, she whirled back around to the cupboard. "We'll need cups, won't we?"

Can he tell I'm nervous? Oh, yeah, the clank of the cups in her hand probably told him she was a trembling wreck. She set them down on the counter by the coffeemaker before she could drop them on the floor. At last the coffee finished brewing, and she poured two cups.

"Well, now," the chief said as Charli set his mug before him and took a seat across from him. He beamed, causing the tips of his moustache to flex upward and revealing a healthy set of chompers. "Thank you kindly for the coffee." Digging in the teaspoon, he added three heaping spoons of sugar and stirred briskly. Charli gawked at the amount of sugar he'd put into his coffee.

He took a sip. "Whooo-wee, but you like it strong, don't you?" Taking the sugar spoon in hand, he dumped another small mountain of white crystals into his cup.

"Uh…"

"That's my kind of coffee."

The small talk was killing her. She was five seconds from blurting out the truth. Was this his secret interrogation weapon, to sit back and wait for a person's nerves to do his job for him?

It's working. Give me a boil on a backside to drain any day. I am so not cut out for a life of crime.

He took another sip, smacked his lips and dabbed his moustache with a napkin. "Well, now. About all this money."

"It was a lot, wasn't it," she murmured. Her coffee mug felt warm as she gripped it tightly with her fingers to steady it.

"Yep. One hundred fifteen thousand, one hundred seventy-six dollars. That is a lot of dough."

"But it's not a crime to donate money, right? So the clinic should be able to use it." She waited for his answer as he crouched over his mug and took another deep draft of coffee.

"That is some fine coffee. Let me guess, imported? You doctors, you like the expensive stuff, don't you? I'll bet it's fresh ground beans."

"No. No. Just from the grocery store. Out of a container." *And about a third too strong.*

The chief frowned. "This stuff? From the grocery store?"

"From the grocery store," Charli concurred. She set her cup down, hard enough to slosh the coffee. He didn't seem to notice.

She repeated her earlier question. "So it's not a crime, right? To donate cash?"

"Nope. Kind of hinky. But not a crime."

She relaxed. "Oh, good—"

"Unless the money was the proceeds of a criminal enterprise. Say drugs. Or a prostitution ring. Cash, well, it worries me."

He didn't look worried. He looked implacable, his forehead smooth, his moustache working back and forth as he sipped his coffee. He drained the cup and stuck it out to her. "Don't mind if I do."

Charli sprang up. "Oh, sure, have some more." It glugged into the chief's cup like black tar.

His cup refilled, she settled back into her chair. Surely now the questions would come.

They didn't.

"So how do you find out?" she asked. "About the money?"

The chief turned a meaty palm upward. "Don't rightly know, but don't tell anybody I told you that. It's above my pay grade, for sure. There's all sorts of forensic stuff people expect you to do these days—the other day, somebody wanted me to fingerprint their car after it got vandalized. Mind you, it was raining that night, and the window was broken out with a brick." He shook his head. "But still, just to shut 'em up, I had to get out my fingerprint kit and dust that brick. A brick! Course there were no prints to speak of on it. And they didn't believe me when I told 'em that without specialized methods, we weren't gonna be able to get any fingerprints off their car. I mean, my lift tape won't even stick to wet metal."

"Oh. So what will happen?" she asked. Her pulse slowed at least ten points. This was going to be okay. He wasn't going to trouble himself with an unsolvable case.

The chief frowned and shrugged. "They turned it in to their insurance company and— oh! You mean about the money. Well, I guess I'll do what I always do when I got a case that's hinky and I don't have the resources. I'll call in the Georgia Bureau of Investigation. They'll come down, print the money, all that."

Charli choked in surprise, and hoped he hadn't seen the reaction for what it was—a confession that she had anything to do with the money. "The GBI?" Her heart felt as though it might be going into v-fib any minute as it thumped way up into her throat.

Print the money? Her father's fingerprints— her fingerprints—were probably on that money. Had her dad ever been fingerprinted in a database that was still searchable?

She was pretty sure her own fingerprints

weren't lurking in the state's database—any time her fingerprints had been taken for background checks, she'd always been assured that they were deleted afterward.

But her father's?

Too late now.

"Not that they'll turn up anything useful. Do you know how hard it is to fingerprint money? Especially *old* money?" Chief Hawkins laughed loudly, his white teeth on display, his chest shaking behind the tightly stretched white polyester uniform shirt he wore. "*CSI.* Bet you feel about all those doctor shows like I feel about *CSI.*"

Charli kept her mouth closed and her fingers tightly laced together.

The teeth disappeared and the moustache's handlebars once again pointed down. "So you didn't see anything, huh?" The question caught Charli by surprise.

She swallowed. Her throat was dry now, in addition to housing a runaway pulse. "No. No, I didn't see anything that evening. Nothing suspicious."

He lifted his chin, drew his brows together and scrutinized her. "Why'd you stop by?"

"I—uh, sir?"

"You have a patient there or something? You work for the clinic sometimes?"

"Not exactly." At least she was prepared for this one. "I was updating them on Luke Chatham, the little boy who got hurt at the fair. He was their patient, but I treated him."

"Sad thing, about that boy. He's doing better, though. Right?"

"Yes."

"And that's all? That's all you talked about?"

She swallowed. Surely this man knew something. Why else would he be in her kitchen, drinking the vilest coffee ever perked? "I'd helped them out a few days ago, and they'd wanted me to volunteer some more. I—I was letting them know I hadn't forgotten them."

He set the coffee aside and steepled his fingers. The chief gave her a hard stare. "Feeling guilty, are you?"

"Sir?" Had her voice come out as choked as it had sounded to her?

"About not helping them more? I wouldn't. They're always coming by the police station with all manner of fundraisers. Sometimes they're peddling something, sometimes they flat out ask for money. They'll hit you up before too long. Mark my words."

Charli breathed out as slowly as she dared. "I expect so," she managed to get out with as little squeaking as possible.

"And you didn't notice anything?" he asked again.

"No." That was true.

"Nobody around?"

Charli shook her head.

"Did you happen to notice the bin under the mail slot? I mean, whether it was empty?"

"Sir?"

"Well, we got this video, and it shows somebody doing something, but I can't assume that it really was the person who donated the money. Not unless I can rule out whether that bin was empty at the close of business. Louredes can't say for sure, but she thinks it was. They don't check it before they leave. So how about it?"

"I—I didn't pay attention," Charli said. She debated on whether to offer a red herring of a clue—after all, she could describe the envelope to a *T*.

But no. She'd stick with the truth, as far as she could.

"Hmm." He pursed his lips, hardly visible behind that extravagant moustache. For a moment, he sat there. He rubbed his palm over his scalp. "Here's what I want to know," the chief suddenly burst out. "I've wanted to ask you this since I got in the squad car and headed over here."

Her fingers wanted to clench into fists. She forced them to relax. The fabric of her tweed slacks was nubby and rough to her flattened palms.

"Yes?" Here it came, some question she could not answer, the one answer that would give her away.

"Can you look at my big toe? It's killing me… been killing me for days. I got this ingrown toe-nail so bad I can hardly walk on it, and the wife is threatening to make me go to her podiatrist."

"Your big toe?" The whiplash change from the money to the chief's big toe momentarily floored her.

"Yeah." The chief nodded. "And that guy— well, he's slow as Christmas, and I figured you could get the job done here."

"Oh." This was it? The thing he'd wanted to ask her? Was this the reason he'd chosen to come himself, to hit her up for complimentary medical care?

He must have taken her silence as a no be-cause he levered himself from the chair and re-trieved his hat.

"Aw, forget it," he said. "It's probably not ethical for you to treat me at home, huh? With all this overtime, I can't take off to go to that guy—"

"No. That's okay, Chief. I understand." Charli didn't hesitate. She moved off her chair and pulled it close to serve as an impromptu exam table. "You sit right back down and take your shoe and sock off. I'd be glad to look at your ingrown toenail."

At least it's not a boil on his backside.

CHAPTER THIRTEEN

"GOT ANY MORE of this week's papers, Neil? We've sold out, and people are asking for more."

Raucous background noise nearly drowned out Ida Cunningham's words over the phone connection. Neil figured the morning round-up session at Ida's Gas-n-Go had come to order. In addition to gas, lottery tickets, cigarettes, soft drinks and any kind of junk food that ever called for preservation with sodium benzoate, Ida ran a short-order kitchen out of the convenience store and had a couple of booths in the corner where the old-timers gathered.

As he stood behind the counter at the newspaper office Wednesday afternoon, Neil tucked the phone between his good shoulder and his ear to reach for his spare box of papers on the shelf behind him. His stash was thinner than he'd remembered. "Ida, I've got…exactly two dozen."

He spread one of the papers out. A big, splashy headline—Secret Santa Brings Gift Early—

stretched six columns wide under the banner. Anchoring the story was a three-column color shot of the heap of old greenbacks, with Louredes grinning with joy as she held one of the packets. Neil had titled a boxed sidebar Who Is Brevis's Secret Santa? and had rounded up the community's various theories of who the donor might be.

This week's edition had been his bestseller yet in the entire year he'd had the paper. Something about Santa and the mysterious money had hit all the right buttons. A few more issues like this, and he'd be more than ready for the lean January to come.

Ida groaned. Neil could swear he heard a head slap on the other end of the phone. "Oh, come on, Neil! You know you've got to have more! Don't hoard 'em! People get mad when they come in here and I don't have a paper. They get riled up and leave without buying anything."

The bell on the door jangled behind him. Neil shoved the box of papers back in its place. "I'm sorry, Ida. I didn't realize they'd go so fast, so I didn't order an extra big print run. You know you could actually subscribe and you'd have access to the digital edition—"

"What? Then I'd have all these yahoos hounding me for that free Wi-Fi everybody's going on about. Plus, you know how many people can huddle over a computer screen? Three. But with a real newspaper, you spread it out and everybody can share. So give me all two dozen—"

"I can give you exactly six. I need a few here, plus I have to save a dozen for bound copies and archives."

She said something decidedly unladylike but all too decidedly Ida-like. "Oh, all right. Bring me the six."

"In a few. I need to make some calls, see if there's anything new on the Secret Santa."

"But I don't have any more papers, Neil!" Ida howled.

"Hey, take comfort in the fact that nobody else has any, either," he told her.

She didn't sound at all cheered up about that, just hung up the phone in a huff.

Neil put the phone down. "Can I help—"

He stopped midsentence as he turned around to find Charli on the other side of the front counter, holding down the worn square of dun-colored carpet just inside the door. He took in a breath before saying, "Hey."

The sunlight streaming in the front plate-glass windows turned Charli's hair a shimmering gold.

She didn't look tired now. She looked...good. Really good. Sophisticated in a trench coat that was cinched at the waist, over slacks and a print blouse, and she'd even tied another one of those frilly scarves her mother made in a complicated way that made her look like a model in a magazine.

She looked like a doctor. While he...

Well, suddenly the old flannel shirt and the jeans with the hole in the knee that had seemed just fine this morning had slid from Brevis's business casual to complete slob.

"Hey," Charli replied, smiling.

"I've been moving the arm." To emphasize the point, Neil pumped his arm, sans sling, and showed her how much range of motion he had.

"Good! Keep at it and you may not need physical therapy." Charli's fingers strayed to her scarf. Her mouth parted—it was such a kissable mouth, Neil thought. Just the right shade of pink, with just the right amount of fullness.

And then he remembered she hadn't made one mention of that kiss on the Ferris wheel. Or the goodbye kiss he'd planted on her before taking the Chathams to Savannah.

He struck what he hoped was a casual lean against the front counter. "Well, skipping physical therapy would be a relief, both in the pain and annoyance department and to the wallet. How can I be of service?"

She nibbled on her bottom lip. Neil marveled at the whiteness of the nicely even teeth as they did precisely what he wanted to do to her mouth.

Get it together, Bailey.

But moving his gaze farther up her face didn't help much. All he saw were those big blue eyes as they darted first toward him, and then downward. Her eyelashes, incredibly long, fluttered against cheeks that were touched with just a hint of pink. He wondered how those lashes would feel if they were grazing his face.

Maybe she is remembering that kiss, he thought.

But she didn't mention kisses or Ferris wheels or compliment his Christmas decor. She just extended her hand and dropped two quarters on the counter. "I came to buy a paper."

Without hesitation, or a bit of guilt, he pulled one out of the half dozen he'd promised Ida. "Good thing you came by when you did, because I'm pretty much sold out all over town."

"Wow, all this fuss over someone who obviously doesn't want the attention," she said. She shifted the strap of her handbag on her shoulder.

"So what's your theory about Santa?" he asked.

"Didn't you know?" Charli gave him an arch grin. "He's a fairy tale made up by masochistic parents."

"No, I'm serious. About this guy." Neil thumped his knuckle on the article.

"Probably just someone trying to do a good deed. Not everyone wants to advertise their generosity to the world. So does this issue cover the latest on the money? Have you heard anything more? Did the clinic get to keep it?"

"Not yet. It's still at the crime lab."

Charli appeared to be on the verge of asking another question.

The door jangled again. Darius Heath burst through, one hand hitching up a pair of overalls that stretched over his wide expanse of a belly. Neil stifled a groan.

Darius was a talker who would park it here all afternoon and wax on about the pros and cons of different lures on trotlines—only slightly irritating on days when Neil had nothing better to do, but hugely annoying when he had something pressing.

Or someone. Like Charli.

Neil was glad to see her face had fallen at the interruption. He'd expected her to step back, let

Darius closer to the counter. But though Neil could see her body turn toward the door, her feet still pointed straight toward him. Neil wondered if that pop-psychology business about the direction of feet really meant anything, or was it pure baloney?

Charli began again. "I—you know, I was curious—"

Darius steamrolled around Charli, nearly knocking her sideways. "Hey, Neil! I netted me a whopper of a catfish! It's bent my hook and weighs nearly sixty pounds! Come on out to the truck, where I got it in a bucket. You can get a picture of me holdin' it."

"Wow! That's a big one. Sure, I'll be with you in a minute, Darius. Charli, I—"

Darius turned around, registering Charli's presence. "Oh, you got the new Dr. Prescott in here! I's just thinkin' about comin' around to see you—this here is perfect timing." Darius looked back over a meaty shoulder at Neil. "Neil, buddy, you know what I say about timing—that only true fishermen have got talent at perfect timing."

"That's right, Darius. That's what you tell me." *Every blessed time you come in here.*

Charli had donned her professional "doctor" smile. "Why, thank you. It's Darius Heath, right? Well, Mr. Heath, call the office and make an appointment and—"

Darius frowned. He reared back and surveyed her from his considerable height. Charli, despite her high heels, barely came to the man's midchest.

"Aw, your daddy never fooled around with appointments. I could just find him on a street corner somewheres, and he'd doctor me. And don't think I didn't forget him, or that I was some sort of deadbeat lookin' for free medical advice, no siree. Many's the string of fish I laid on his back doorstep, yes sir! He got his money's worth. Told me my fish were the best-tastin' fish he'd ever eaten."

Charli's head dropped in a slow incline, then rose again. "I seem to remember that," she replied.

In an instant, Darius was pushing down the straps of his overalls and had his plaid shirt splayed open and slid off. He stood in the middle of the newspaper office clad from the waist up only in a stained undershirt that smelled strongly of fish. This he jerked up, showing a mound of doughy white belly fat.

"See here?" Darius pointed to a straight line of blisters around his waistline. "I got in some kind of poison ivy." Darius's version of the word *poison* came out *pie-zun*. "But glory be if I know how. Since your daddy found that mela-mamma cancer on me and sent me to that cancer doctor, I been real good about wearin' long sleeves and hats and all. It burns and itches and pains me somethin' awful. So what is it, Doc? Can you tell me what plant I done got into so's I can avoid it? And maybe I can go over to the county extension office and find out what to spray on that demon vine to kill it."

"Umm…" Charli bent low to inspect the angry scarlet line of blisters Neil could clearly see even from behind the counter. "Mr. Heath, I can't be positive in this light, but I believe you may have a good case of shingles."

"The shingles!" Darius leaped back, bumping into the counter with such force he knocked over the stack of newspapers Neil had sitting there. "That ain't the cancer come back, is it?"

"No, no, it's not—why don't you stop by my office so I can get a better look under my exam light."

The door jangled again, this time Olivia McBain. "Gracious!" the prim little librarian gasped. "Put your clothes back on, Darius Heath! Before I get a switch to you!"

"Miss McBain, I's just gettin' Doc here to look at my very important skin disorder.…"

The librarian soured her lips and sniffed. "I don't care if it's jungle rot, Darius. You can't be taking your clothes off in public. You're not six anymore, you know."

Darius began to dress himself, hanging his head. "Yes, ma'am. The doc was just here, and I just thought—"

"You didn't think a thing, that's what you didn't do. Now, if you had something on your face—this little mole here, for instance…" Olivia jabbed a finger against a mole at the corner of her mouth. "Dr. Prescott, don't you think I should have this removed? Because of the risk of cancer? I mean, it's on my mouth, so easily irritated."

With a sinking heart, Neil saw Charli take a step back toward the door. "You know, I think you'd better come in so I can have a look—"

Darius broke in. "Doc's got a newfangled exam light, she does, and it shines on it and tells you if you've got the cancer. I'm gonna go by and have her shine it on me."

Charli had taken two more steps back. "Call Marvela, Miss McBain. She'll fix you right up with an appointment, and we'll see exactly what's going on."

And then she bailed on Neil, leaving him with two less-than-satisfied patients—and her paper still on the counter.

CHAPTER FOURTEEN

OUTSIDE ON THE SIDEWALK, Charli dearly hoped Neil would run interference for her until she managed to get to the sanctuary of her car.

Charli had clicked her car's key fob to unlock her door when her phone buzzed. She answered it, and Lige Whitaker greeted her with his usual Southern charm.

"I know you're busy, but do you mind stopping by my office, Charli? I need to go over something with you."

"Which office? You only have, what? Two?" She couldn't help but tease her father's friend a bit. He had a finger in every pie in town, it seemed.

Lige, as usual, didn't take offense. "Three, actually. One at the farm, one at the bank and then one at the hospital, and that's about three too many. Today I've got my hospital hat on, so come on across the street. I guess you're at your dad's—I mean, your—office?"

"Actually, no, I was downtown. I'll be there in a bit—five minutes or so?"

"Sure."

Five minutes later, Charli poked her head into the small office Lige kept at the hospital, just off the conference room.

"Am I in trouble?" she asked.

Lige peered over reading glasses and waved her in. "Come in, come in. Shut the door behind you, and pull up a chair."

She obeyed, worry bubbling up within her for the first time. It wasn't like Lige to call anybody into his office. Usually, if he needed to speak to people, he simply stopped in their office or shop. It was part of his "no pretensions" persona. And if it had something to do with the day-to-day running of the hospital, the hospital administrator would usually handle it. Lige was generally a big-picture sort of guy.

So why was Charli here?

He didn't enlighten her for a moment or so, just continued scrawling signatures on paper and reviewing what looked to be an Excel spreadsheet.

He was like no other hospital board chair she'd ever seen, that was for sure. Charli could smell hay and cigarette smoke waft off him. From the long fingers of his left hand dangled the source of part of the odor—a forbidden half-smoked cigarette with a long gray bead of ash. Lige must figure the hospital's strict no-smoking rules didn't apply to him.

Then he sighed and stubbed out the cigarette in a battered plastic ashtray. He pushed aside the paperwork. "That'll keep. How are things going?"

Was the question small talk or was this the reason for the meeting? She folded her hands and tried not to let her nervousness show. "Busy. I can see why Dad wanted someone to help out with the practice."

"Chuck was a great doctor. There's been some talk that we should rename the hospital after him, in fact, for all he did for the community. He was proud of you, Chuck was. And yeah, he was looking forward to handing it off to you." He beamed. "I'm glad you're busy. I was a little worried you'd find it hard to get established here quick enough to suit you. Some doctors—the new out-of-towners who come in from med school—they complain, say there's not enough volume, and then they're outta here for greener pastures. Got to pay off those student loans."

"Those loan balances do tend to grab your attention once you graduate," she allowed.

"So your dad didn't leave you any money to help with that?" Lige asked.

This was bordering on too personal for Charli, even if Lige had known her father for decades. "You knew my dad. You said it yourself. He wasn't much for business."

"True, true." He leaned forward and removed his glasses. "I take it you're not too busy to do me a special favor? Not a favor, actually, because I'm willing to pay for it."

"What sort of favor?"

"Nothing too big. It shouldn't take up much of your time. In fact, your father helped me out like this now and again."

"If I can help, you know I will," Charli told him.

Lige rubbed his chin and nodded approvingly at her. "That's what I like, someone who remembers who her friends are. That's why it's refreshing to have a hometown face back here."

If his words were supposed to be taken as a compliment, they had the opposite effect. They made Charli uneasy. She found herself regretting her offer to help him.

I did say "if."

"So what's this project?" she asked.

"You know I've got a lot of workers coming

in. It's onion planting time. Some of 'em aren't feeling so pert."

That was all? "Sure. Send them to my office. Marvela will block out some appointment times—"

He cracked his knuckles. "See now, that's not what I had in mind."

"I beg your pardon?"

"Your dad, now, he would work with me. He'd either drive out to the farm or they'd come by his office after hours."

Charli stared at him, perplexed. "Lige, I don't see what the problem is. If they're uninsured and you're worried about containing costs, I'll do my best. Or better yet, why not send them to the community clinic. I mean, they cater to migrant workers and speak Spanish better than I could ever dream of."

"I don't think you quite get it, Charli." Lige's jaw tensed, and she could see his eyes had lost their twinkle. "I want you to do this. Just like your dad did. And I'll pay you. Just like I paid your dad. We don't need to be bothered with any paperwork."

The tiny office seemed to close in on Charli, the room rank with the smell of Lige's cigarette. She could focus on nothing but his face, tanned and wrinkled from years in the sun. She'd never felt intimidated by him before, but suddenly, though he sat across from her behind a cheap desk wearing his trademark chambray shirt, she was afraid.

Because she knew. She knew where that hundred thousand dollars in her father's safe deposit box had come from.

"Lige, if you're asking me to treat patients, I'll be glad to do that. I'll even be glad to do some indigent care work for you. But I won't cover up whatever it is you're asking me to cover up for you."

He laughed. Fifteen minutes earlier, that laugh would have completely taken in Charli. But now? When she'd seen the hard light in his blue eyes?

"Charli, I'm not asking you to do anything unethical. I mean, honestly. We're not bilking Medicaid here. We're not defrauding an insurance company. I'm just paying you to take care of my workers. Your dad did it."

"Did he cover up a TB outbreak for you?" she asked.

It was a rash question for someone in her position to ask, but she had blurted it out without thinking.

His chuckle came a few seconds too late to fool her. "Charli, what's the big deal here?

You're seeing conspiracy theories everywhere. So your dad and I had an arrangement. So sometimes he bent a few rules for me. What's important is the patient gets care, right?"

She stood up on knees that trembled. "I think you'd better get someone else to see to your farm workers, Lige."

He came around the desk, blocking her way to the door. "Charli, here's what I think. I think you've got the wrong idea. And I would hate for you to go off half-cocked, spouting stuff to people. I mean, I don't know that your dad actually reported all that income. I'd hate to see your mama have to deal with the IRS. Besides…it would be awfully hard to pay for it now that she's donated it to the community clinic."

"She didn't—" Charli clamped down on her words, but the damage was done.

"Doesn't matter who did, Charli. I can't help it if your dad didn't report income I paid him. I thought it was a little strange he wanted to be paid in cash all these years…."

"You liar." She spat the words. "You paid him in cash—just like you were hinting at paying me. Why did he do it? What did you have over him?"

"Who said I had anything over him? Maybe he was more pragmatic than you, Charli. Maybe

he understood that money was money, especially when he had a wife who spent it like
water."

He folded his arms across his chest. He was
so close now that Charli's nose twitched from
the overpowering stench of the cheap cigarette
he'd been smoking. She lifted her chin.

"The doctor I knew—the man I knew—
wouldn't have done this for money. And I won't,
either."

His mouth twisted, and he shook his head
in disgust. "You young kids. You don't know
how to work with people. You think you got all
life's answers handed to you with that medical
degree. Well, think again. You don't work with
me, I won't work with you. And your mama will
be mighty disappointed when that hospital isn't
named for your dad."

*He thinks that will get me to do his dirty
work?* "Dad wasn't much for ceremony. Thank
you, but the hospital doesn't have to go to that
length. Plant a tree instead," Charli told him in
a terse voice, and pushed past him.

"I'd give my offer some more thought, if I
were you."

The words were addressed to her back. She
heard the flick of a cigarette lighter before she
had taken another step.

Charli glanced back over her shoulder to toss another, "Thanks but no thanks," but what she saw in his face stopped her.

His eyes—cold, sharp, unrelenting in their intensity—didn't leave her face. His next words were as gruff as before. "You need to think about people beyond yourself, Charli. You need to think about all the folks who depend on you. Your mama. Marvela. Your nurse—what's her name? People who cross me—*doctors* who cross me—find themselves without a job and without references. And their staff? Their families? They're the ones who suffer for somebody else's pigheaded self-righteousness. Now that you got none of Daddy's slush fund left to pay off your student loans and help folks out, you *might* want to remember that."

With that, Lige rounded the desk, lowered himself into his chair and turned his attention to the paperwork on his desk. Charli couldn't get away from him fast enough.

It took Neil a solid half hour to persuade Darius to go bug someone else, and that was only after, in a rash moment of weakness, promising the man to do a half-page article on all of the lures Darius had invented. Ever.

In the meantime, Ida had already called twice

for the papers. "I need 'em now! Or you can save 'em for catfish wrappers. What sort of business sense do you have, boy?" she snapped the last time she'd called.

So Neil flipped the closed sign on the door, ushered Darius out ahead of him and twisted the key in the lock.

In the car, bracing the steering wheel with his cast, Neil dialed his contact with the Georgia Bureau of Investigation.

Brian Mulford answered on the first ring. "No."

"What?" Neil tried to push a note of aggrieved injury into his question. "I call you to—"

"You call, nothing. You call to get the dirt on somebody or something or wheedle me into running a tag or do a criminal background check. Buddy, you owe me about five pizzas for all the free work I've been doing for you. How many *Georgia Press* awards have I won for you?"

"Three. Give up the badge and the gun, and you can be a reporter, too," Neil told him.

"Then what would I use to shoot aggravating newspaper guys like you?"

"And if you shoot me, who would make you

look good on the front page? How many promotions and pay raises have I earned you?"

Brian bellowed with laughter. "All right. Five. You win on that score. I guess we're even. You do have a way of paying me back dividends. So what's up?"

Neil made the turn onto the main drag and drove out to near the county line. There, in the middle of nowhere, sat Ida's Gas-n-Go, a mecca for gossips and junk-food lovers alike. The parking lot was overflowing with pickups and SUVs, all featuring gun racks and hunting logos. Neil had made the mistake of going hunting just once—and embarrassed himself by pleading for the life of the deer he was supposed to shoot.

"The video from the community clinic," Neil started as he pulled into a parking space. "You heard anything back on that?"

"Weird case, huh? Somebody wants to donate a hundred big ones, they can come find me and give me some charity." Brian started listing all the ways a hundred thousand dollars would come in handy, from bass boats to a year's supply of pork rinds.

Neil cut him short. "Well, anything pop on the video? Or something else? You know, fingerprints on the money?"

Brian scoffed. "Are you serious? Man, don't believe what you see on TV, okay? Yeah, we got prints on the money. Partial prints. Smudged prints. Thousands of 'em. Anything *usable?* What do you think, genius?"

"I take that as a no."

"And you would be a winner."

"So nothing, huh?" Neil saw Ida, standing at the door of her establishment, hands on her generous hips, hair sticking out like Medusa's snakes. He levered himself out of the car, only banging his hurt arm once.

"Well…" Brian's voice took on that note of self-importance he always used when he was in the possession of anything resembling a clue.

"Give." Despite Ida's frantic waving, Neil stopped halfway to the convenience store's entrance. Trying to hear anything in Ida's establishment was a fool's errand.

"Not for publication, right?"

"You've got a witness?"

"A witness? Is this even a crime? Giving away a hundred grand is not exactly a crime, least not according to the Georgia code. So feel free to—"

"Brian, Ida Cunningham is about to clock me if I don't get her extra papers into the Gas-N-Go in, like, thirty seconds, so *feel free* to dispense with the drama."

"Oh, man, I'd give anything to have some of her chicken tenders right about now. Or one of those onion things she makes."

"Brian, you don't spill what you've got now, I'm going to tell Ida it was you who delayed me, and you'll never get her chicken tenders again."

The threat worked. "Go after a guy's weak spot, won't you," Brian grumbled. "Okay, our tech guys have managed to do a little magic on the tape. And we may have something."

Ida had a spoon in her hand now, and she was miming some fierce motions about what she would do to Neil with that spoon if he didn't hurry up. Neil gave up on the drama-free version of Brian's story and headed to deliver Ida's papers. Maybe if he were still on the phone, Ida wouldn't abuse him so badly.

"What?" Neil stopped again as he got to the door. Ida took him by the jacket lapels and dragged him across the threshold.

"Boy!" she blasted. "I get to keep *all* the money from my papers this week, because you are an aggravating—"

Neil stuck his finger in his ear, his cast straight out, and pressed the phone closer to the other ear. "What did you say?" he asked Brian again.

"I *said* the person on the video is either a really small guy or a woman."

"How do you know?"

"'Cause videotape—even scuzzy black-and-white overused tape—doesn't lie. Our tech guys have done the measurements."

Someone came in the door behind him and collided with his cast, sending a radiating pain up into his shoulder. But it had nothing on the stomach-churning feeling that shot through him. He couldn't explain it, that feeling.

"Brian. I need to see that video."

CHAPTER FIFTEEN

"Patrons, thank you for shopping at your local IGA, but our store will be closing in fifteen minutes."

As Charli heard this, she yanked a grocery cart from the corral and swore under her breath. Even the blueberry yogurt was beyond its sell-by date, and she had to eat something besides hospital food, Twix and granola bars.

After the horrid meeting with Lige Whitaker, she'd dived into seeing patients just to distract herself from the doubts he'd given her about her dad. Lunch had been a hastily in-haled Twix with an orange juice—the orange juice was good for you, right? She'd fitted that two-course meal in between a screaming toddler with an almost-perforated eardrum and Mr. Hank Tolleson's hemorrhoids.

Who said primary care physicians didn't lead a glamorous life?

And she'd intended to get out of the office early for a change, so she could figure out what all Lige's garbage had really meant, and if there was a way to get beyond it. Marvela, however, had slapped down a whole host of insurance paperwork for her to review, and Shelly, her nurse, had dumped about ten thousand orders for home health and medical equipment and—the saddest part of her job—hospice orders.

Plus today was payroll day, so she had to sign off on the staff hours so Marvela could write out checks.

How had her father done this for over four decades without going crazy? Maybe that was the explanation for why he'd taken Lige's money. Why he'd hidden an outbreak.

Charli would have raced right through the produce section if she hadn't been spotted by Julianne Brantley, who was thumping a head of cabbage.

Julianne, whose lipids panel was scarier than the first installment of *Nightmare on Elm Street,* held up the cabbage. "Hey, Doc? See? I'm following your orders! Gonna start eating those vegetables you're so keen on. What are you getting?"

Honestly? Charli had been planning on picking up a few frozen dinner entrees. Faced with having to live out her own sermons, she brought the cart to a shuddering, squeaking halt.

Charli surveyed the small selection of basics the little store carried. This store was the only grocer in town, and an independent to boot, so prices were much higher than in the megamarts a half hour away—and the selection much more limited. Bagged lettuce. Tomatoes that looked pink rather than red. Bell peppers so expensive she'd have to take out a loan. Broccoli. Potatoes. A fairly good selection of fruit, thanks to it being the Christmas season.

Christmas made her think of Neil, which made her think of how unsubtle she must have looked in the newspaper office.

So does he think I'm just after the story or after him?

"Doc?" Julianne waved her hand in front of Charli's face. "You in there?"

"Oh!" Charli snapped her attention back from the tiny newspaper's office in her memory to the quandary at hand. "I was thinking about how expensive all this produce is. If health insurance companies wanted to get us healthier and spend less money, they'd do better to pay for part of the expense of eating right."

"You got that in one, Dr. Prescott. This cabbage is about the cheapest thing going. I was wondering if you could write me a prescription for it and I could file it on my insurance."

"I wish I could. It would save everybody money in the long run."

Charli grabbed a couple of bags of prewashed lettuce, some of those expensive bell peppers and a pallid tomato, along with a bag of carrots. To the cart she added some bagged mandarin oranges and a head of broccoli. Yes, all of it was more expensive than junk food, but in the long run, it was cheaper than poor health. Tonight it would be quick and fast and that was what she was after.

"Whew, Doc, you're eating high on the hog now!" Julianne told her as Charli wheeled toward the bread aisle. "That broccoli costs almost as much as steak, at least per pound. I could eat a lot cheaper if I just bought me some of those boxed dinners."

"I'll either pay it now or pay it later," she called over her shoulder to Julianne. "Like I told you this morning in my office."

"Yeah, well, I'll wait, just get this cabbage now. My sister-in-law was telling me about some Mexicans who've got a vegetable stand. They have a greenhouse and everything, and they got some pretty tomatoes. Buy local, isn't that what everybody's saying now?"

"A vegetable stand?" Charli stopped her cart, despite another ominous warning the store would be closing in ten minutes. Surely they wouldn't lock her in here without taking her money first.

"Yeah, out on the main highway, south of town. It's run by some folks Lige Whitaker keeps around all year."

Charli's stomach twisted at the mention of Lige's name. She'd tried to put their meeting out of her mind and, thanks to her schedule, she had—mostly.

"I'll have to check it out," she told Julianne. She hurried away—ostensibly because of the lights flickering on and off in warning, but mostly because she didn't even want to think about Lige Whitaker.

As Charli rounded an endcap, she saw a big display of powdered cocoa, complete with marshmallows. Again, she had an image of Neil, with his dimples and his warm brown eyes and his apparent belief that hot cocoa could fix anything. Charli took a peek left, and then right, didn't see Julianne or any of her patients behind her, and quickly dropped the box into her cart. It wouldn't be as good as the real thing, but it would be a tolerable substitute.

Two loaves of whole-wheat bread, a sack of frozen boneless skinless chicken breasts, a jug of one percent and four fresh cartons of blueberry yogurt later, Charli arrived at the checkout. The high school girl who was ringing up her order glowered at her. "You didn't hear the announcement about the store closing?" the girl asked.

"I'm sorry. I didn't think it would take me long to grab these few things."

"Well, I wish people realized that when they stay longer, we gotta stay longer, and I've got a chemistry final to study for."

Charli winced. *I so remember those days.* "I am sorry. I hope it goes well. Do you like chemistry?"

"It's okay." The girl darted her eyes around, probably to ensure the bag boy had not yet returned from carrying out the last customer's groceries. "It's kind of neat, actually, but boys around here don't want to take you out if they think you're some kind of genius nerd."

Charli remembered this phenomenon, too. "Oh, I wouldn't worry about that. High school's not forever." The girl's tag had a smiley-face sticker plastered beside the name Jen. "Jen, while they're still scratching their backsides in a hunting stand and living with their mom, you could be enjoying driving around in a cute little BMW sports car that you earned with a megabucks job at a pharmaceutical company." *But*

*don't go into family practice medicine. You'll
never pay off the med school bills.*

Jen froze for a moment, the head of broccoli
halfway to the scales. A bemused smile hit her
expression like a ray of sun on a cloudy day.
"You think I could do that? Like, work for a
pharmaceutical company? Maybe find a cure
for cancer?"

"If you're good in chemistry. And biology."

"I never thought about that. My mama wants
me to go to cosmetology school. She says everybody needs a haircut. She tells me I don't
need to be worrying about getting straight A's
and I should work as many hours here as I can.
B's are good enough, she says, for cosmetology school. My friends call me lucky." The girl
rolled her eyes, weighed the broccoli and keyed
in something on the cash register. The rest of
the groceries beeped quickly by the scan bar.

Charli shook her head in commiseration.
"Mine thought I needed to be in beauty pag-
eants so I could learn charm. That's kind of like
putting someone in the Daytona 500 so they
could learn how to drive."

The subject of mothers reminded Charli of
her worries about her mother. Her mom had
been eerily silent all day—no phone calls, no
messages, not even a surprise visit to the office.

Charli had tried to get her on the phone after the meeting with Lige. But the phone had rung straight to voice mail.

Had Lige called her mother? Peddled some of his garbage to her? She didn't want her mother worrying—and truth be told, Charli didn't want to have to explain how she gave away a hundred grand of money that didn't belong to her. Because in years past, her mother's favorite self-medication for stress was a buying binge.

A buying binge.

Macon. I told her to go to Macon with her friends! Did I send her into temptation?

Charli blinked at the largish total that appeared on the cash register's computer screen. She slid her debit card through the checkout's card reader and prayed she had enough money in her account. When she saw Approved flash up on the screen, she nearly did a happy dance.

Despite med school and an M.D. after her name, Charli was a long way from that BMW convertible she'd dangled in front of the cashier. *I'm encouraging her, that's all. We need more girls in math and science.*

Jen bundled up her bags and handed her the receipt. Her face was glowing with hope and dreams. "Thank you! Thank you!" she said effusively. "You're that new doctor, aren't you?

Well, if you can do it, go to medical school, I mean, so can I. I mean, not taking care of sick people. I am *so* not a nurse. But that chemistry thing, working for a pharmaceutical company, I could do that. I can see that."

Charli was caught up short by the cashier's words. It occurred to her, too late, that despite not feeling like one at all, she was now a role model. Great. Something else to live up to. Fresh veggies and inspirational tidbits? Forever? She didn't feel worthy of the frank admiration in the girl's gaze.

Especially when, a few days earlier, Charli had wiggled out of a police interview by plying her skills with ingrown toenails. "Good for you, Jen!" Charli told her, and scurried for the automatic doors.

A cold gust of wind cut through even the wool coat Charli was wearing. The groceries would be okay for a few minutes while she drove by and checked on her mom. It was cold as a refrigerator out here, after all.

The lights at her parents' house were dim. A few low lights from the living room lamps filtered out.

It looks so different now. When her father was alive, every light would be on at this time of night, and by this time of year, at least according to Neil, her father would have turned it into a twinkling fairyland of Christmas lights—tasteful tiny white lights, not resembling Neil's over-the-top display one whit, she suspected.

Funny how Neil's lights were growing on Charli.

Growing up, the holidays had been a stressful time for Charli. Too many fights about money, too many times her mother had blown scads of cash for just the right present. Her father had wanted to ignore the holiday—and that suited Charli just fine, then and now.

Charli pushed away the sadness that welled up inside her and hurried to the front door. She could see the glow of a computer through the study window at the front of the house. As she climbed the front steps, through the living room windows, Charli could make out her mom's figure glide through the room. She rang the doorbell.

The door opened. "Why, Charli." Her mother's eyes darted from Charli's face to somewhere over her shoulder, then back to Charli. "I wasn't expecting you."

Weird how her mother didn't seem all that happy to see her.

"I hadn't heard from you all day."

Her mother's lips pursed in annoyance. "You're always saying I should let you work."

Can't win, can't win, can't win. Charli stifled the urge to scream with frustration. "I appreciate that, Mom. I was just...worried."

Violet opened the door wider with slow, dragging footsteps. "I suppose you'll want to come in."

Okay. This is officially the Twilight Zone. My mother always wants company. If she doesn't want me to come in, I definitely need to.

Inside, nothing outwardly appeared to have changed. The house was still neat as a pin, with every knickknack dusted and in its prescribed place. Charli followed her mom to the kitchen, where beside a beautifully decorated, uncut chocolate cake lay the makings of a cup of tea. Her mother's favorite porcelain china cup, lemon, tins of herbal teas and sugar were out on the granite countertop of the island.

"Want some?" her mother asked. "This is my test sample. I just got finished decorating it. I'm practicing some new designs for the cake I'm donating to the Christmas bazaar."

"Sure."

While her mother busied herself with slicing the cake and preparing Charli's tea, Charli nosed around as unobtrusively as possible. She was lucky her mother remembered her preference for Darjeeling and insisted on digging it out of the back of her cupboard.

Sidling over to the basket of mail under the phone, Charli took a sneak peek.

There it was, a corner poking out from under the power bill. A credit card logo. Charli's heart skipped a beat. A quick look told her that her mom was still busy with finding the tea. Charli took a finger, slid the power bill aside enough to see what it was.

Congratulations on your new Chase credit card! Please keep this—

"Charli! I said, do you want honey or sugar?"

In confusion, Charli blurted out, "Honey?" and her mom took that for her answer. Crossing the kitchen to the island, Charli accepted the cup her mother offered her. She tried to think of a way to broach the subject of the card with her mom.

Directly. That was the way to go. No beating around the bush.

"Mom, you're not having trouble, are you? With shopping?"

"Me? Oh, no. Charli, why do you think that?" Her mother took a long sip from her cup. "Oh. You must have seen that credit card paperwork. Jed thought I should build up some credit. But don't worry. It only has a thousand-dollar credit limit on it. I can't get into any trouble with that."

Charli picked up a wedge of lemon and squeezed its juice into her tea. Should she demand to see the paperwork? Should she call Jed?

It makes sense. Mom does need some credit history. And a thousand-dollar credit limit is small enough.

"Okay," Charli said at last. "You'd tell me if you were in trouble, right? If you felt like things were slipping?"

"Oh, sure, honey." Her mother's smile was wide and easy, tinged with a little indulgence. "But you don't have to take up where your father left off. He didn't want you to have to worry about me. That's why he set up this elaborate allowance thing with Jed. Besides, me being accountable—well, that's what support groups are for, too. I won't stop going to the meetings. Aren't you proud of me? A credit card holder for the first time in years!"

Laying aside the lemon on the cup's matching saucer, Charli framed her words carefully. "I am proud of you, Mom. You've really seemed to settle in the past few days."

"It's hard." Charli's mother's fingers tightened on her cup. "I miss him terribly. I know you do, too."

"I do. Sometimes at the office, I think I'll go crazy. I keep wanting to run down the hall, stick my head in his office door and ask him what he thinks about something," Charli admitted.

Her mom let out a long sigh. Her forehead puckered with faint worry lines. "Are *you* all right, honey? You're working so hard, and you've had so much stress."

Tell me about it. Lige—I can't believe Lige. I thought I could count on him.

Her face must have given her away. Her mother pounced. "Something *is* worrying you! Is it work? Is something wrong at the hospital?" her mother asked.

"It's just that—everybody expects me to be *him*. Everybody expects me to be just like Dad." Charli blurted out the first thing that didn't have to do with money or donations or Lige Whitaker. Well, not directly, anyway.

Her mom set her cup down, took Charli's from her and wrapped her in a rare hug. Charli stood stock-still, not daring to move for fear of breaking the spell. The fierce, quick embrace made tears well up in Charli's eyes.

As her mother pushed her to arm's length, Charli could see it had affected her mom in a similar way.

She stroked her palm against Charli's cheek.

"Don't try to be your father, Charli. You be you. If I've learned anything through all that counseling, it's that you have to be true to yourself."

"Who am I? Who was Dad? I hear so many things—I keep thinking that maybe I didn't know him at all."

Her mom stepped back, got her cup and took a sip with fingers that shook. "Who am I, Charli? Who's anybody? I don't think we know those answers. He wasn't perfect, but who is? Your dad was a good man, a good husband, a good father, a good doctor who did a lot for this town. But you know that, don't you?"

Charli started to tell her mother about the money, about Lige. Her mom stopped her by saying, "Oh, listen to us, all down in the dumps." She sniffed back a tear, laughed and said, "I guess we are tired. Go on. Get some sleep. I'm fine, Charli. Really. But thank you for worrying."

CHAPTER SIXTEEN

NEIL TOLD HIMSELF Rudolph needed some additional staking to be sure he didn't blow over. Not to mention the extra set of lighted netting he'd bought to stretch over his boxwoods.

Okay. So he was coming along really slow on stretching that netting, and those boxwoods were the hedge that divided his property line from Charli's. And yes, he could have done it before dark.

But while he was out here, there was no harm in checking every once in a while to see if Charli's car was in her drive.

Even if *every once in a while* meant every five seconds.

He'd seen the video. Despite the GBI's magic, the quality was still blurred and grainy, and the dark night hadn't helped. Plus, the Secret Santa had been determined not to show her face.

Yes. *Her.*

It couldn't be Charli, could it?

Sure, the figure walked a little like Charli,

but it couldn't be her. But then, just for a second, the video had captured a flicker of something long and flowing. In the video, as grainy as it was, it was almost unidentifiable. Unless you'd seen it.

And he had.

One of Charli's scarves. One of a kind, practically speaking, because he'd not seen anyone else in town wearing Violet's creations—not even Violet herself.

Brian had noticed his interest in the flicker. He'd badgered Neil about it, but Neil had stood firm. Until he was sure—absolutely sure—he wasn't going to say anything to anybody.

And to be sure, he had to talk to Charli.

He heard a car turn onto their street and willed himself not to look up. It wasn't her. She was working late or at her mother's or—

It was her. Suddenly, Neil went all thumbs in his good hand. He plucked at the netting on the hedge like it was a banjo and he was playing at a square dance. The car stopped midway up her drive, even with him, and her passenger window slid down. She leaned over.

"Hey," she called. "My apologies for abandoning you to Darius and Miss Olivia. What's my penance?"

"Hmm." Neil pretended to contemplate her

question. He tapped his chin in what he hoped was a good approximation of judicious consideration. "I think you owe me a cup of hot cocoa. To smooth over my hurt feelings."

"Sure—but I haven't had supper yet. What about this? I have about three sacks of really healthy stuff one of my patients guilted me into buying from the IGA. How about I cook us a quick supper?"

Neil was surprised at her offer. "Sure…"

"Oh, wait. It's practically nine o'clock. You've probably already had supper. You're a normal person." Charli's face fell.

"No, actually, I had a late lunch, so I hadn't really gotten around to eating." Neil buried his fingers in the hedge and crossed them. No point mentioning the slice of convenience store pizza he'd scarfed down on his way home from the paper. "Well, nothing healthy, anyway," he amended.

"Great! Let me get this unpacked and put away—"

"I'll help. Many hands and all that."

Groceries unloaded, and supper preparations under way, Neil found, when push came to shove, he could tear lettuce and turn the chicken she was grilling. She'd taken away the knife when she'd seen his clumsy attempt at cutting tomatoes one-handed.

He kept trying to figure out a way to bring up the video. Tonight, though, Charli seemed brittle and superficial and resisting any sort of serious conversation. He found himself wondering if she'd actually wanted him to accept her invitation.

But she had looked disappointed at the prospect of him having already eaten.

When he offered yet again to try to chop something, Charli shook her head firmly. "I'm being completely selfish," she told him. "The last thing I want tonight is another patient."

So he pulled up a chair. "How shall I sing for my supper, then?" Neil asked.

Her lips curved and those golden eyelashes fluttered his way, for the briefest of seconds, before she went back to slicing a carrot.

"I thought I was supposed to be providing some sort of community service," Charli joked.

"Ah, yes, that. Darius is going to be the death of me one day. If I come into your office completely bonkers, you can diagnose me as Darius-overdosed."

"I was going to ask you..." The knife blade speeded up, and Neil wondered if she'd picked up her expertise from wielding a scalpel or from cooking lessons. Charli used the back of her forearm to push a strand of hair from her forehead.

"Ask me what?" Neil's stomach tightened. Was she going to bring up the donation? Would she confess that she was the Secret Santa?

"Er…" The strand of hair had fallen into her face again. Charli laughed and tried to toss it back.

Neil rose from his seat and gently tucked the silken strand behind her ear. She froze, the knife still in her hand, her face angled toward him. Those pretty pink lips had parted ever so slightly.

He should just blurt it out, just ask her once and for all if she was the Secret Santa, and if so, where on earth she'd gotten the money.

But he didn't. He couldn't take his hand away, instead letting it trail along her jawline. Somehow, this touch felt more intimate than the kiss on the Ferris wheel.

Charli let out a breath that sounded shaky to him. He could see her throat work in a nervous little gulp. The pulse at her jawline pounded away—matching his.

"Wow," she whispered. "You sure know how to distract a girl. You won't ever get your supper at this rate."

"You know, I don't think I'm hungry, after all," he murmured back. He lowered his mouth toward hers, slowly, slowly—

And then, just as their lips met, Charli jerked away. "Oh, no! The chicken!"

The knife fell from her hand with a clatter against the wooden cutting board, and she leaped for the pan of chicken. Snatching up the crispiest one with a pair of tongs before it turned to complete charcoal, she practically threw it on the plate.

"Here, let me turn the unit down." Neil leaned over and adjusted the flame under the skillet. "I'm sorry, it's my fault. I was supposed to be watching the chicken, and I was, um, otherwise occupied."

Her face was flushed—more from embarrassment than the heat of the stove, he thought. She'd never looked prettier to him.

"So much for my cooking abilities." Charli put the last piece of chicken on the plate and surveyed the damage. "Are they even edible?"

"Sure. I like my chicken blackened."

She closed her eyes and blew out a breath of exasperation. Opening them, she stared down at the chicken. "This is the reason I'm not a natural in emergency medicine," Charli told him. "I can't multitask well enough."

"Hey, if you'd been able to multitask during that moment, you are not the girl for me," Neil tossed back.

"Well, yeah, about that…" She squared her shoulders. "I probably shouldn't be kissing my patients."

"Fine. You're fired."

She did a double take, her face suddenly the color of chalk. "What?"

"I meant—I was trying to joke." Neil shoved his good hand into his pocket and wished he could do the same with the other one. "I'll find another doctor. Because…well…because…I wasn't able to multitask, either."

"I don't know if it's that simple." She was nibbling on her bottom lip again, clearly not realizing how crazy that drove him.

Focus. She's sweet and she's got that vulnerable yet strong thing going. As Dad would say, she's cute as a speckled pup. But you've got to ask her about that video.

The blasted words wouldn't come. But he did manage to step back and give himself some breathing space.

Charli promptly closed the gap. She laid a hand on his chest, turned those beautiful blue eyes up to meet his and said, "I have a lot on my plate right now."

"I'll say."

His doubts about what she might be keeping from him must have spiked his words with sarcasm, because she jerked back. When she would have turned from him, he pulled her around, gently.

"I'm sorry," he said. "It's just—this Secret Santa business. It's got everybody in a froth. Folks are expecting me to unmask Santa. To reveal the identity of whoever left that money."

"Not everyone, surely." Charli said. She turned back to the vegetables and once again began chopping them. "You know, I've been thinking. Maybe you should respect Santa's privacy. If he'd wanted to have his name attached to the donation publicly, he could have done so. Chief Hawkins told me it wasn't a crime to donate the money, even that much money." The bell pepper fell into neat little strips of green under her knife, which rocked back and forth with unrelenting accuracy. In one quick and efficient move, she piled them atop the carrots. The chicken came under assault next.

"Santa picked the wrong town if he wanted to remain anonymous. The whole community is buzzing about it. Ida at the Gas-n-Go says they've got a pool already on likely suspects."

Charli carefully sliced away the blackened

edges of the grilled chicken and swept them into the trash. She turned her attention back to the salvaged chicken, lining it up precisely before she started running her knife through it and answering over the thump of the blade against the cutting board. "But what about Santa's wishes? He must have had his reasons, right?"

He? He is a she. Unless the GBI's tech folks are mistaken. "Okay," Neil said aloud, knowing he was stringing Charli along if she was the Secret Santa. "I'll bite. Why all the cloak and dagger business? Why not give the money to the clinic on the condition of anonymity?"

Charli shrugged. She picked up another carrot and peeled it with quick, strong strokes. "You got me. But I'll bet the reason seemed good to Santa."

Okay, now Neil was needling her. He knew it. But she knew something about where that money had come from. Had she been a messenger for the money? Had it been her dad's dying wish to donate something to the clinic?

And why couldn't he have done that publicly? Or at least, if he wanted to do it anonymously, in the usual manner, not sticking it through a mail slot.

"You know...the GBI has been digging through the evidence," Neil told her.

The knife in Charli's hand came down at an awkward angle, and Neil could see she'd almost cut herself. She waved him off as he sprang up to check on her.

"Sorry! I'm all thumbs tonight," she joked.

"More cutting like that and you won't have thumbs at all," he said. But his comeback was reflexive. What he'd said had surprised her, that was clear.

"So…" Three more whacks and the carrot was history. "What did they tell you? Chief Hawkins didn't seem to think it would be a high-priority case."

How was it he could still want to kiss her when he was convinced she knew more than she was telling him? Or telling the police?

"For one thing, there were no usable prints on the money."

Did her shoulders slump? And was it relief or disappointment?

"Yeah?" She scooped up the carrot and tossed it into the bowl of lettuce, then started in on another bell pepper. She didn't seem to be paying attention to the level of vegetables in the bowl—just chopping mindlessly to keep her hands busy.

"Yeah." Neil shifted in his chair to get a better view of her face. From the side, it was perfectly calm, no hint of anxiety.

Maybe you're imagining things, buddy.

"And they analyzed the video tape. Very interesting," he said in his most casual tone. Did Charli's chin jut out? Her lips had compressed, but was it the conversation, or was she concentrating on her chopping?

"Videotape?" She asked it calmly enough. "So did they catch him in the act?"

"Yeah. About that." Neil's heart rate went into overdrive as he was about to deliver the next piece of information. He wanted to see her reaction. "The GBI doesn't think it's a him at all. They think it's a woman."

Charli's tongue darted out and touched her upper lip. She brought her forearm up to her face again, but there was no irritating strand of hair this time.

"A woman?"

"Yeah. In a trench coat. With an umbrella."

"How could they determine that? Some sort of CSI reflection analysis?" The pepper would be pureed, the way Charli was going after it.

"No, measurements. Based on comparisons—her height compared to the door, and the proportions of her hips to her waist. Plus... there was a scarf."

"Wow. They can do miracles with videotape. Next you'll be telling me they have a picture of Santa's—well, Mrs. Claus's—face."

"Nope. No picture. No clear shot of her face."

Neil held his breath as he waited for her to respond. She didn't. She concentrated on using the knife to scrape up the pitiful bell pepper slices into a pile and toss them into the bowl.

"Charli, *were* you—"

She cut him off with the most beautiful, dazzling smile. "Hey, enough shop talk for you. I think I've got this. All that's left is for me to toss it together and get out the salad dressing. Mind putting some ice in the glasses? Oh, and we'll need plates and flatware. Try that cabinet over there. And then I'll tell you about *my* day."

CHAPTER SEVENTEEN

AFTER SHE'D BID Neil good-night and sent him across the hedge a final time, Charli collapsed into a puddle of limp exhaustion.

I'm so not cut out for this, she thought, rubbing her eyes.

I should have told him the truth.

Well, at least part of the truth. Maybe she could have told him her dad had wanted to donate the money—

No. Neil would have asked why her dad had waited. Or where the money came from.

Where the money came from. Blast you, Lige Whitaker. My dad was a good man—a hard man, but a good one. I don't know how you made him do this, what hold you had on him, but he couldn't have done it for the money. If he had, wouldn't he have spent it, not socked it away in a safe deposit box?

No, if she came clean about the Secret Santa being her alter ego, she'd have to explain exactly what had happened. And that was something she still didn't know herself.

Maybe before this morning, before that awful confrontation with Lige, Charli would have been able to.

She rubbed her eyes and considered her next move. Maybe she could tell Neil. She'd swear him to secrecy and ask his advice—

No. He was the type who felt honor bound to protect the purity of news and the people's right to know. She could predict he'd talk about a "breach of public trust," or something like that.

Well, he's right. They should know. And if I didn't have Mom to worry about—not to mention a gajillion dollars in student loans to pay off—I'd march right over there and tell him now.

Or would she?

What would Neil think of her if she did tell him? Would he still think she was an honorable person? Would he understand why she hadn't gone to the authorities at once?

Charli yawned. Getting up from her chair, she stumbled on weary feet to her bedroom. Neil's Christmas lights slanted through the closed blinds, right onto her pillow.

Light. It had a nasty way of showing the worst dirt you were trying to hide.

MARVELA SLAPPED ANOTHER minitower of charts onto Charli's desk. "I am so sorry, honey, but these need signing off on, too, and now if you don't mind," she said. "We can't bill until the chart is complete. Speaking of billing…"

Charli slumped back in her chair and stared at the ceiling. A brown water stain made a perfect concentric circle around the heating and air vent cover.

Terrific. A roof leak. At least the hospital authority owns this building.

But thinking about the hospital authority immediately led to thoughts of Lige Whitaker.

"Are you in there?" Marvela's voice brought Charli back to the moment. Charli raised her gaze to Marvela, who had taken off her purple-pink framed bifocals and was shaking her head.

"Honey, you are dead on your feet. You have *got* to get some rest."

"How did my dad manage all this?" Charli asked. "For every patient I see, I'm pushing a forest's worth of paper."

"Welcome to modern medicine, honey. You've been working in hospitals where they've got armies of staff to handle billing and insurance. Here, it's just me. And I could use some help."

This was not the first time Marvela had said

something similar—not even the first time that day. Charli bent her neck in first one direction and then another to work out a crick that had lodged there. "Oh, Marvela... You see our cash flow. How am I going to afford to hire another person? Huh?"

"Well, what about part-time? Somebody who could answer the phones and handle the front desk, in the afternoons, when it's busier?"

"Who would we find that was willing to put in those few hours?" Charli reached for the next chart on her pile and flipped it open. "You have anybody in mind?"

"No." Marvela's voice sounded as dispirited as Charli felt. "Maybe we could put an ad in the paper?"

The paper. Neil. A shiver ran through Charli as she thought about the night before, when he'd come so close to kissing her. She'd willed him to kiss her, long and sweet, and hold her....

At which point, she'd burned the chicken. And compounded her bad cooking by lying to him.

I will not think about that videotape. I will not. Nobody can tell it's me.

"Marvela, I don't know. We'd have everybody in the county applying, and when would I have time to go through all those applications?

I might fit them in between one and two in the morning."

Marvela muttered something that didn't sound so pleasant and headed for the door.

Another happy customer. Charli was racking them up these days, and she particularly hated to disappoint Marvela, who'd been nothing but a mother hen in fuchsia to her. At least she had groceries in the house again. It had been nice to have a slice of bread to jam in the toaster—

"Wait, Marvela!" The thought of the grocery store had jogged Charli's memory. "Do you know a Jennifer—maybe Jen, for short?—who works at the IGA?"

Marvela turned around very slowly. "Yes. Yes, I do. Her parents are Bobby and Sue Isley. Pretty good kid. Why?"

"She's got a head for chemistry. And she seems…" Well, customer service hadn't been her strong point, not at first, anyway, but Charli wanted to encourage any girl to better herself.

"You mean, ask her? About working part-time?" Marvela's beringed fingers came together in a prayerful little clasp in front of her ample bosom. "You mean it? You'd hire her?"

"Maybe. Why don't you call her in and interview her? See what you think? She wants to go to college and major in chemistry, so she's motivated."

Marvela's shoulders lifted, her back straight. "Oh, sure. I can certainly do that. Interview her, I mean. I was always telling your father I could handle all the staff hires, at least at the initial level."

Oh, my word, but I'll bet you did. And I can imagine how Dad reacted to that. "Sure," Charli told her, trying to smother her laugh at what her father's control-freak reaction would have been. "You will be the one to work with her the most."

The phone rang before Marvela had a chance to get back to the front desk, so Charli snatched it up. "Family Medicine," she said into the phone as she read over a chart before making a note on it.

"May I speak to Dr. Prescott, please?" A man's voice, somewhat officious. Could be a telemarketer.

"Speaking." She skimmed down the page, flipped to another, decided it would do and signed off on the chart.

"This is Special Agent Brian Mulford with the Georgia Bureau of Investigation. The GBI is reviewing the cash donation made to the Broad

County Community Clinic. I was wondering if I could talk to you?"

Charli clutched the phone in suddenly sweaty fingers and gasped like a dying fish. This was one phone call she wished she'd left to Marvela. Marvela would have demanded he set up an appointment. Had the sound carried over the phone line? "Yes?" she responded, more of a question than an answer.

"Yes, ma'am. Well, we'd like to ask you a few questions. Are you free now?"

BREVIS COMMUNITY BANK popped up on the newspaper office's caller ID. Neil picked it up, expecting to hear Nora Evers or one of the other ladies at the bank reporting a discrepancy in the paper's night deposit.

"Well, well, Neil! How's that paper of ours coming along?" Lige Whitaker boomed over the phone. "Ya know, if ya ever need to refinance that loan of yours, let us take a look at it. I'll bet I can get you a sweet deal."

"Thank you, but I'm happy where I am for now." Not for the first time was Neil glad that he'd taken the prior owner's advice about not applying for a loan with Lige—because that's really who the Brevis Community Bank was, in the end. Or the Broad County Hospital. Or any of the many endeavors Lige ran here in Broad County.

And you didn't want someone who could call in your loan to be involved in so many activities and news stories as Lige was here in Brevis, even if he was a pretty easygoing person. It could lead to untold numbers of conflicts of interests.

"Can't blame a man for tryin', now, can you?" Lige had apparently moved on from banking to the real subject of his call. "I wanted to tell you, the boys and I met last night—"

"The hospital authority met? Without notice? That's an illegal meeting, Lige. You know that."

"Oh, pshaw! Even you with your stuffed-shirt attitude won't quibble about this one. The authority voted to rename the hospital after Chuck Prescott. Figured you'd want to know. Seems right, doesn't it?"

Neil collapsed back into his chair. To be honest, it didn't exactly make sense, though Prescott had fought beside Lige to keep the hospital doors open. Plus, Prescott had been the one doctor Lige had kept around for years.

The timing, for one thing, was off. The authority had met at least once before in the weeks since Prescott's death. Why had they waited until now?

And it was unlike Lige, who watched every penny, to okay a potentially expensive name change for a hospital on such a shoestring budget—he'd fought against one previously, complaining about the wasted letterhead, and the expense of signage.

"That's—that's very generous, Lige. I'm sure his family will appreciate it."

"Yeah, yeah, that Violet, she's a piece of work, isn't she?" Lige seemed to have lost interest in the subject at hand. For a moment, silence reigned.

Lige broke it by saying, "Well, Walt's gonna get you a press release. And I've told young Dr. Prescott, so you go on over there and get a quote from her, okay?"

Without so much as a goodbye, Lige clunked the phone down, leaving Neil listening to a dial tone.

Hmm. Lige hadn't seemed all that fired up about the name change. Maybe Violet or Charli had pressed the hospital authority to do it? Maybe it was a rare revolt by the other members of the hospital authority?

Or maybe it had something to do with the Secret Santa? The timing, coming right after the donation, was at least suspicious. Neil had long ago learned to suspect coincidences.

"Neil? Buddy?" Dawn's voice wafted over the cubicle divide. "You're awfully quiet. What's going on over there? A break in the Secret Santa case?"

Neil exhaled. Dawn didn't know the half of it. He considered again telling Dawn that Charli might be Santa. But he could be wrong, and information that wasn't substantiated wasn't news—it was gossip and speculation.

He drummed his fingers and decided to keep mum. For now. "Dawn, you're my buddy and my pal, but honestly, you're beginning to sound like the managing editor I quit on because he nagged so much."

"Just hoping for a raise."

"Remember. I'm your boss."

She laughed. "I do. Promise. Every year on Boss's Day. Don't I get you something?"

Neil muttered in the affirmative and punched in the number for the Brevis Family Medicine office. "Hey, Marvela." He tried to inject the right amount of friendly casualness into his voice.

"Hold on a minute, won't you, Neil?" Marvela didn't bother to cover the phone as she hollered, "Oh, no, you don't—we did not order a thing from any company named Christmas Wishes! I know, because Dr. Prescott has said she doesn't want a tree this year. So you don't put that thing down!"

"Marvela! Marvela!" Neil shouted into the phone to get her attention.

"Neil, can you call back? This delivery guy is insisting that we ordered something—big old box that'll take up half the waiting room!"

"Uh…uh, about that, Marvela." Gee. What had seemed like a good idea at the time now suddenly didn't. "I bought it for her."

"You what?" Marvela's attention was pulled away again. "No, you don't, you sorry sapsucker! You can't leave that there! You come back here— oh, last time I ever work that fellow in without an appointment. What were you saying, Neil?"

"If it's a big package from a company called Christmas Wishes, I ordered it for her. But it was supposed to come in a small box—oh, no. They probably got it wrong and put my order and her order in the same shipment."

"Well, she forgot to tell me, and I want you to know, Dr. Prescott has an excellent memory." She sniffed.

"I—I didn't exactly tell her about it. It was going to be a surprise. You know, she doesn't have any decorations up at her house—not even a wreath. They were supposed to deliver it to her house."

"Something about a signature. They were trying to be nice. Neil, I don't know that she's gonna like this. She won't even let me put up a tree. And you know Dr. Prescott—Dr. Prescott's daddy—he set quite a store by Christmas."

"I know. I was trying to help. I'd hoped she'd changed her mind, because her part of the order is a tree—a predecorated one."

"Well, go, you! I think that's great. So is that what you were calling about?"

"No. Lige called me to tell me that they were naming the hospital in memory of Charli's— Dr. Prescott's—dad."

"Praise be!" Marvela sighed happily. "Oooh, that's so great!"

"Yeah, well, I wanted to talk to Charli—Dr. Prescott—about it."

He could hear Marvela's long nails tapping against her front teeth. "That could be a problem. Dr. Prescott's in a meeting with the GBI."

Whoa. Brian hadn't told him they would be interviewing Charli. Had Neil's interest in the fact that it was a woman—and the scarf— tipped Brian off? Or had the GBI found out something else?

"The GBI? Do you know which agent?"

"I couldn't say," Marvela told him primly.

"As a matter of fact, I've probably said too much already."

"Hmm. Do you think she might have a few minutes? Long enough to get a quote? It's about Dr. Chuck Prescott, and how he served this community."

"Well…" Marvela wavered.

He threw in what he hoped was the clincher. "And I'd come take that package off your hands while I'm at it."

"Can you come right now?" she asked.

Thank goodness for delivery screwups. Neil sprang from his chair and told her, "I'll be there in five minutes!" Without even telling Dawn, he was out the door.

In four minutes and thirty-six seconds precisely, Neil was walking in the front door to Charli's office. A large squat box sat in the midst of the waiting room's cheerless blue low-pile industrial carpet, way too big to be the small Christmas tree Neil had ordered for her. A toddler had decided the carton was a great climbing apparatus, and the child's mother was having little success in talking him down.

"Trey! Get off that thing before you break it! I mean it! I *will* tell your daddy when we get home!" the young mother yelled in between prodigious nose blowing and sneezing.

Marvela propped up on the dividing counter. "Well, aren't you a sight for sore eyes? Did I exaggerate?"

"No, you did not," Neil admitted. "That's definitely not just Charli's tree."

The reclaimed toddler wriggled out of his mother's arms once more as she dissolved into a fit of sneezing, and was busy scaling Mount Carton again. Marvela's brows pulled together and down, leaving her looking like the grouchy receptionist she pretended to be.

"I wouldn't be so all-fired-up to get it moved, but I don't want a little kid to get hurt using it as a jungle gym. Where's your help? The delivery guy had a hand truck, and he struggled with it. With two good arms."

Marvela gave his cast a speculative look. Just then, the door to the back area opened, and Brian Mulford came out with Charli behind him.

Brian was all decked out in a jacket and twill pants, a sure sign he was spending the day doing interviews. "Thank you for your time, Dr. Prescott—" He broke off as he spotted Neil standing by the carton. "Oh, hey, Neil! How's it going? Man, you gotta come out strong if you're gonna get into a fight."

For a moment, Neil was confused, but then

he realized Brian was referring to his broken arm. When he'd driven over to the GBI regional office to see the video, Brian hadn't been there to notice Neil's cast. "Oh, I broke it putting up Christmas lights."

He couldn't help but focus in on Charli, who stood behind Brian, her hands jammed in the pockets of her lab coat.

But her face, though pale and a little dark under her eyes, betrayed no anxiety. She smiled first at Neil, then waved the mom and the toddler to the back. Neil couldn't quite hear her words to the pair as the mom gathered the kid up and headed through the door.

"Still making Georgia Power happy, huh, buddy?" Brian slapped him on the shoulder. "Those linemen like the Christmas bonus your light bill provides."

"I'll have you know, I've already collected over four hundred bucks in donations to the Toys for Tots drive with my Christmas lights," Neil said. "I fully expect to collect a thousand total this year."

Charli's eyebrows skyrocketed. "That much! Wow! I guess I don't sound like I have much in the way of Christmas spirit with all my complaints, huh?"

"I don't take it personally," Neil told her. "I'm here to take the package off your hands."

"This big old box contains more lights? Where is there any space? And if I get any more illumination through my bedroom windows, I'll need sunblock and shades." In way of explanation, she added to Brian, "We're neighbors."

Brian shook his head. "Better you than me. Especially from November to January."

"So?" Charli prompted. "Or… You didn't buy this for my front lawn, did you?"

"Well…" Neil couldn't quite meet her eyes. He could imagine what she'd say when she found out that part of the box's contents were for her. "Part of it is mine. But part of it is yours. Since Rudolph fell and I set him up on my lawn, my roof is looking a little plain…."

She wagged her finger at him. "Nuh-uh. No way. With that arm, you are not climbing up any ladders. Doctor's orders."

Brian guffawed. "Oh, listen. You hear that?" He cupped his ear. "It's all the guys down at Georgia Power boo-hooing over their lost revenue. What is in the box, anyway?"

Neil didn't take the bait. Brian needled everybody, but he was a big kid himself when it came to the Christmas season. "Well, lucky for me, Brian, what the good doctor tells me, I don't have to listen to."

Charli put her hands on her hips and laughed. "Oh, yeah? I never figured you for a noncompliant patient."

"Remember, I fired you."

The remark was probably ill advised, because Marvela dropped something with a loud clunk behind the counter, a sure sign she was paying more attention to their conversation than her work. And Brian's eyes grew round and speculative.

Charli's fingers came up to her mouth, and her lab coat moved as she took in a sudden breath. She blushed. The most beautiful pink Neil had ever seen.

Brian frowned and started to speak, then broke off, seeming to discard whatever he had been about to say. He scrutinized first Neil, and then Charli. Neil could almost see lightbulbs going off. He could only hope, for now—until he decided whether to tell Brian about his suspicions—that the GBI agent was wondering whether Charli and Neil were seeing each other.

Brian's mask of professionalism firmly back in place, the GBI agent gave Charli a little wave. "Thanks, Dr. Prescott. I'll be in touch. Neil.

Call me." This last was a little pointed. Brian nodded to Neil and headed for the door.

Alone—except for Marvela, who hung persistently within earshot—Neil and Charli stood there, not speaking. Neil found himself desperately missing the ability to crack his knuckles.

"Well." Charli's breathy one-word attempt at breaking the silence didn't have the desired effect.

The phone rang in the background, and Marvela made an irritated noise before picking it up.

"What did Brian want?" Neil asked.

"Oh, nothing. He just wanted to go over the same stuff that the chief did. Had I seen anything the night before the donation? Did I notice if the bin was empty?" She waved away the questions.

"Did he mention anything more about it being a woman?"

"No, not really. He just said it was routine to ask witnesses what they'd seen—and I pointed out that I really wasn't a witness."

Maybe you're actually something more. Where did that money come from? And why all the secrecy?

Neil didn't ask these questions. Instead, he said, "Lige Whitaker called me with some information about your dad."

Charli's eyes widened. "What?"

"He's announcing that he's renaming the hospital in memory of your dad."

Neil took in the way Charli's nostrils flared and eyes tightened, how she covered that flash of anger quickly. Obviously, this wasn't welcome news to her.

Neil added in the silence that followed, "He told me he'd already let you know. You seem surprised."

"I—I thought he'd changed his mind." The words came out flat.

"Did you or your mom suggest it?" Neil asked.

"No!"

Neil was relieved by her strong response. *Maybe I've watched way too many Oliver Stone movies. Maybe the two things don't have anything to do with each other. But why the hostility when I mentioned Lige?* "Oh. I'll be doing a story on it. Do you want to give me a quote?"

"I—" She rubbed her forehead. "Maybe you'd better hold off. I'm shocked that the hospital board is doing this. It's not something we asked for, and they may wait. Or change their minds. It could be that the community wouldn't want to rename the hospital. I haven't even mentioned this to my mom, and I don't— I'm really not sure how she'll take it."

Her response was as perplexing as Lige's announcement had been—certainly not the one Neil had been expecting.

"It's quite a tribute. And I can think of nobody who deserves this more. Your dad gave his life to this town," Neil pointed out. "Lige made it sound like a done deal—said the hospital was sending over a press release about it."

Again that flash of hostility at Lige's name. Charli's words came out careful and slow. "Yes, it is an honor. But can you wait? Hold off? Let me be the one to tell my mom?"

"Sure. How about I talk to you tonight?" Neil glanced back over his shoulder. Marvela was still tied up with the phone conversation. Now that he didn't have Marvela eavesdropping, he felt a little emboldened. "So what do you say?" he asked Charli. "Want to help me uncover Santa?"

Charli's shoulders jerked, and her face went a half shade paler. "Santa!" Then her expression cleared. "Oh! The box. Santa? That's what's in the box?"

What are you holding out on me, Charli? You're a nice woman from a nice family, and I can't imagine that it could be so awful. But where did that money come from? Tonight, I will ask you. Directly. And I'm not going to take evasion as a response. "Yeah. That's the part of it that's mine. Yours is a tree. Predecorated. Folds up for easy storage. But Santa's life-size—hopefully not true to scale as far as pounds. He goes on my chimney. The kids will love him."

"I'm wondering how you plan to get him on the roof, since you are down to one arm these days," she said.

"Oh, but you told me I needed to use the arm more."

Her lips twitched at the corners. "But *you* said I was fired, and that you didn't have to listen to my advice," she pointed out.

"Touché. So…how late *are* you staying tonight?"

"Really late if I don't get back there and see the rest of my patients." Charli wriggled her shoulders as though she were working out some stiffness. "Be careful, Neil, on the roof. Get your buddy Brinson to help you."

"Worried about me?" Even as he still tried to puzzle out if Charli was indeed the Secret Santa, or knew who was, the idea of her concern sent a buzz through Neil. He liked having someone—not just *any* someone but Charli in particular—care about his well-being. He wanted to touch her. He wanted to pull her into his arms and kiss her senseless. With her eyes all soft and warm, she looked as though she wouldn't mind if he did. But there was Marvela, and more than that...

Charli wasn't telling him the truth about her role in the Secret Santa story.

"I worry about all my patients," Charli said, her mouth curving. "Even the ones who are crazy about Christmas."

"But I'm not your patient. Not anymore." It was so easy to be with her when he didn't think of all she wasn't telling him.

Her lashes did that slow dip against her flushed cheeks that he'd figured out meant she was pleased but embarrassed.

"I have to go. I'll...I'll see you tonight," she said, tagging on with good humor, "And get that thing out of here. It's taking up way too much real estate. I might start charging rent."

"What about the tree? Don't make me take it, too."

She looked torn, but finally she nodded. "Let Marvela at it—she'll put it up here. Thank you—I know you're trying, Neil. It's just— It's hard, okay? Christmas is just hard."

She didn't bother to explain. With a flap of her lab coat, Charli beat a hasty retreat.

CHAPTER EIGHTEEN

ONLY A DRIPPING FAUCET and the squeak of Charli's desk chair broke the silence in her office. The night sky was dark when she lifted her head from the pile of finished paperwork and stretched. Done. She could go home, get some sleep…and do it all over again tomorrow.

And sometime soon, she was going to have to make the complete switchover to computerized charts. But not, thankfully, tonight, or this week.

She had enough worries to keep her brain churning.

Charli knew she hadn't dived into catching up on all the paperwork Marvela had left for her because of a good work ethic. She'd been procrastinating about facing Neil.

Part of her hadn't. Neil Bailey was, with those dimples and those eyes, sweet. Okay, so he was still pushing Christmas, but she could tell he would have taken no for an answer on the tree. She could see herself falling for the likes of Neil, the gentle, caring guy who seemed to want her to be happy.

But, she had to remember, that was only half of who Neil was. The other half of him was the reporter who'd been asking way too many questions about the Secret Santa. And she was surely going to slip up and say something if she stayed around him. He would charm a confession right out of her mouth—and that would be the end of any feelings he might have for her.

Grabbing her bag and her keys, Charli headed for the car and for home. On the short drive, she considered what she'd say to Neil.

I'm sorry, but I don't have time for a relationship now. Maybe later?

Only Charli didn't want Neil later. She wanted him now.

I'm a lying, deceiving accessory after the fact. You still want me?

I'm bound by ethics not to even muddy the patient/doctor boundary.

Ha. That ship had sailed.

No. She should focus on the essentials, what he might ask her, be on guard and not let his charm wear her down.

The fact that he knew the GBI agent worried her even more. She'd danced around that interview with all the grace of a gorilla doing the waltz. Brian Mulford hadn't been satisfied with her answers, she knew. Still, Charli hoped Mulford would buy the "sleep deprivation" excuse for some of the dingbat answers she'd floated by him.

And what about Lige going ahead with renaming the hospital? That was the way to put the screws to her. She'd called her mother, only to find out that Lige had already personally given her mom the glad news. Her mom had been over-the-moon happy, and now Charli was loath to jeopardize the renaming plans.

But she wasn't going to find herself in the same boat her father had been in. Lige must have had something to hold over her father's head. That's the only way her dad would have covered up a TB outbreak—and who knows what else that translated into cash payments of a hundred thousand dollars.

Forget it. Deal with what you can. One thing at a time. The best plan was to avoid Neil. *And don't dwell on how disappointed you are at the prospect,* she ordered herself as she turned off the highway toward home.

The traffic on their street was thick and clogged with cars. Wow. Neil's new decorations must have lived up to his hype. Or maybe people really had their minds on Christmas by now?

Once parked in her carport, Charli gave in to the urge to at least look at Neil's lights…even if she wouldn't see him. She crossed the strip of lawn to the lighted boxwoods that divided their properties. Neil's lights *were* a winter wonderland, all sparkles and designs—reindeer bobbing their heads up and down, the silhouette of a trio of carolers lit in red and green, big Christmas ornaments and candy canes, elves and roly-poly miniature Saint Nicks, even a Christmas star…. Everything to do with Christmas.

Huh. No Santa on the roof.

She saw a shape hanging alongside the chimney, but in the shadows formed by the face of the chimney and Neil's bright-as-daylight illumination, she couldn't make out what it was.

Oh, no, it couldn't be!

"Hey! You made it!"

Neil's voice wrenched her gaze from the roof to lower down, where to her relief Neil was safely on terra firma. He jogged over to the hedge.

"Oh!" Charli's hand flew to her chest, where she felt her heart pounding under her breastbone. "I thought for a minute— I saw that shadow and I thought you were stuck on the roof."

"No. I got Brinson to help me, like you suggested. I've been waiting on you. I didn't think you'd ever make it home!" He caught her hand and tugged at it, guiding her through a well-worn break in the hedge.

Her pulse quickened—not just at his touch, but also at his words. Charli had liked the sound of them. It was as though he was making sure she had a soft place to land after a hard day.

"You can thank insurance companies and the government for the delay," she said. Breathless. She was breathless as he wrapped his arm around her and walked her to a spot in the far corner of his front lawn.

"I don't want to thank them at all." He pulled her up against him, her back to his chest, the better to position her in the exact optimum spot for whatever he was going to show her. Neil propped his chin on the crown of her head. "I guess I don't like sharing."

Neil's body was warm against hers as she leaned against him. For just this minute, she could pretend her father was still alive, she'd never found the money, she'd never misled Neil, that he was just a guy, and she was just a girl.

"Okay… So what is it?" She looked up to see his face, which was alight with excitement and anticipation.

Neil took advantage of the moment. His

mouth met hers. She turned in his embrace and gave herself to the kiss. It was everything a kiss should be: warm, sweet, hungry. Charli didn't care how drivers were honking their horns. She didn't heed the wolf whistles from lowered car windows. She didn't care about anything except making this moment last.

Neil pulled back. "Wow. That makes up for all the waiting. Can we try it again?"

Charli put her hands to her cheeks. They were flaming hot. "Oh, I— We—"

"Don't think. Don't. I'm not. I'm calling a halt to all thought processes—logic and worries and doubts. Let's have this. Right now. See? I even tied up some mistletoe so you'd have an excuse." Neil pointed up.

She followed his finger. Sure enough, a bunch of mistletoe, with its pearly white berries, hung from the limb of the birch tree that anchored this corner of Neil's lot.

From the street, someone yelled, "Kiss the doc again! I'll donate twenty bucks to the Toys for Tots till!"

"Well, now…" Neil gave her a stern look. "We can't *not* help the kiddies, can we?"

Gently, he took her hands in his and pulled them away from her face. "Hey, don't make a one-armed man have to work so hard," he chided.

Charli took a deep breath and said in as serious a voice as she could muster, "For the children." Standing on tiptoe, she pressed her lips to Neil's.

And there she was, on another roller coaster ride. She'd been kissed before, sure. But she'd never been kissed like this, not ever in a way that felt so right, as though she were coming home.

"Buddy, that's worth a U.S. Grant!" somebody hollered.

The spell broken, Charli stepped back to see children running up the sidewalk to Neil's Toys for Tots collection bucket, stuffing wadded bills into the slot.

"Wow. We did good tonight," she said.

"Don't look so smug," Neil told her, chucking her on her cheek. "It's not like you didn't enjoy it."

"Oh, no. It was hard work." Charli burst out laughing, unable to keep a straight face.

"Okay, are you ready to see it?" Neil asked. "Because as much as I want to kiss you some more—for the children, of course—I really think you may have had enough kisses for one night."

"Yes, we must watch the dosage of kisses very closely," Charli agreed. "They do seem to be addictive."

Exhilarating. Intoxicating. Blame it all on those endorphins that are running like mad through my body.

Neil turned her back around. "This baby has a remote control—which is good, because I wouldn't relish climbing up and down a ladder to turn it on. I've been waiting for you so you could be the first to light 'im up."

Into her hands, he plopped a small rectangular piece of electronics. "M'lady. The honors are all yours."

"Okay..." She stared at the remote control. "I'm assuming this big red button is the one I press, and that it's not a self-destruct switch."

"You assume correctly. Have at it."

Charli pressed the button, and suddenly, the chimney flared to life. Santa in all his glory looked as if he was about to climb down the chimney with a sack full of toys.

"Well, what do you think? Does he look like he's checking his list to see who's been naughty or nice?" Neil asked.

She'd known it was a Santa. Neil had told her that. She'd even looked for a Santa on his rooftop when she'd arrived home.

But seeing the merry figure on Neil's roof sobered her. Neil's Santa reminded her of what Neil had called her in the paper—a Secret Santa. Everything came flooding back to her—and suddenly, standing here in this innocent wonderland of lights, with Santa looking down on her, it was all too much.

And Charli knew beyond a shadow of a doubt she would not make Santa's nice list at all.

WHAT DID I DO?

For the life of him, Neil couldn't figure out what had gone wrong. One minute, Charli had been relaxed and happy.

The next? She'd jumped the hedge as if he'd lit her shoes on fire.

She'd made the flimsiest of excuses and taken off. Her compliments on Santa had been lukewarm. She'd turned him down flat on his offer of hot cocoa. She'd denied that a thing was wrong.

She was tired. It was late. Thanks, but no, thanks.

Neil hadn't even had a chance to ask her, once and for all, if she was the Secret Santa.

Feeling a little flat, he made his way into the house. His grandmother's mantel clock was striking nine o'clock when he shut the front door behind him. Outside, the traffic was thinning out, people heading home to put their sleepy, pajama-clad kids to bed.

Will I ever have a kid to share Christmas with?

Neil picked up a framed photo of his mom, eternally young. It had been taken the year she'd died. She was sitting with Neil in Santa's lap—his dad, he knew now—planting a big kiss on the guy in the red suit's cheek. Her hand rested on a six-year-old Neil's shoulder.

It was his favorite picture of his family. To him, it summed up everything about her—her love for his dad, for him, for Christmas.

His dad had waited years to remarry, telling him how once you'd found your soul mate, it was hard to settle for second best. And while Neil's stepmom was great, she could never be the ebullient grab-life-by-the-horns type of woman his mom had been.

Which was fine, too. His mom might have changed if she'd lived. Probably would have—she'd been so young. He was older now than his mom had been when she'd died in that car wreck.

What wasn't fine was the longing that Charli had set off in him, a longing to share Christmas—

life—with not only the world at large, but with one person in particular.

For the life of him, he couldn't understand how his emotions were overtaking his logic. He knew—with a reporter's nose for a story—that she was hiding something, lying by omission at the very least. So how did she make him forget that?

And just when he'd thought she might trust him enough to tell him the truth, she'd turned tail and run.

Something was worrying her. Beyond grief. Beyond overwork. Did Charli blame herself for not saving her father? Did she have bad memories about the holidays in particular?

Or was it this donation business?

Why was she lying? Not just to him, but to everybody? What could possibly be so bad she had to hide it?

Neil put the picture of his mom down. Time for bed. A glass of water and an ibuprofen, and he'd be ready to toss and turn.

In the kitchen, he filled a glass with tap water...and thought about Charli.

I can offer you tap water, or tap water.

Man, but he loved her self-deprecating sense of humor.

Neil tossed the pill into his mouth, washed it

down with his water and turned to put the glass in the dishwasher.

A movement outside caught his eye and he leaned close to his kitchen window to get a better view. A truck had pulled up into Charli's drive. He knew that truck.

Lige Whitaker.

Now what was Whitaker doing at Charli's this late at night?

The truck's headlights switched off. Whitaker came around, opened the passenger door and the crew cab door and jerked his thumb over his shoulder.

In the big puddle of illumination from the street light, Neil could see two Hispanic men stumble out. One of them, an older guy with salt-and-pepper hair and a moustache, was bent double. The other guy, younger by a good ten years, didn't look so hot, either, even if he was semiupright.

Lige pushed them up Charli's drive to her back door under the carport. As he hurried them along, he cast a furtive glance over his shoulder toward Neil's kitchen windows.

Neil was suddenly glad he hadn't bothered to turn on the kitchen light.

Lige Whitaker was up to something. That was for certain.

The older Hispanic man nearly fell. Lige picked him up by the collar and nearly booted him the remainder of the way to Charli's door.

Now Lige was banging on the back door with his fist.

Should he go over and see if Charli needed help?

The door opened. Charli's mouth fell open, then compressed in anger. She shook her head vehemently.

Lige jabbed a finger at her and then at the two men with him. Charli shrank back. Her head-shake this time was more hesitant.

That was it. Neil was going over there to see what Lige was trying to bully her into.

But as he started to turn, to head for Charli's, he saw her put her hand to her mouth, considering. Then she nodded.

Opened the door wider.

Let the men in.

Looked out just as furtively as Lige had a few minutes before.

Then slammed the door shut.

CHAPTER NINETEEN

CHARLI YANKED THE BELT of her robe tighter around her waist. She surveyed the two men who'd collapsed into her kitchen chairs and whirled around to face Lige Whitaker.

"What exactly do you expect me to do here at my house?"

"Chuck always kept stuff at his house. I'd take sick ones by his—"

"No." Charli swallowed hard. She didn't want to hear how she'd been snookered into doing the exact same thing her father had done. "No. These men, if they're as sick as they look, they need to go to the E.R."

Lige put one hand on a hip and eyeballed her. "They're illegals."

Good grief.

"The hospital can't turn them down based on their status. You of all people should know that."

"Sure. But maybe I don't want some nosy tri-age nurse to know my business and who I've got working for me. All it takes is one busy-body do-gooder to put a call in to immigration, and suddenly I've got a raid on my hands. Then even the legal ones scatter."

This man couldn't be for real. She worked her jaw to keep from yelling at him.

In as even a tone as Charli could manage, she bit out, "Hospital. Now. I'll treat them in the E.R., like I'm supposed to."

"You could have already seen to 'em in the time we've spent arguing."

The sickest man made a retching sound. Charli snapped her head in his direction to see him turn a shade greener. He grabbed his abdomen and moaned something in Spanish. Poor fellow. A pawn in Lige's army. He needed to be on a nice, clean hospital bed, getting pumped full of IV fluids. It angered her that Lige was delaying their care simply to yank her around.

Charli turned back to Lige. "And you could have already had them at the E.R. in the time it's taking you to attempt—and fail, I might add—to persuade me to treat them."

"Oh, you're gonna fix 'em up. You're bought and paid for. A hundred grand's worth. You can suck it up, and the hospital won't have to. Save the taxpayers money. Plus, your mama already thinks the hospital will be named after her hero." With that, Lige yanked a chair from the table, spun it around and straddled it, resting his arms on the back.

When he mentioned the money, nausea to rival the sick migrant worker's welled up in Charli's stomach. "No," she said. "You paid my father. That has nothing to do with me."

Lige sneered. "I like the way my money's getting me a buy-one-get-one-free."

Charli decided she'd call his bluff. "You can't reveal anything about that money without revealing why you paid it. I think that's called a standoff."

Lige raised an eyebrow. "Who said anything about talking about the money? It's easier to fire you. Suspend your privileges at the hospital. Evict you from your office. With no privileges, you're going to find it hard to keep your patients—oh, I mean, your *daddy's* patients. And I'll make sure no other hospital around here takes you on."

She drew herself to her fullest height and wished desperately he had not caught her in her robe. Something about bare legs and the thin pajama shirt she wore under the robe left her feeling defenseless and vulnerable. "On what grounds? I've done nothing wrong—"

"Pshaw. I don't have to go to much trouble.

You're peer-reviewed at the hospital. Somebody won't mind doing me a favor."

Charli folded her arms across her chest. The man was a snake. "Then whoever you'd get to do *that* favor? Why don't you dial him up to help you out of this jam?"

Lige scratched his chin. His tobacco-stained nails made a rasping sound against his salt-and-pepper whiskers. "Who else do I have such prime leverage on? Not just that business with your daddy—and you want to protect his memory, don't you? You don't want people asking questions. But I know for a fact you were the one who donated that money. So all I got to do is start a whisper about how you were the one who donated it. Suddenly, people are going to wonder where you got all that cash. People are funny about cash. Especially big piles of it. They tend to jump to conclusions. And then when I say, 'I had to suspend her privileges for the good of the hospital,' well, they'll be ready to believe the worst."

"Do it." She made her voice firm, hard. "I won't repeat my father's mistakes. I'll start over somewhere else. Your reach can't extend that far. I'll dig ditches to pay my student loans back. Plus, I'll make sure people know why you really fired me."

He threw back his head and roared with laughter. The man's teeth were as yellow as his nails.

How could I have ever thought he was my father's friend?

Lige's raucous laughter dribbled to a chuckle. He wiped a tear from one eye and shook his head. "Oh-ho, aren't you high and mighty on those fine principles of yours. First off, who are people going to believe? You've got an honest face, I'll grant you that. But I have a lot of credibility in this town, and a lot of people owe me favors. Plus, you'll be trashing your daddy's memory and stressing out that mother of yours. And you still won't have a job."

Charli was on the brink of telling him she'd take her chances and dialing 9-1-1 when he smiled.

In the blandest of tones, he asked, "Why not think about it like this? If you won't do it to protect your own backside, then think about your mama. How much trouble would the IRS make for her if I just happened to anonymously report all that income?"

The sickest Hispanic man dashed for Charli's kitchen sink and retched into it. She gagged at the smell, but went over to him, patted him on the back. The man looked at her with desperate eyes. He muttered something in Spanish in a pleading tone.

Poor guy. He's caught in the middle of this, and all he wants is someone to help him feel better.

Charli rinsed out the sink, walked him back to his chair. The man settled and gave her a grateful look; she turned and pulled a gallon jug of bleach out from under her sink cabinet. A generous glug of chlorine cut the odor and began the disinfecting work.

"Don't bring my mother into this—" she began.

"Yeah, well. She's got other fish to fry besides the IRS. She's already come to me, asking me for a quiet little loan. I guess she's run up some credit card debt, and that Jed Cannady, your dad's attorney, he's not letting loose any of your dad's money." He chuckled. "I do like a predictable woman. Too bad you gave away all the money you could have used to solve her little problem. So, what's it gonna be?"

Hot anger boiled up inside Charli. How dare her mother put her in this position? There was no money. Jed had been crystal clear that the terms of the will specified that the annuity would come in regular payments, that he would pay the household bills out of the annuity, and then whatever was left was her mother's allowance.

And Charli? With her own student loans and bills, there was no way she could help her mother out of a jam.

Charli had asked her mom if she was having trouble—and she'd smiled and told her she was just rebuilding her credit. How could Charli have been taken in by her mother's reassuring lies?

But Charli's anger was tempered with a flash of pain and guilt. She knew exactly what had happened. Her mother had wanted to give the perfect gifts for Christmas—just like she always had—and she'd spent all of her allowance. And then she'd done what she'd always done— found a way to buy something right now, and left it to her family to figure out how to pay for it later.

I hate Christmas.

Charli steadied herself against the doorframe, stared at the tableau before her and came to the decision that seemed all but inevitable.

Is this how her father had felt twenty years ago? Had her mother put him in a similar position?

Lige regarded her with complacent satisfaction, and a tad of impatience. "Well, okay, then. You getting with the program, or what?"

"We'll have to go to the office," Charli told him in a low voice.

Lige cupped his hand around his ear. "What's that? I don't think I quite heard you."

He'd heard her. Sadist that he was, he wanted to twist the knife.

She grimaced, bit back bile that had risen in her throat. "I said, we'll have to go to my office. I don't have anything here but my first aid kit. You drive them. I'll follow in my car. When did they get sick? And do they speak any English?"

CHARLI HEARD A TAP on the front door of the office. She ignored it, rolling over and burying her head under her father's pillow. She breathed in the last vestige of her father's cologne from his couch.

You did it to save Mom, didn't you, Dad? That was the only reason someone with your integrity would have gone along with a cover-up. You did it for the same reason I did. For Mom. But then once Lige had you he wouldn't cut you loose. You couldn't bear to spend the money—except maybe to help people out.

The two migrant workers were gone now. She'd patched them up and pumped them full of IV fluids, exactly what she would have done at the hospital.

Well, no. At the hospital, she would have had access to a full lab that would have given her quicker results. Drawing blood here and using the stool samples they'd given her, she'd have to wait for send-out lab results.

Tonight, she had been flying by the seat of her pants. Vomiting, diarrhea, stomach cramps... sounded like a garden-variety stomach bug, albeit one on steroids. From what she could understand in their broken English, they were the sickest of their families. Bad meat? Poor refrigeration? Could be anything.

At least they were gone—asleep, presumably, in their beds.

But most importantly, Lige was gone, too.

Man, she wanted a shower, both a literal one and a figurative one.

The tapping came again, louder, more insistent. It had to be the security guard who patrolled both the hospital and the offices across the street. Charli shoved back her shirtsleeve and saw that it was half past two. Great. Four hours and she'd be due at the hospital for morning rounds. Should she even bother going home to bed?

Straightening up, she stuck her feet into the

flats she'd shoved on earlier. Might as well tell the security guard she was alive and well and then she could at least head home to grab that shower and change clothes.

The man at the door, however, wasn't a security guard.

It was Neil. And he didn't look happy.

Perfect. Coming up with explanations on the fly during the wee hours of the morning was exactly what she wanted to do. This day had gone from a zero to a negative five on the jubilation scale.

Charli unlocked the door and waved him in.

"Well, why on earth not come on in? Arm hurting? Stomach cramps? Coughing? Or maybe a sore throat? I think I got more sleep during residency than I have the past month."

Neil stood just inside the door, his back ramrod straight, his arms by his side. "I saw you leave. And when you didn't come back…"

She averted her eyes to the floor. The poor philodendron plant in the corner drooped as badly as she felt.

How much had Neil seen? How much had he understood of what he'd seen?

"Welcome to my world. Doctors' hours, you know."

Neil crossed through the vestibule to a chair

and sat down. "I don't want to keep you long, because you look dead on your feet. So we can make this quick. But I'm not leaving until I know what Lige wanted tonight."

Charli pushed the inner door back open. "You might as well have saved yourself the trouble. Because I'm sorry, but no can do. Patient confidentiality."

"Those guys should have been at the E.R. There's no reason you had to treat them here in your office. If it's an emergency, people go to the emergency room."

Neil had a keen grasp of the obvious, she had to give him that.

"Guess Lige wanted the best," Charli ground out bitterly.

"No. Lige wanted something else. Secrecy. Charli…" Neil leaned forward with an imploring expression on his face. His eyes were dark and serious. "Charli, why go to this trouble for him? You didn't want to. I saw that tonight."

"You saw a lot tonight, didn't you." It was a statement, not a question. Charli felt the restraint on her temper loosen. She made an effort to pull it back, hold her tongue from saying anything that could cut.

"I saw enough. He was… I've never seen him like that, Charli. You can't let him bully you.

You have to stand up to him. Does he expect you to provide concierge medical service for him 24/7? In exchange for him naming the hospital after your dad? Or…is it something more?" Neil's tone was laden with judgment.

What did he know? Then her fear gave way to anger. She didn't have time for this—not when she had to clean up her mother's mess. "This is the last conversation I want to have at almost three in the morning. It is what it is. I'm a doctor. Those guys were sick. They came to me for help. I helped them. End of story."

"Yeah, but in the morning they could have gone to the community clinic."

Yeah. Because I gave the clinic the money I could have used to bail my mom out of debt. She twisted her attention back to evading Neil's questions and logic.

"In the morning," Charli said, "those two guys would have needed a hospital. So I saved the taxpayers some money on indigent care. That a crime?" Charli folded her arms over her chest and leaned against the door to keep it propped open. "Out, Bailey. I need sleep in the worst way."

"It's not simply that you're the new man on the totem pole, is it, Charli?" Neil's voice was heavy with sorrow. "He's got something on you, doesn't he? It has to do with that donation, doesn't it?"

Charli winced, remembering in Technicolor detail Christmases past, when her father and her mother would have raging fights over debt—lots and lots of debt that her mom had racked up in a seriously short period of time.

If I could wring my mother's neck right now, I would.

She tried to cover it as best she could. "You obviously don't know much about the politics of small-town medicine if you go all conspiracy theorist on me after just one night call. This is my life, Neil. This is what I do. Tell me you haven't gotten up at two in the morning to go cover…I don't know. A fire, maybe. Or a break-in."

Neil shrugged. She could see the tug of emotions on his face. He wanted to believe her. And that broke her heart.

He wanted to, but his next words told her he didn't.

"Sure. And tonight, if you'd gotten a call from the E.R. about those guys, it would be a good comparison. What you did tonight was the same as if I'd agreed to go do a feature story on Darius's fishing lures at 9:00 p.m. It doesn't make sense…unless…unless…"

Charli's pulse jumped the way it always did when she was faced with something unpleasant and inevitable at the same time. The pieces were all there. And Neil was smart. Give him time and he'd put them together in the right way.

"Did you know Lige was bringing them?" he asked. "Is that why you hauled off so quick tonight?"

She yanked at her ponytail in frustration. It hurt too much to think of how happy she'd been with Neil mere hours before. Charli could have had that chance if her father, her mother, hadn't blown things for her with their bad decisions.

Correction: if *she* hadn't blown things. She should have gone to the police immediately when she'd found those patient notes, told them about the money. But now she no longer had the money, and she had no firm proof that Lige was involved. It would all come down on her dad—which would leave her mom to face questions from the IRS and the police, at exactly the moment her mother was already stressed to the point she was burning up credit cards.

Charli squared her shoulders. This was her burden, and Neil couldn't help her, might not want to help even if he somehow could. "I hauled off, as you so elegantly put it, because

I'd seen Santa and I had been on my feet all day. And I'm *still* on my feet."

But he wasn't paying attention to her answer. Instead, he frowned in concentration, his lips moving silently as though he were retelling himself a story that didn't make sense. "You didn't know, did you? You left…because I guess you didn't want to be with me. Because something scared you. And then Lige showed up—" Neil broke off. "Just tell me what it is. What's wrong? Maybe together we can fix this."

The fetters on her frustration snapped loose. "What's wrong? What's *wrong?* The fact that everybody keeps asking me what's wrong! Oh, and why can't I be more like my dad? And, oh, by the way, nobody told me I'd be running my own office and cleaning up after my mother and trying to keep my dad's patients—all while I'm still dealing with losing my dad! And then—" The anger blazed out and to her horror turned into tears.

Then Neil's arms were around her, clumsy because of the hard cast, and she allowed herself to lean into him and the comfort that he offered her. This was what life was supposed to feel like, his arms around her, a balm, protection and strength. She could almost believe he could save her from anything.

"It's okay, Charli. We can get through this."

The spell was broken. Neil *could* rescue her from anything—anything but herself. Charli jerked back.

There could be no "we" with her and Neil. There was only her, and she was all alone in this. She had to be alone in this. She wouldn't get him involved in the mess she'd created.

She would, with enough sleep and enough mental space, figure out how to neutralize Lige Whitaker. She would get her mother help. She would come up with a way to deal with the fall-out from the donation.

But it was her problem. The last thing she wanted Neil to see was the hash she'd made out of all this. Right now, his nearness, his gentleness, made it hard to withstand the temptation to confess all.

If she could just fix this—if she could just deal with Lige's threat, Neil would never have to know and maybe she'd have a chance with him.

What was she saying? Did she even believe such nonsense? Any sort of a relationship needed to be grounded in trust—she knew that from her own parents' marriage. But if she told Neil the truth…he probably wouldn't have her, anyway.

She rubbed her fingers against her forehead. "Neil. Please go. Okay? Please?"

He backed away as though she'd slapped him. Raising his hands, he said, "Sure. Fine. I was just offering to help."

"I think I can manage on my own."

A pulse worked in Neil's temple. A muscle flexed in his jaw. "You know where I am if you change your mind."

With that, he pushed open the door and left, a cold breeze whistling around her in his wake.

CHAPTER TWENTY

NEIL SAT IN HIS CAR, watching for Charli to emerge from the hospital. He felt a bit like a stalker, but Charli was in trouble.

Trouble with Lige Whitaker.

And it had something to do with that donation. Neil knew it to the marrow of his bones.

His cell phone buzzed, and he put it to his ear without letting his eyes stray from the hospital doors. "Neil Bailey."

"Hey. Got your message," Brian told him. Neil could hear what sounded like coffee burbling in a coffeemaker, and then Brian pouring a cup. Neil would kill for some java right about now. "What's up, Bailey?"

"Those video cameras. What sort of range did they have?"

"To the clinic? You still hot on the trail after the Secret Santa?"

Brian's words surprised him enough to pull his focus from his surveillance.

"You mean you aren't?"

"Case is still officially open, but we've got word from the top not to prioritize it. Got a political corruption case in another county, and the boss is catching heat from the *Macon Telegraph*. See how you media guys just make us go around chasing our tails?"

"So…your talk with Charli…"

"You done got bit by the love bug, have you?" Brian laughed. "It's all 'Chaaaarli' when you say her name."

"I might have," Neil admitted. He didn't know what scared him more: the fact that he was falling for a woman he couldn't trust, or the fact that he was practically stalking the woman he wanted desperately to be in a relationship with.

Something about Neil's frank confession must have given Brian pause. The GBI agent cleared his throat. "I don't want to tell you what to do. You know her better than I do, obviously. But she was lying her— She was lying, Neil. All throughout that interview. Why she would do it, I don't know. And you know something, don't you? You saw something on that video that makes you think she's involved. Me? Before I got any cozier with her, I'd be asking her if she donated the money, and if she did, where all that cash came from."

Some nurses in candy-colored scrubs got out of their cars, stood for a moment at the employee entrance of the hospital and, laughing, headed in for their shifts. Neil wriggled to find a more comfortable spot in his Corolla. He was hungry and thirsty and sleepy. A cop he would not make. "What do you mean *I saw something?*"

"Man, you're as lousy a liar as she is. Look…" In the background, Neil heard doors opening and shutting, what sounded like bacon frying in a pan. It took Brian a few seconds to decide he was going to spill what was on his mind. "She's hiding something. It may not be a crime. It might not put her in jail. But…it would sure make me think twice if I were looking to take her out on a date."

Just then Charli came out the door. She was wearing a lab coat, slacks and a sweater, sensible shoes. She didn't cross over to her office, but got into her car and backed out.

"Thanks, Brian. I owe you."

"I'd say it was my pleasure…but it's not. I hate to be a dream crusher, Neil. Just be careful with her, okay?"

"Sure. Careful's my middle name," Neil said, eyeing Charli as she turned south onto the highway. "Gotta go, Brian." He hung up before Brian could finish his goodbye and waited for Charli to get a little ahead of him before he followed her.

What are you doing, Bailey? She obviously doesn't want you nosing into her business. And you're nuts if you think you can have a relationship with a woman who has secrets stacked up like cordwood.

A yawn cut short his mental argument. He slid the driver's side window down to let in some air. The chill morning breeze made him more alert, but it did nothing to settle the confusion crowding his brain.

Neil was certain Charli would spot him in her rearview mirror. The morning commute in Brevis, after all, mostly consisted of school buses and a tractor or two, with a lot of farmers in their pickups heading out to Ida's for a sausage biscuit.

But either she didn't recognize his car—not likely—or she had her mind on other things. Charli drove on out of town.

With a sinking heart, he realized she was driving toward Lige Whitaker's place.

Brevis proper fell away. Neil followed Charli past a handful of houses on larger lots outside of town. Beyond this, the scenery dwindled to nothing but pine trees interspersed with wide fields sprigged with Vidalia onion transplants. Broad County lay at the edge of the official area where the Vidalia onion could be officially grown. And Lige Whitaker? He was the Vidalia onion king of Broad County.

Neil could see many workers bent over almost double as they set Lige's spring cash crop in the ground. The work was done by hand—painstaking, backbreaking, mind-numbing. One of these poor fellows, on a good day, could plant maybe a half acre of transplants.

Lige was getting a late start with his onions, probably because the weather hadn't cooperated earlier and the fields had been wet. Maybe that was why he'd barged in on Charli the night before. Was he desperate to get his crop in the ground?

Ahead of Neil, Charli touched the brake and turned without a signal. Perhaps she hadn't been checking her rearview mirror. That wasn't like her. She always used her turn signal—even if it was to turn in to her own drive.

Now Neil faced a choice. If he turned and followed Charli down the narrow dirt track that paralleled one of Lige's fields, she'd surely see him. But if he didn't, he might as well have not followed her at all.

Well, he'd come this far. He yanked on the

steering wheel and felt the car's front end bounce in the deep ruts of the farm track. On one side, small tree branches in the field's fencerow nearly scraped the side of his car, while irrigation hoses and rows and rows of transplanted onions boxed him in on the other.

For a couple of minutes, Charli kept motoring on. But as Neil had known it would, his luck ran out. She came to an abrupt halt in the middle of the pig path. There was no cover, no hidey-hole.

He put the car in park and opened the door. What would he say to her?

Charli scrambled out of her car. She twisted to face him as she stood in the V of the open door. Her eyes narrowed and her mouth formed a thin line. "Just what do you think you're doing, Neil?"

Neil drew in a deep breath. He left his Corolla running and walked over the uneven ground to the back bumper of her car. Anger radiated from her in palpable waves. He could see it in the grip of her fingers on the door and the tightness around her eyes. He ventured no closer.

"Following you."

"Spying on me, are you?" she asked harshly.

"Making sure you're okay. What, more house calls for Lige?"

Charli turned her head and focused on something near the fencerow. Neil could see her face had flushed. She looked as though she was about to cry. For a moment, Neil thought he'd broken through to her.

But her back straightened and she lifted her chin. "I need to check on my patients."

"Wouldn't need to drive out here if you had 'em in the hospital where they belong."

As soon as the words were out of his mouth, he regretted them. Who was he to judge whether Charli had shortchanged their medical care? The woman he'd come to know would have insisted they stay in the hospital if they needed it.

"I'm sorry. That wasn't fair," Neil said.

"You're right. It wasn't." Her eyes held a wounded, angry light.

"Look, I want to help. I know—" He held up his hand to forestall her protest. "You say you can take care of this on your own. But I'm convinced you need help. I'm on your side, Charli."

She laughed. The sound was bitter and harsh. "You don't even know what side that is."

She had a point there. "Okay. So tell me."

Charli covered her face with her hands. "You're not going away, are you?"

"Stuck like glue." He risked walking closer to her. She dropped her hands to her sides in tight little fists. He could see the uncertainty on her face.

"Okay. But please, Neil, this isn't for publication, promise me that."

"I can't—" When she would have turned and got back in the car, Neil hurriedly said, "Wait! I can promise this—I won't put anything in the paper unless we've talked it through first. I may not agree with you, but you won't be ambushed. I swear."

Her shoulders sagged in resignation. "Promise?" When Neil nodded, Charli said, "Well, you're right. I'm not doing this out of the goodness of my heart. I mean...those farm workers last night—yeah, they needed my help. They were genuinely sick." Charli shook her head. "They're illegals, but you figured that out."

"Most of 'em are around here. But why you? Most of the illegals go to the clinic—and if they're sick enough, they'll brave the hospital's E.R."

Charli turned her palms up in the classic "who knows" gesture. "He doesn't want to advertise the fact that he has illegals working for him, maybe? I don't know. He showed up at the house last night, demanding I take care of them."

He sucked in a breath at her evasiveness. "No,

Charli. We made a deal. You would tell me what was going on. Am I going to have to drag it out of you, bit by bit?"

"It's my mom," she blurted out. "She's—she's got this problem. She's a compulsive shopper."

"I don't understand." How did Violet figure into all this? What ammunition could a spend-thrift woman be for Lige Whitaker? "So she likes to shop?"

"No. It's not *normal* shopping, Neil." Charli looked as miserable as he'd ever seen her, and he'd seen her in plenty of misery since he'd first met her. "She can run up debt—thousands and thousands of dollars of debt—in a heartbeat. And I don't have that kind of money. My dad arranged it so that she gets her household bills paid and gets an allowance, and there's nothing left over. She doesn't have access to the bulk of his life insurance money. Because he knew he couldn't trust her. So…" She rubbed her eyes and pinched the bridge of her nose. "This is so humiliating."

Neil reached to touch her, but she snatched her arm away. "I can't— I can't—" she cried.

He wasn't sure what had proven impossible for her—telling her story or bearing his touch. Part of him wanted to tell her, "Forget it. Share it when you're ready. I can't stand to see you in this agony."

The other part? He knew the agony was only beginning if Lige had some kind of hold on her. So he waited.

Charli stared out into the distance, her mouth pinched. In a low, clipped tone, she said, "She got a credit card. How she did it, I don't know, but she did. She lied to me, told me it was just a thousand-dollar credit limit, said that Dad's attorney had suggested it to…" She laughed harshly now. "To rebuild her credit. But this is exactly what she'd do—like clockwork— every single Christmas when I was little. She'd sneak around, open either a store account or get a credit card without Dad knowing about it, and then she'd run up the bills until the plastic smoked. I thought…I thought she was better. She hasn't done it in years. But I guess, what with losing Dad…"

Neil frowned. "But…how does that figure in with Lige?"

"She asked Lige for money. To bail her out. I guess Jed—Jed Cannady, Dad's attorney and executor—wouldn't or couldn't give her the cash."

Neil whistled softly. "So he tells you to treat

these guys or he won't lend you the money. Man, that's cold."

"Tell me about it. I don't have a choice, Neil. He threatened to fire me, send me packing without references, and I told him, do it. But… Mom—once she gets stressed, it's like it unleashes this person you'd never, ever imagine. She's not a bad person. It's not as though she means to do it—or even that she needs the stuff she buys. She gives it away, mostly. It's a compulsion."

"If she has a problem, don't you think you need to deal with it straight on? How long… has she been—"

"Years. I don't want to talk about it, okay? I'm doing the best I can." Bitterness shot through her words. "My dad took care of her, made sure she was okay, and he…did things to get her out of jams. Every cent got paid back. So no harm, no foul, right?" Charli attempted a smile.

Her reference to her dad doing "things to get her out of jams" caught Neil's attention. Now that he really listened to what she was saying— rather than focusing on her teary eyes—he saw a gaping hole in her explanation. "What else have you done, Charli? To get your mom out of a jam? I mean, you're a doctor. You could go to the bank, borrow the money yourself. It's not like you're a credit risk. You could even go to another bank, not this one."

The pleading turned to anger. "I've done nothing illegal, if that's what you're insinuating."

"No. I'm not insinuating. I'm telling you I've figured it out. You're the Secret Santa. Aren't you? It was you who gave that money to the clinic? So how come you had access to that money, but you don't have enough money to tell Lige to take a hike?"

Charli blanched. "Okay. So I went on a little shopping spree myself—dropping all my dad's spare cash on the clinic. It's not a crime. And I don't want this spread in the papers. Maybe I did it in an unorthodox way, but I wanted it to be private. I didn't want anyone to know. I didn't even tell my mom. The clinic is a good cause. You said it yourself that it needed to be saved. So I did good, right?"

Only, she sounded as if she was trying to convince herself as much as him.

"And yeah," she went on. "I'm a doctor, but I'm loaded down with student loans. The only way I can pay them off, not to mention my mom's newest debt, is if I can write some of them off by working in Brevis—or another underserved area. And Lige? He's threatening to fire me. Without references. Do you know how hard it is to get a job as a doctor without references? How will I pay any of the mountains of debt I owe without a job? Not even counting what my mom has probably racked up."

"Charli, you can't live like this. You know it's not going to end—blackmail never does. Go to immigration, turn his sorry carcass in—"

"I can't. I just can't!" The cry tore from her. "You don't understand. Not right after Dad— She's so fragile right now." She laid her head on the roof of her car and wept. Neil reached out to touch her, remembered how she'd snatched away from him a few minutes before and held back…out of fear that she'd shut him out again.

CHAPTER TWENTY-ONE

CHARLI RAISED HER HEAD from the crook of her arm and scrubbed at her eyes. She sniffed and wished desperately for a tissue to blow her nose.

"It doesn't matter. I *know*." She cut short his protest with a wave of her hand. "I have to deal with it—with Lige, with all of it—sooner rather than later. I have to deal with my mom. But right now?" She turned and dared a look at Neil. "Right now, illegal or not, those poor guys need to be checked on."

"Well, I'm not letting you go alone. You can use at least some moral support."

Charli's heart lifted. He still wanted to be near her, despite her having a crazy shopaholic for a mom and doing Lige's bidding, not to mention being the Secret Santa.

Of course, she still hadn't told him about her dad covering up outbreaks and deaths for Lige. Or that she hadn't told the whole truth about where the money for the clinic had come from.

But for now, she wanted to feel Neil's strength. "Okay. All right."

"I speak Spanish. Would that help you out?" he asked.

Part of the weight she'd been carrying moved from her shoulders. It would be a relief not to rely on a game of charades to glean medical history. "Yeah. Yeah, it would. Last night I was relying on Lige to do the translating...and, well, I figure he's not the most trustworthy translator. I decided I was better off without him."

Neil rolled his eyes. "Tell me about it." He turned and headed back for his car. "I'll follow you."

About a half mile farther on, the dirt road emptied out into a shantytown of trailers at the edge of the onion field. Charli parked the car and got out, taking in the scene before her.

The newest trailer had to be thirty years old, with cardboard blocking off a broken window. The oldest? It was a remnant of a trailer frame, with blue tarp covering the roof and a stovepipe stuck out the front window. Aluminum foil and towels seemed to be the insulation material of choice to stuff in windows.

An old school bus with its paint peeling and the school system's name blacked out rested at an angle on two flat tires. Here and there clothes flapped on clotheslines, but for the most part, there was no sign of life.

At least not human. A skinny dog skulked away from Charli's approach, darting behind the trailers. No grass grew here, only sprigs of frostbitten dog fennel that had sprung up in the narrow spaces between the trailers. The sturdiest, most carefully maintained structure was a hoop greenhouse. Charli could see lush green plants through the translucent plastic and marveled that these people would house their plants better than themselves—or was that Lige's greenhouse?

The whole settlement resembled something Charli had seen on the disaster relief trip she'd taken to Haiti while she was in med school.

The sound of a car door slamming made her turn around. Neil strode up to where she stood, his mouth drawn in contempt. "Well, this explains why he wants illegals. If he had them on legit work visas, he'd have to provide better housing for them."

"It's awful, isn't it? Do they even have running water?" Visions of typhoid came charging through Charli's imagination. She'd known migrant workers lived in subpar conditions, but she wouldn't even call this primitive. She shook her head. "Let's find Hector and Luis."

Neil trailed after her as she took off for the nearest trailer. "I take it that was the pair you treated last night?"

Charli just nodded. She didn't have time to offer color commentary. She was due at the office, and she'd already taken way too much time trying to explain her situation to Neil. She climbed a set of rickety steps and knocked on the trailer's dented door.

It opened a crack. Suspicious brown eyes stared out at her. *"Hola,"* Charli greeted the person. *"Soy la doctora Prescott."*

The eyes blinked, no less suspicious than they had been thirty seconds previous. But then, somewhere deep in the trailer, came a groan and the all-too-familiar retching sound from the night before.

"Hector?" Charli asked. "Luis?"

The door opened a sliver wider. *"La médica?"* The eyes turned out to belong to a short round woman in a tight pair of jeans and a faded sweatshirt, with worry and fatigue marring her features.

"Sí." Charli held up her medical bag. *"La doctora."*

The woman threw open the door and let loose a torrent of Spanish. Helplessly, Charli looked over her shoulder at Neil. "Did you get any of that?" she asked.

Neil said something in Spanish, and the woman spoke more slowly. He turned to Charli. "She says for you to come in, that her teenage daughter is very ill. She says Hector and Luis are a couple of trailers down."

"Oh, no. Is it the same thing Hector and Luis have? If it's the gastroenteritis, they all must have eaten some bad food." Charli crossed the threshold and saw an interior more in keeping with a third-world country than any place in the U.S. Naked plywood had been nailed across what had presumably been a sliding glass door on the backside of the trailer. The linoleum under her feet was buckled and cracked, mended in some places with wide strips of duct tape.

Still, in the corner stood a ragged plastic Christmas tree decorated with tinsel and multicolored lights. A motley collection of irregularly shaped presents waited under the tree.

Charli quelled her dismay at the living conditions she saw and fumbled in her medical bag for latex gloves. She handed a pair to Neil. "Here. Put these on. They're probably going to be tight because they're mediums, and you have bigger hands than me, but it's better than nothing."

"You think it's contagious?"

"I'm not sure, but safety first," she said, snapping the latex gloves into place.

The woman directed them with a finger to a mound of covers on a couch with its stuffing spilling out of soiled upholstery. Again she rattled off a quick burst of Spanish.

"She says the place is cursed. That it's bad luck. They haven't been here long, but the girl's gotten sicker the longer they've stayed."

Charli negotiated her way through the narrow path between the Christmas tree and a chunky coffee table loaded with candles featuring religious scenes on them, lit and burning. She squatted down beside the teenager, who was as round and soft as her mother. The girl's dark hair was matted, her skin pale and damp despite the chill air in the trailer.

It took a long time to manage an exam, what with Neil having to translate. But at least she could trust his translation. Again, the symptoms were intense stomach distress, nausea, vomiting, diarrhea—severe, bloody diarrhea.

"What is it?" Neil asked.

"I'm thinking *E. coli*. That's three people who are sick. Ask her if they all ate the same things, maybe a cookout where hamburger was served?"

Neil asked, listened to the woman, then volleyed the mom's answer back. "No. She doesn't let her daughter hang out with those guys—the younger one has been making eyes at her girl, and so she keeps her away."

The woman started again, hands on hips, anger lighting her eyes. Neil listened for a moment before telling Charli, "She says that lots of people are sick here, or have been, all with the same sort of thing. Ten, maybe fifteen. They've been here a few days, and they got sick when they first arrived. Some became sick, improved and then got sick again."

Charli frowned. "It has to be some form of *E. coli*. Probably STEC."

"STEC? What's that? It sounds bad."

"Shiga-toxin producing. Basically, you eat or drink something—or touch something and, say, lick your fingers—that's contaminated and the bacteria produces toxins that inflame the lining of your intestines. So that's where the bloody diarrhea comes from."

"Hope you've brought along the economy-size packs of Imodium," Neil joked.

"Tell them not to use that—some Pepto-Bismol is okay, but anything else can prolong the illness."

"Prolong it! The girl's been sick for nearly a week. She can't go without something to—"

Charli shook her head. "It's *very* important that they stick with something like Pepto and not Imodium—the body needs to be able to clear the infection. Usually this is self-limiting. There's not a lot we can do besides push fluids and watch for complications."

The mother interrupted again with what sounded like a question. Neil started in on Charli's answer.

"She keeps saying the place is cursed," he told Charli after he'd finished relaying her instructions to the mom.

"It must feel like it." Charli straightened up. "Let's go find Hector and Luis…and while I'm here, I might as well look in on some of the sicker ones. Maybe I can figure out the common denominator."

From trailer to trailer, they worked in tandem. Charli saw the same thing over and over, in varying degrees of severity. Squalid living conditions, horrible stomach ailments. Lige had lied about the scope of the problem—no surprise there, but she was still shocked. By the fifth trailer, Neil had lost any urge to joke.

"This is awful," he said when they were finished. "Something is making them sick."

They stood outside, after having stripped off yet another pair of gloves, breathing in fresh clean air. Charli squirted a generous dollop of hand sanitizer into Neil's cupped palms. "I wouldn't touch your face," she advised, "even with this stuff and the gloves."

"I'll probably burn these clothes," he said, a small amount of his humor restored for a moment. "What's causing this?"

Charli shook her head. She rubbed the alcohol-based cleanser into her skin. The winter air chilled her wet hands. "I don't know. They were all pretty adamant that they'd not eaten any of the same food."

"Could somebody have brought it in? The bacteria, I mean?"

"Sure. Sometimes you don't even present with symptoms, but you can still be a carrier." She moved her shoulders to relieve the ache between them and yawned. If she stood still, with the hovel behind her, all she could see was a peaceful countryside. Across a fence, cows drank from a placid watering hole and munched contentedly on winter ryegrass that was an improbable shade of green in a landscape of dun brown.

To be a cow, with nothing to do but stuff your face and loll around all day. No patients to see. No compulsive-shopper mother. No father who died and left you with a hundred thousand problems.

Beside her, Neil stood quietly at first. "Fifteen. That's a lot. Especially with no common thread," he said. "You have to call DPH."

She jerked around to face him. "What?" Call the Department of Public Health? On illegal workers Lige wanted to keep under wraps? That would be *just* what Lige had in mind.

"Yeah. I mean, this could be serious," Neil told her. "I covered an *E. coli* outbreak from a fast-food restaurant in Macon when I was a reporter for the *Telegraph,* and DPH was all over it."

Charli's palms went sweaty, despite the cold. "That's a little different situation, Neil. That's a threat to the entire population. This—this is self-contained. And besides, I don't know yet that it is *E. coli.* It could be viral."

"But aren't you supposed to? Report it? An outbreak? And isn't this an outbreak? With this many cases?"

She closed her eyes, worked her jaw. Yes. Any cluster of cases needed to be reported to health authorities at once. She couldn't believe she was rationalizing reasons not to do so in this case.

Unable to look him in the eye when she said it, she faced the cows again. One big guy, the color of the rust that was covering almost every piece of metal here, was almost shoulder deep in the water. Apparently, he didn't mind an ice bath.

Yes. Yes. She should call DPH. It was the right thing to do. These people were sick, and it was complicated, and the easiest solution was to turn it all over to the state and let it be their problem.

Easy if she wanted to get fired and likely never work in medicine again. Easy if she wanted her mother to have a nervous breakdown.

Maybe she could manage this. After all, what could DPH actually do? She could take care of those who were sick—push the fluids, keep them quarantined. These folks didn't tend to mix with the general population, so it was doable.

It's not like it's TB.

She exhaled a shaky breath. How to convince Neil? "Neil…it's… It—it would just go down in some database of statistics. Fodder for boring PowerPoint presentations. It's not like they're going to actually come out here and be able to do anything I haven't already done," she replied at last.

"You're afraid of Lige, aren't you?" Neil stepped in between her and the pasture. "Charli, you can't let him blackmail you. You could lose your license."

"It's a technicality," she insisted. "Not everything gets reported right away. I'm doing the care. And if it gets worse…" She hefted her medical bag's strap on her shoulder.

"Worse? Do you hear what you're saying? Charli!" Neil waved his cast-covered arm toward the trailers behind her. "These people are sick! They're depending on you—"

"They're *depending* on me not getting them deported, too," she said. "I'm doing exactly what the community clinic would do—treat now, and ask questions later. You think well enough of *them,* so why don't you cut me some slack?" Charli stalked toward her car.

"I can't believe you're doing this. I mean, I know it will be tough for your mom—"

She whirled around. "Look, buddy. You have no idea what tough is. Don't make me out to be a villain for thinking of my mom first, especially when she's in such a fragile state. I think I know what's best for my family."

"And for them?" Neil jabbed a thumb toward

the settlement. "What about them, Charli? Are you thinking about what's best for *their* families?"

For a long moment, she stared at him, her mouth agape, speechless with fury. "Are you kidding me? Do you *seriously*—" She let out a shuddering breath and glared at him. "I am thinking of their families. I came here, first, with barely an hour of sleep, without calling my mom, without checking on her. I just made a two-hour house call, gratis. While I have paying patients waiting, in my office, getting madder by the minute. I handed out supplies and advice and samples to those folks back there. *And* I took stool samples. *And* I'll send those samples and pay for them myself, though God knows where I'll get the money to pay for it. So yeah, I *am* thinking about them. I'm a doctor, Neil. I think I know what I'm doing, thank you very much."

And with that, even if she hadn't convinced Neil, she'd done a good job convincing herself. She left him standing in the cold, barren landscape and headed for all the responsibilities still awaiting her in Brevis.

CHAPTER TWENTY-TWO

NEIL RUBBED A TOWEL over his head, then tossed it into the bathroom hamper. A hot shower had made him feel marginally more sanitized, but it hadn't cleared his head.

He couldn't banish the image of what he'd seen that morning.

Correction. You can't get over the idea that Charli is bought and paid for by Lige Whitaker.

Sure, the story of her mom's shopping addiction—that could explain some of the weirdness. A lot, actually.

Clean clothes on, he followed the scent of coffee into his kitchen. He leaned against the kitchen sink and surveyed Charli's house next door.

What would he do if someone wanted him to kill a story and threatened his family?

Yeah. He could see how Lige was swinging a big hammer. But people would get over the idea that Violet was a compulsive shopper, wouldn't they? It wasn't like she was secretly a raging meth-head.

The main thing Charli's story didn't explain was the money. Where had it come from? Why hadn't Charli used it to pay off her student loans, or to at least create a slush fund in case her mother ever got in a jam?

Neil could not wrap his head around that question. Had Charli accepted a donation to the clinic from Lige? Had she somehow rationalized that maybe it wasn't a bribe if it didn't go directly to her?

Tired and weary from no sleep, Neil cut short his foray into the deduction business. He was not much good at it lately. And besides, he had a paper to put out. On less than two hours of sleep.

At the paper, Dawn ambushed him before he'd even got to his desk. "Just where have you been, Clark Kent? You haven't answered your phone, you didn't call in and you didn't even send me a text."

"I—" Neil considered what to tell her. He couldn't believe the intense loyalty he still felt for Charli. What he'd witnessed this morning was the biggest exposé of the year. It would not only sell papers and win him a caboodle of press awards, but it might actually do some real good.

So why wasn't he blurting it all out to Dawn?

"I can't say," he muttered. "I'm working on something."

"Well, I sure hope so. Because, as the stick you appointed me to be when you hired me, I'm telling you, aside from that six-inch article you've got on the board of education, you have zip for the front page, and it's already Friday. Got anything else on the Secret Santa? People are asking me if we'll have it in this week's edition."

Neil groaned and collapsed into his chair. Why had he made such a big deal over the Secret Santa's identity?

"Well?" She made a big show of tapping her foot. "C'mon, you can tell Auntie Dawn. What's got you so...un-Neil-like? You're usually focused and gnawing on something like this until the bone crunches into splinters."

"I don't have it," he told her.

Oh, you have it, Bailey. You have it. You just don't want it. You don't want to hang Charli out to dry.

"You don't have it, or you don't have proof?" That was the reason Dawn made such a great copy editor. She quibbled over exact language. She wanted it precise.

He wasn't sure what to say. If he told her he knew who the Secret Santa was—after all, Charli had confessed to it—Dawn would harangue him until he revealed Charli's identity or fired Dawn, sold the paper and quit small-town journalism.

"The GBI is dropping the case," Neil said. "They've got a higher priority corruption case in some other county, so they're not pursuing it."

Dawn flipped her palms faceup. "See? There's your story. GBI loses focus. Santa still on the lam."

"She's not on the—" Neil clamped his mouth shut.

"What did you say?" Dawn reached around into her cubicle and yanked her rolling office chair around. Plopping down in it, she folded her arms. "Am. Not. Moving. Not until you spill."

He stared at Dawn, started to make up some story out of complete moonshine so she would go away and leave him alone in his blue funk and not guilt him into writing the story he'd seen in stark reality a half hour before.

Neil realized what he was thinking.

What he was about to *do*.

Turn a blind eye on a story because it involved a woman he cared about.

"I can't believe it," he muttered.

"Believe it, dude. I can sit with the best of them," Dawn shot back.

"No...I wasn't talking about you." Now for the life of him, Neil couldn't figure out which was more unbelievable—that he was willing to throw his ethics over for Charli or that Brian was more right than he'd known in their morning phone conversation. Could Neil have fallen this hard for Charli so soon?

If not, then why does this hurt so much?

"Neil?" Dawn prompted. "If you weren't talking about me, what were you talking about? You're pale as cotton, my friend."

"I—I was about to do something—the same thing...I was judging somebody else for." The admission was a humiliating one for Neil to make. He'd always been so proud of the way he stuck to his guns and wrote straight down the middle of any issue.

"What is going on with you?" Dawn had lost her playful stubbornness. Now she leaned over and touched his shoulder. "You okay?"

He winced at the concern in her face. Dawn

felt sorry for him? When he'd been about to make the mistake of his career?

Still, the answer to Dawn's question was a big fat *no*. He was not okay. But if he didn't write what he knew, if he held back on what he'd seen this morning, on what he'd heard from Brian, how was he different from Charli?

CHARLI HAD SPENT the past seventy-two hours since going out to Lige Whitaker's farm in almost nonstop activity. Friday had been taken up until way past closing with patients, then she'd trucked it back out to the farm to check on the workers. Saturday and Sunday, she'd divided her time between the migrants—more people sick, but none critically ill—and catching up on all the paperwork she'd let slide. Plus, she'd had to do two admissions in the hospital for her paying patients.

Even so, Charli was failing miserably in her effort to catch up on everything she'd let slide—including her mother.

Charli hadn't realized her mom had taken a powder until sometime late Sunday. That's when she noticed that a) her mom wasn't answering her calls and b) aside from one call that had gone to voice mail, her mom hadn't called her, either.

Nope. Her mom was gone.

No note. No phone call. Just a breezy voice mail assuring Charli that she'd decided to "take a little trip for a change of scenery!" No destination, no clue as to where that change of scenery was. And Charli's desperate calls back? They went unanswered. Violet was gone.

Her mom had done this before. One Christmas, to escape Charli's father's wrath over debt, she'd used a secret credit card, and Charli and her mother had spent a weekend—and several thousand dollars—in a luxury hotel suite in Atlanta. Charli had been six and thoroughly charmed over the room service and "girls' weekend" her mother had dubbed the Escape. Her father? Not so much.

It hadn't been the last time, either.

Lige had told Charli about her mother asking him for a loan. It stood to reason that he'd told her mother that Charli knew she needed money. And that bit of deduction had paradoxically made Charli less worried about her mother. Charli figured that when the credit limit tapped out on whatever card her mother had managed to get, she would turn up, broke, sad and full of remorse.

Just please let it be a very small credit limit, Charli thought grimly.

She didn't have time to worry. Her two-hour foray just that morning at Lige's farm, to again check on his workers, had put her even more behind on everything. Irate patients had to be rescheduled, labs had to be checked and the hill of charts on Charli's desk had morphed into a small mountain range.

Charli was grateful for the packed schedule, the hustle from room to room to room. She didn't have time to think about Neil or her mom or how she still hadn't made that report to DPH about a probable STEC outbreak.

Who am I kidding? That's all I'm thinking of.

She took a stealthy peek at her cell phone, which was lying beside the chart of her current patient. She should call DPH. She should try her mother. She should call Neil again. But he hadn't called her. No text message. No email. No voice mail. No missed call.

No Neil.

She wanted to shake the phone until it produced the desired, "Hey, I got your forty-three calls and messages with all your apologies, and I accept."

But what if he didn't call her back?

Those calls—okay, not quite as many as forty-three, but a lot more than a few—had netted her nothing. Voice mail on his house phone.

A cool and distant, "He's not available, but I'll leave another message," from Dawn at the paper this morning.

Charli had made one bad choice, and that choice had led her further than she'd wanted to go and kept her longer than she'd ever dared imagine it would.

She pulled her focus back to the chart in her hand and tried desperately to remember her patient's name. She should remember this dearly familiar face, with its kind, twinkling blue eyes. The woman had taught her English in sixth grade. There it was. Roerden.

"Very good, Mrs. Roerden, everything looks good—"

"You got the test results back, then?" Mrs. Roerden asked.

Charli flipped through the chart and saw a note to call the labs about the delay. She cursed her forgetfulness. Tugging at her earlobe, she said, "I'm so sorry. I don't have those results yet. Not all of them. Let me call the lab."

Picking up her cell phone—and checking in vain for any sign of Neil's relenting—she dialed the lab's number. The person answering grumbled at first, then realized she was talking to a doctor and got radically nicer.

It irritated Charli to think the woman was

civil only because Charli had an M.D. after her name.

On a sticky note, she jotted down the lab results the tech gave her, asked for them to be faxed as soon as possible and was about to hang up when the woman said, "Oh, by the way, we got that rush order for you on those stool samples."

Charli felt her fingers go numb as they gripped the phone. "Yes? Good. You can fax—"

"Looks like you have a pretty big STEC outbreak. You reported it to DPH yet?"

"STEC, huh? I thought as much." Charli swallowed. Hearing it from the lab made it real in a way she could no longer deny. She risked a glance at Mrs. Roerden, who sat on the exam table with the heel of one shoe flap-flapping against the sole of her foot. "I'm with a patient now. Can you fax me those results so I can review them?"

Her heart hammered away in her chest as she tried to finish up with Mrs. Roerden without completely losing it. What she wanted to do was run to the fax machine and yank the results off the tray.

Mrs. Roerden slid off the table. She straightened her clothes and reached over to give Charli a motherly pat on the arm.

"Dear, you needn't be so nervous. You always were an anxious little thing. Remember? When I had you in English, I told you that you were going to have ulcers before you were forty? Relax. Your patients will forgive you if you're not perfect. Didn't we forgive your father for all those times he had less than a stellar bed-side manner?"

"Oh, Mrs. Roerden…" Charli had to blink away tears. The sweet patience of the woman almost undid her. "You have no idea what that means to me. Most people—I miss my dad, don't get me wrong, and I was looking for-ward to working with him—but…most people around here seem to think he walked on water."

"Your father?" Mrs. Roerden laughed. "I think somebody has been in an awfully big hurry to install stained-glass windows."

Charli reached for the tissues she usually saved for patients to use. "I don't understand. What do you mean?" She blew her nose and tossed the tissue in the trash.

Mrs. Roerden waited for Charli to finish rins-ing her hands in the sink before explaining. "Oh, it's a saying my mother used. It means… What does it mean?" She cocked her head to one side and fiddled with the string of pearls at her throat. "It means that when somebody dies, people are quick to forget all the qualities that made the person human. I don't want that. And I'll bet your father wouldn't, either. So don't go putting in stained-glass windows. He was just a man, Charli. Oh, listen to me, calling you by your first name as if you're still in my classroom. I mean, Dr. Prescott."

Charli squeezed her teacher's hand. "You of all people can call me Charli. I would have never made it through English 101, much less med school, if you hadn't hammered grammar into my head."

"I'm proud of you, dear. To think someone I taught grew up to be a doctor! Well, that is an accomplishment!" Mrs. Roerden beamed and went out the door.

Charli watched her go with a sinking heart. If Mrs. Roerden knew the corners Charli had cut recently, would she think so highly of her?

Her nurse, Shelly, rushed up to her in the hallway as Charli dragged herself to the next patient. Shelly had a sheaf of papers in her hand and a frazzled expression on her face.

"What is it?" Charli asked. She took the papers and glanced at them. It was the lab results from the migrants. There it was, clearly spelled out, as she'd expected—STEC, or more precisely, good old *E. coli* O157:H7.

Charli resisted the urge to ball up the papers. How long did she have to figure out a good way to neutralize Lige's threat to her mom? Not long. She had to call DPH. This was mandatory. And if she remembered correctly, the lab was required to report this to DPH, anyway.

Lige would have to like it or lump it.

"What a day!" Shelly blew a strand of hair out of her eyes. "Can you take out five minutes to talk Julianne Brantley down off the ledge? Her granddaughter is in the E.R., and Julianne is insisting you come in and admit her. I'm sorry, I know you're behind, but Julianne has completely lost it."

Charli tore her attention from the labs. "Her granddaughter's how old? Six? Seven? Was it an accident? Didn't I give her booster shots?"

"Yeah, you did. Last week. No, two weeks ago. It wasn't an accident. The kid has some kind of gastroenteritis thing going on. Bloody diarrhea, vomiting, the works. And—get this— a nosebleed that just won't quit. Julianne says she's limp as a dishrag. I mean, I get she's upset, but honestly, you're stacked up here, and she's called fifty gajillion times, or it seems like that, anyway. You want me to tell her to let the E.R. doc handle it?"

Charli pressed a hand to the wall for a brace.

Her lungs had failed her, or else there was no longer any oxygen in the room, because she couldn't seem to draw a good breath in. "Did you say gastroenteritis? And a nosebleed?"

"Yeah. Weird, huh? Julianne's more freaked out about the nosebleed—"

Charli shoved the papers back into Shelly's hands, snapped, "Reschedule everybody," and tore out past her for the door to the hospital.

CHAPTER TWENTY-THREE

NEIL SAW CHARLI run across the highway from her office to the hospital, her white coat out behind her. A driver slammed on the brakes to avoid hitting her, a squeal piercing the air. But Charli never looked.

Well, I can't tell her now.

No, he couldn't chicken out. Since he was running the story of the migrant workers in Wednesday's paper, he at least owed it to her to tell her first. That was what he'd promised her.

He flipped the blinker light from right to left and pulled into the hospital parking lot. The automatic doors to the E.R. had swallowed up Charli by now.

Neil followed her with steps that felt as though he had lead for soles. He would wait on her inside and catch her when she headed back to the office. Because if he didn't go ahead and tell her, he'd remember all those voice mails she'd left and be tempted to hit the delete button on the story.

•

Knowing he was susceptible to such temptation drove him crazy. He couldn't live with himself if he backed off on his own personal code: no matter who was the subject of a story, it went in the paper just as it happened. He'd already broken that once, not revealing Charli as the Secret Santa. No more.

Inside, the E.R. waiting room was deserted except for Julianne Brantley and Charli. Julianne had grabbed hold of Charli's arms. "They won't listen! That man won't listen! She needs to be in a hospital, and he's saying it's a virus—"

"Shh, shh—slow down, Julianne." Charli made soothing noises that had the opposite effect on the woman.

"I will not calm down! I will not! That's my baby in there!" she raged.

"Let's step over here—"

"No! No! Everybody's been trying to 'handle' me and calm me down and tell me that I'm overreacting, and I'm not!"

Neil took a step back, meaning to go back out on the portico in order to give Charli space to deal with the crisis at hand. But his movement had attracted Julianne's attention.

"Neil! You do something! You own the paper! This hospital is trying to send my baby home and she's bad sick! They won't keep her—" Julianne dissolved into sobs that racked her body.

Charli turned to see Neil. Her face, already pale and drawn, went at least a shade and a half whiter.

Neil lifted his hand. "This can wait," he mouthed. Again he started for the door, and again, Julianne saw him. "No! You've got to—somebody's got to—" She collapsed onto the floor. Charli bent down and tried to help her back up.

Neil closed the gap between them and added his strength to the efforts. Together, Charli and Neil managed to settle her in a chair.

Neil sat beside Julianne, while Charli knelt down and took Julianne's hands in hers. "Listen to me," Charli said. "Listen. Are you hearing me?"

For a long moment, all Julianne could do was shake with sobs. Finally, though, some of Charli's calm seemed to penetrate. Julianne took a couple of deep gasping breaths and nodded.

"That's good. That's good," Charli told her. "I need to go and assess her. But I *believe* you. I *believe* that she is critically ill and she needs help. I won't let them release her until I am sure she's out of danger. I promise."

Julianne's sobs came harder again. "Thank

you! Thank you! Oh, you don't know what this means—"

"Now, this is important, Julianne. I need you to focus. I need you to think back." Charli slid a sideways glance at Neil. Her mouth twisted into a grimace.

"Anything," Julianne rasped. "I'll tell you anything you want to know."

"Have you had anything at all to do with Lige Whitaker's farm workers? Maybe had them help you around the house?"

Neil drew in a sharp breath. He started to speak, but Charli held up her hand.

The question made Julianne sit back. She shook her head. "No. What does Lige Whitaker have to do with my Bethie being sick?"

"Okay, okay," Charli said. She furrowed her brow, concentrating. "Have you or your granddaughter eaten at any restaurants in the past couple of weeks?"

"No! No! We've been trying to do what you said, Dr. Prescott, and quit the eating out. I've been making nice green leafy salads at home. And she likes 'em. She says it makes her feel like a big girl." Again, what little calm Julianne had managed deserted her.

Charli stiffened. "Oh, my Lord." Her bottom

lip trembled. "Julianne, you— Where'd you get that lettuce? The tomatoes? For the salads?"

"Right here. I bought it from the vegetable stand that I was telling you about. You know. Buy local. It was good fresh lettuce. And the tomatoes were very nice. You don't think— Oh, my gracious, I'll just die if I gave her something that made her sick."

Charli lifted a trembling hand to her forehead. "I—I've got to go see your granddaughter. I could be wrong. Let's pray I am."

She stood up, but looked almost ready to fall. The last time Neil had seen her this shell-shocked was when her own father was dying in this very hospital.

The door to the treatment area opened and a man in scrubs Neil didn't recognize came out. "Mrs. Brantley, the nurses have told me you wanted to see me before you—"

Julianne came out of the chair with the ferocity of a wildcat. "You're fired!" she spat. "I've got my own doctor here, and I want her to examine my granddaughter." She sat down heavily, crying with what looked to Neil to be an equal mix of fear, relief and righteous anger.

The doctor rolled his eyes heavenward. "Sure, fine." He reached over and extended a hand to Charli. "Dr. Warren Teglia. And you are…?"

"Dr. Charlotte Prescott. I'm their primary care physician. I think you should be aware—"

He interrupted Charli. "Sure, the child is sick, very dehydrated, but you know these things. She's already been symptomatic for a few days, so she's probably through the worst of it. We've pumped her full of fluids and she's good to go. Take a look at her. You'll see. I did a thorough exam."

Neil saw Charli's back go rigid, her jaw jut out, at the condescension in the man's tone.

In a crisper voice, Charli asked, "I understand she had a nosebleed? Along with gastrointestinal distress?"

The doctor shrugged. He stepped a few feet away and motioned for Charli to follow him, which she did. However, he made no real effort to lower his voice. "Yeah. Nosebleeds. Kids have nosebleeds." He shrugged again. He made an effort to clear the put-upon expression on his face and school it into a mask of patience. He began ticking off a few salient details on his fingers. "The grandmother said the nosebleeds stopped after about ten minutes. No history of unexplained bruises. No history of bleeding disorders or clotting issues, if that's what you're getting at. Plus, she's a girl, so it would be a rare thing for her to have a bleeding disorder. The kid needs some Pedialyte and bed rest, period, and she can do that at home. I don't like admitting kids. They do better at home."

Neil felt Julianne about to come out of her chair again. He put a soothing hand on her, though he, too, wanted to deck the man.

"Remind me—what's gastroenteritis plus bleeding issues? In a kid?" Charli snapped.

Teglia blinked. "If you're thinking HUS as a complication of STEC, I'd already asked the grandmother about fast food and undercooked beef."

Neil tried to figure out the medical lingo. Whatever HUS was, it had lit a bell of recognition in Charli, and he certainly recognized the term *STEC*.

But as Charli was about to speak, Teglia cut her off yet again. "So it's not that, most likely. Yeah, I'll send the labs off, but I'm not really expecting anything. And the grandmother's raising the kid, by herself, on a fixed income—she can't afford a hospital stay to cover our butts." Teglia blew out a breath and reached over to pat Charli on the shoulder. "Look, no offense, but I've been doing this for years, and you look like you're fresh out of med school. Let me give you some helpful advice. Maybe you should just chill—"

Charli picked Teglia's hand off her and practically shoved it away from her. Her eyes blazed. "Maybe you should *just* stop. I hope you're not this condescending with all of your patients and their families." She pushed past him. "I've wasted enough time with you. I need to see my patient."

The door slammed behind her. The E.R. doctor stood there for a minute longer. His brows flexed up and he made a little "hmm" noise. He approached Julianne and Neil with some visible trepidation. "I am sorry if I offended you or if you think I wasn't thorough. Of course it's your prerogative to have someone else assess your granddaughter. But it's my opinion—from years of experience in emergency medicine, mind you—that she's got a self-limiting viral infection that will get better on its own. Now, I have other patients. If you'll excuse me." With that, he disappeared behind the door to the treatment area.

In the quiet of the empty waiting room, Julianne sniffled. "Dr. Prescott sure told him, didn't she?"

Neil sat beside the grandmother, unable to say anything. Sure, Charli had taken on the other doctor. She'd stood up to him.

But if she'd stood up to Lige Whitaker with

that kind of backbone, maybe Julianne's grand-daughter wouldn't be ill in the first place.

CHARLI RUBBED THE BACK of her neck and looked at Bethie Brantley's labs. Not good. Not good at all. "Lainey, any luck getting a bed in a children's hospital?"

Lainey ducked her head. "I've tried. They're saying they don't have a bed yet—not in Macon or Savannah or Augusta. Everybody's full up. They keep telling me maybe tomorrow."

Lainey's words made Charli want to weep. "What about Egleston or Scottish Rite? She can't make it until tomorrow. Her kidneys are failing. If she goes into multi-organ failure, we'll lose her. We may lose her, anyway. Her condition is beyond this hospital."

"I—I tried, Charli." Lainey's face was pinched with misery. The whole hospital had watched the child deteriorate in the hour since she'd arrived. "Thank you for taking a piece out of Dr. Jerk. Boy, I would have paid money to see you tear into him."

If I'd done my job, I wouldn't have had to.

Charli pushed away the thought and gritted her teeth. "There will be no dead babies on my watch. I graduated with a few pediatricians who are at Egleston and Scottish Rite. Let me see if I can swing something."

She checked on Bethie one more time—critical but stable. The small figure seemed so weak and listless as she lay in one of the four beds in the hospital's tiny ICU, despite the IV fluids and packed blood they were pumping into her. She would need dialysis, and pediatric dialysis needed to be handled by a children's hospital with a stellar pediatric nephrologist.

Julianne sat slumped, asleep beside Bethie's bed, her head on the mound of blankets, her hands tightly clasped around the girl's pale fingers.

When Charli moved the covers to place her stethoscope against Bethie's chest, Julianne stirred. The grandmother looked up, her face alight with hope. She waited until Charli had listened to the child's labored breathing, decided it would do for now and straightened up.

"Did you—"

"No, no bed yet." Charli placed a hand on Julianne's shoulder. "I'm going to try to call in some favors in Atlanta. I know it's a long way for you to travel, and you said you didn't have any family there, but she really needs to be in a children's hospital, okay? I wouldn't send her unless—"

"Oh, Dr. Prescott, she'd be dead by now if it weren't for you. You tell me what to do and I'll do it. I don't care if you send us to a hospital in Timbuktu."

Julianne's faith in Charli cut like the sharpest of scalpels. Charli flinched and turned away. "I'm going to call. I'll let you know what I find out."

She walked outside where the cellular reception was marginally better even if the air was colder. Leaning against the rough concrete of the building, and trying to ignore the biting wind, Charli thumbed through her contacts. Who could help her? Who did she know who could find a bed for such a sick little girl?

It was almost Christmas, the worst time in the world to be sick. Doctors were away on month-long vacations and kids packed the hospitals with respiratory infections and the accidents that always happened around the holidays.

The crunch of gravel pulled Charli's focus from the phone. She looked up to see Neil. For a moment her heart lifted. Seeing him made her think surviving this awful night was possible. He'd been there for her so many times. She ached to throw herself into his arms and let him hold her.

And then she saw there was no smile on his face.

"How is she?" he asked.

Charli stopped herself before putting her hand to her mouth. "Not good. I'm trying to find a bed for her at CHOA—Children's in Atlanta. Either their Scottish Rite or Egleston campus. We need to airlift her out of here. I have the chopper. Just no bed."

Neil hunched his shoulders forward. He folded his arms across his chest, and Charli's gaze fixed on his cast. The night she'd met him felt as though it had been a million years ago. That night, she'd been worried about proving she was a good doctor to her father.

And now? Now Charli knew good doctors weren't only up on the latest techniques and treatments and doses. They weren't necessarily politically correct. Good doctors made the hard decisions. Not like her. Not like her father.

"What's HUS? Julianne said you'd pretty much confirmed HUS, but she couldn't remember what it stood for."

Charli ran a hand over her head. What was the point in arguing about Bethie's privacy when she'd already broken so many, much more important, ethics rules?

"Hemolytic uremic syndrome. It's a complication of STEC—of *E. coli.* About fifteen percent of kids with STEC get HUS. It…" Charli closed her eyes, pictured the textbook definition and tried to figure out a way to explain it minus the medical jargon. "The body gets rid of red blood cells too quickly, and that clogs up the kidneys. Bethie's part of the fifty percent of kids with HUS who need dialysis—she needs everything a children's hospital can throw at this thing." Charli tried not to think of what would happen if she couldn't find a bed for Bethie.

"She's going to make it, though, right? You got it in time?"

Charli stretched her neck and considered the question. Her heart wanted to say, "Absolutely! Yes!" But she'd seen how sick Bethie was…and HUS was serious.

"I…I honestly don't know, Neil. I'll feel a lot better if we can get her to CHOA."

Neil's face visibly paled. His brows drew together and he swallowed hard.

"She wouldn't be here, Charli. If…"

At his words, echoes of her own thoughts, a tear trickled down her cheek. She dashed it away. "I've called DPH. They're bringing in a team. You were right, Neil."

"Yeah. Well." He stared into the concrete wall hard enough to bore holes in it.

"I know you're angry. So say it. Go ahead. Tell me you told me so. Tell me it's all my fault." She reached out a hand to his arm.

Neil stepped back and stared at her with flat eyes. "Just so you know. The migrants are going to be on page one this week. Do you want to give me a quote?"

As she had the night she'd stood listening to the doctors run the code on her father, Charli knew the bitter taste of regret. Her heart physically ached at the finality in Neil's tone, the disappointment in his eyes.

Whatever she and Neil might have had was gone, and gone before she'd even realized the prize she'd held.

With as much dignity as she could muster, she lifted her chin. "Only that I am aware how my decisions—or rather the lack of my decision to act—endangered the lives of many people. And…I am…" Her throat closed up. "So sorry."

Neil didn't bother to hide the contempt that twisted his mouth. There would be no more dimples for her, she knew, no more admiring glances, no more laudatory articles about her prowess as a doctor. He gave her a stiff half nod of his head. "I appreciate the quote." With that, he spun on his heel and walked to his car.

CHAPTER TWENTY-FOUR

"THE STATE MEDICAL BOARD has confirmed it's investigating a south Georgia physician who covered up an outbreak of *E. coli* that has led to at least eleven people sickened from a migrant-run farmer's stand—"

Neil punched the radio knob off with a stab of his finger. He didn't need to hear another state news bulletin about Charli. He'd written it. It was his article that had blown the whole cover-up. The only things he'd left out of the story were her mother and the part about the Secret Santa—that was the least he could do for her.

He parked the car in about the same place he had when Charli and he had come to the farm only a few days before.

Only a few days? Today was just Thursday, and he'd broken the story early, putting it on the news wire so the dailies could pick it up.

It felt like it had been forever. It felt like Charli—the woman he'd hoped had been Charli, anyway—had been ripped from his heart. Neil stiffened his resolve. He didn't need the woman she'd turned out to be. The Charli who had turned a blind eye and allowed an outbreak to explode unchecked was not the Charli he'd fallen for.

The migrant settlement looked even more ramshackle and deserted than it had before. Mainly because it *was* deserted.

Every single family here had disappeared into the mist, vanished. It was of huge concern to the state officials because they still hadn't pinpointed the cause of the outbreak.

Sure, they'd figured out the common denominator had been the migrants, who had grown the vegetables sold at the farmer's stand, and the vegetables had sickened Bethie Brantley and at least ten other people in addition to the workers. But had someone brought the bacteria in? And if so, was a public health risk compounded because the migrants had taken the source with them?

So now, Neil waited for the rest of the team sent in from the state to leave their vehicles. They'd asked him, since he'd been the one translating for Charli, to walk them through and give them some context.

Stretching and joking, taking last swigs out

of their coffee travel mugs, the doctors piled out of an SUV with state license plates.

Didn't they know that lives were at stake?

Maybe they were as cavalier about this as Charli had been. She had made her choice to hide from the truth, and she apparently was still making it. Charli, for all practical purposes, had vanished, too. After she'd gotten Bethie a bed and had her airlifted to Scottish Rite in Atlanta, Charli had locked up the office and disappeared.

Neil opened the car door and trailed behind the state health people, his camera in hand. They began an exhaustive tour of the run-down trailers.

"So this was where they said the Patient Zero was?" asked one of the doctors, a tall thin lady whose pants were a quarter-inch too short for her, even in the flats she wore. Neil had learned she was an epidemiologist who had a string of letters after her name.

"Yeah. We started at the first trailer, and the families kept pointing us to other people who had been sick. Best I could understand, one of the guys who lived here in this trailer was the first to come down with it," Neil told her. He looked around at the space originally designed to be an open kitchen/dining area/living room.

It was still crowded with stained folding cots—eight, if he'd counted right.

The tiny bedrooms had been outfitted with rough bunk beds that slept another half dozen in all the spaciousness of a prison cell, but a whole lot less weatherproof. "Though, I guess calling this place a trailer is a bit generous."

"Too right," the woman said. "Appalling. They didn't even have a roof over their heads—I count three buckets in here alone to catch leaks."

When they went back outside, Neil listened as the doctors bounced ideas back and forth on the origin of the outbreak. He scribbled madly to get everything down for the next edition of the paper. The poor migrants weren't the problem—Charli had been the problem. If she'd done what he'd advised her, the sick could have been treated without spreading the infection to the produce stand they ran.

His coverage of the whole incident had unleashed a firestorm of xenophobic rage. What he'd written with the intent to arouse sympathy for the poor suckers who'd called this place home had generated the opposite effect.

Readers wrote fiery letters, demanding that the community clinic be closed and that zoning ordinances be passed to prohibit settlements such as Whitaker's. Neil could have cheered that last one, but those who pushed for the ordinance really wanted to run every Hispanic person out of town on a rail.

The AP and state and national news organizations had picked up the story. Even CNN had been down to get some video. Already, major newspapers and internet blogs had called to offer him jobs. Other weekly editors had given him congrats for his bravery about taking on the system in the interest of public health.

Still, Neil couldn't help but feel guilty. He'd made all this splash on the poor unlucky fate of Bethie Brantley. Maybe he should have called DPH himself when he realized Charli wasn't going to.

"Hey, is that—that's a herd of cows!" One doctor in the team shadowed his eyes and peered across the fence at the watering hole.

"Why, yeah," Neil couldn't help saying. "We have cows around here. Lots of 'em."

Now the whole team became extremely fixated on the cows. Even as they crossed the field to the fence, one of them was counting the number of cows around the watering hole. Another was snapping pictures like mad on a small digital camera he'd tugged out of his pocket. A third was walking a straight line from the fence to the greenhouse.

Neil couldn't figure out what all the excitement was about. He lagged behind them in order to compose a photo of the doctors as a group. As he was about to hustle over to join them, the slam of metal caught him up short.

Neil turned to see Lige Whitaker rounding the hood of his truck and striding over to him.

Talk about someone coming out fighting. First thing Lige had done was very publicly suspend Charli's privileges at the hospital. Next, he'd issued a typewritten statement asserting he'd had no knowledge of Charli's failure to report the outbreak to the DPH.

Who knows? Maybe Charli had overreacted. Maybe Lige hadn't come right out and threatened her.

Funny, though, how Lige dodged every one of Neil's phone calls and visits.

"You and your camera. Off my property," Lige told him. "You're trespassing."

"I don't think so. You allowed the DPH access, didn't you?"

"Last I heard, you weren't employed by the DPH. Unless you're folding up that slanderous thing you call a paper—"

"Libel. It would be libel. And it's only libel

if a) you can prove it's not true, b) I knew it wasn't true and c) I was malicious in intent," Neil corrected him. "And the DPH asked me to come along."

"Go to—" Lige sent a fist toward Neil's jaw, but Neil swept up his arm—the one with the cast—and stopped the punch with a block to Lige's forearm. The older man stepped back, his mouth slack, and rubbed his arm.

"It's nice to be nice," Neil told him. "But I don't have to if you insist."

"You, smearing my name, practically accusing me of ordering Charli Prescott to cover up this mess."

"You didn't? You want to go on the record with that?"

"I most certainly did not. Charli made her own decisions. All I did was take two sick guys to her house one night for treatment. She's the one who covered it all up. I guess it's because she's partial to those illegals. And now look! All my help, sick and well alike, has run off and I can't get my crop planted. I'm on the hook for a million plus!"

"Right." Neil wanted to deck the man. This was the guy who had stolen Charli from him, and part of him still believed that, without Lige, she would have never contemplated such a cover-up. "You didn't have a thing to do with it. She decided, on her own, that it would be better to keep this under the radar. Because she has a soft spot for migrant workers." Neil didn't bother to keep the sarcasm from his words.

"It's just like I explained it to that CNN fellow. She donated all that money to 'em, now, didn't she? Could have helped tax-paying legal citizens here by donating it to the hospital, but no, she had to go give it to freeloaders. And you—you son of a—"

Lige's focus suddenly moved from cussing Neil out to the group by the fence. "What are they doing? That's my wellhead they're messing with. And my greenhouse!"

Lige stomped off toward the fence. Neil followed, frustrated that Lige hadn't finished what he'd been saying. Had Lige known all along that Charli was the Secret Santa? Maybe Lige had indeed given Charli the money, a payoff to keep her quiet.

Neil came up to the team in time to hear sharp words being exchanged. He was amazed to see that Lige was so angry he'd dispensed with his usual "aw shucks" charm that Neil now realized had been a mask.

"Heck, yeah, I put this wellhead here! I drilled this deep well my very own self, like my daddy taught me. How else do you think I could irrigate this field? And that one over there, too." Lige snapped at the epidemiologist with the alphabet soup after her name.

"And these irrigation lines...they go to what?" the epidemiologist asked.

"To these onion fields! Weren't you listening? And to my greenhouse there. And I gave them ungrateful illegals free water out of it!" He shook his head and reached into his shirt pocket for a pack of cigarettes. It took him two tries to tap a cigarette out of the pack, his hands were shaking so badly.

Neil quietly raised his camera and captured the scene, really liking the way the confrontation gave the photo's composition energy.

The epidemiologist nodded at Lige and scribbled some notes down on her clipboard. She delivered the next question in the blandest of tones. "Uh-huh. And was this greenhouse the source of the produce at the farmer's stand?"

"Is that a crime? Can I help it if those sorry good-for-nothings brought some dread disease here from wherever they came from and got snot and spit all over my vegetables when they were running my stand?" Lige's fingers still trembled with agitation as he thumbed a lighter to the cigarette he'd stuck in his mouth. But a deep draw of the cigarette seemed to calm him.

The epidemiologist pressed on. "Did you get clearance from the health department, Mr. Whitaker? For the well? And were you in compliance with state regulations concerning the sale of fruits and vegetables?"

"Missy, I *am* the health department in this county!" Lige ground the words out around his cigarette and jabbed a finger into his breastbone. "You're talking to the chairman of the Broad County Hospital Authority."

The woman didn't look a bit browbeaten by Lige's tone. She raised an eyebrow at her fellow team members. They nodded at her unspoken message.

"What?" Lige's confidence seemed shaken. "What are y'all saying?"

"Mr. Whitaker, by order of the state, we're closing this well and anything watered from it, pending testing."

"No, by God, you're not." He jerked the cigarette out of his mouth and leaned within inches of the woman's face. "I need that water! It's my right! And those fields are my livelihood! You can't do that, not in the United States of America!"

She stepped smartly back, careful not to

touch him. "See those cows over there, Mr. Whitaker?" the epidemiologist asked, sweeping a hand in the direction of the herd across the fence. "See their watering hole?"

"Yeah? They gotta have something to drink." Lige folded his arms across his chest, his cigarette dangling from his fingertips. "What, you gonna kill my cows now, too?"

"No. But we will need to check to see if you've sold any of those cows for beef without proper inspection. That watering hole backs up to your wellhead."

"So? So?" Lige spat out the word. "You think you're so smart with your college education and your state car and your—"

"Sir." The epidemiologist broke in, implacable, totally unscathed by his abuse. "That wellhead is a straight shot down, a sure path for any contaminants. And I'd bet dollars to doughnuts those cows have contaminated that watering hole, which contaminated the well, which… well, you can follow the logic."

Neil's breath caught as he began to understand the epidemiologist's train of thought. His mouth went dry. Nausea roiled in his stomach.

"No! Nah, no way, no how!" Lige's voice went reedy-thin with rage. "It was that Prescott woman! She covered up those migrant workers!

She didn't let me know how sick they were! If I'd known she was hiding the truth, well, I'd have turned her in myself!" Whitaker shouted.

The epidemiologist's mouth curled in disgust. She shook her head. "Mr. Whitaker, you have it wrong. It wasn't the migrant workers or Dr. Prescott's failure to report the outbreak that caused all of this misery. If I were you, I'd get a very good lawyer, because an army of personal injury attorneys are going to be gunning for you."

"Me? They should be suing *her!* She's the quack in all of this! She's the doctor!"

"Sir." The epidemiologist's tone was careful, measured and completely contemptuous. "From our review of the records, that little girl became ill before you took the migrant workers to Dr. Prescott for care. She became ill at about the same time they did. So, no. It wasn't Dr. Prescott's failure to promptly report the outbreak. Your total lack of compliance with and utter disregard for state regulations? *That's* what caused that little girl to almost die."

Lige Whitaker turned a sickly shade of green. He looked as though any second he might retch.

And Neil? Neil felt the same way.

Sure, he'd reported the facts as he'd known them. But in his anger with Charli, he'd made sure to choose words that would vilify her. He had crucified Charli. He had hung her out to dry, spread her face across the nation's newspapers and television sets as the woman who had caused all this sickness.

When, actually, she'd been as much a victim as Bethie Brantley and all those poor miserable migrants.

He'd exploited someone's mistake for his own purposes. Sure, he'd thought he was on the side of right—no, he'd been certain of it. But no matter what his motivation, Neil had been happy to trash Charli's reputation with no thought to the possibility that he'd erred in his assessment of the situation.

Was he any better than Lige Whitaker?

CHAPTER TWENTY-FIVE

CHARLI STOOD AMID crowds of people of all ages in the lobby of the Westin, in Savannah, surrounded by gingerbread houses like she'd never seen before. She didn't have time to appreciate the artistry it must have taken to create an elaborate gingerbread version of Savannah's Cathedral of Saint John the Baptist, though.

She was looking for her mother.

After she'd finally got Bethie on the helicopter for CHOA, it had taken Charli two days and at least a dozen humiliating phone calls to various people in her mom's address book, but finally, finally, one of the ladies had miraculously known where Charli's MIA mom had vanished to.

The Westin Golf Resort and Spa. In Savannah.

Classic move, Mom, Charli thought bitterly. *You picked another ritzy resort to blow your credit card to smithereens.*

Her mother's friend hadn't seemed the least

concerned about Charli's mom. She'd brushed away Charli's fears with a laugh and told Charli, "Oh, she mentioned something about a girls' trip to Savannah with Brenda Arthur and another friend—now, who was it? They were going to the Westin."

It fit the Violet Prescott Charli knew to a T: elegant surroundings, dolled up for Christmas in one of her favorite locations, Savannah. If Charli hadn't been so swamped with catastrophes, she might have realized this was exactly where Violet would have bolted.

As it was, now that Charli was here, she hadn't spotted her mother, and the desk clerk hadn't admitted to a Violet Prescott or a Brenda Arthur having registered at the hotel. Privacy? Or had the reservation been made in the name of the third musketeer?

Charli couldn't think, not with all the hubbub of excited kids around her—or the gingerbread villages. All the exhibits made her think of was Neil—everything Christmassy made her think of Neil.

He was gone. She had lost him. She needed to focus on the things she could still salvage from the wreckage she called a life. Charli took a deep breath and watched as people milled around the villages.

Clustered around tables with fake snow and lights, the visitors oohed and aahed over the intricately decorated gingerbread creations.

Charli didn't know what to expect whenever she finally did track down her mom. At first, Charli had been sure her mom would bounce back to Brevis pretty quickly. Maybe Charli had been foolishly hoping her mom hadn't been lying about the thousand-dollar credit limit.

But she'd been gone for four days now, and all Charli's phone calls had gone to voice mail, with no return calls. It spoke of guilt for sure—an unwillingness to face Charli or her debt.

Who knows how many cards she managed to get approved, or how I'll pay for it? The first person she'd talked to was Jed, who'd admitted that he'd agreed with Violet about applying for the Chase card. But he'd been genuinely shocked to hear that Violet had applied for a loan at Lige's bank. He'd taken the whole thing hard, blaming himself for not doing a better job of looking after her mom.

Charli had spent the past two days desperately searching for anyone who could tell her where her mother might have gone to ground.

At least she wasn't in Brevis—after the one hundred and twenty-nine messages on her cell phone and various reporters looking for her, she'd stopped answering anything but the state medical board's calls or the numbers of her mother's friends or support group members.

Neil had even called a time or two. She had erased the messages without listening to them. Hearing his voice, as cold and impersonal as it had been that last time, would have hurt too much.

And then Charli spotted her. Amid all the gingerbread admirers, there was her mother, her head thrown back, laughing along with three other ladies. They looked very much the part of ladies of the club, with their designer hand-bags, their coiffed hair, shopping bags dangling from wrists.

Shopping bags. Charli groaned. She could finally understand the depth of her father's an-tipathy for all things Christmas if this is what the season did for her mother.

No. Her mother had done this to herself. Just like Charli had put Bethie's life in danger. It was your own choices that got you.

Charli pushed through the crowd, trailing her mother through the exhibit. She moved past an elderly lady and a little girl, which reminded her all over again of Julianne and her grand-daughter.

"Mom!" But her mother was too engrossed

in what someone was saying about a particular entry in the gingerbread contest to hear her. Charli grasped her mother's arm, causing her to whirl around.

"Charli! Look, girls! It's Charli! Oh, this is wonderful! I'm so glad you decided to take time off to join us."

"Mother." Charli hated the way the word came through gritted teeth. "Where have you been? I've called everyone I could think of."

"Honey." Some of the joy faded from her mother's face, replaced by a wary defensiveness Charli knew all too well. "Is something wrong?"

"Something—" Charli choked on her anger. "You disappear off the face of the earth, and I don't have a clue where you are? And you ask—"

"But I left a message. Charli, I left a message on your phone. I told you."

"That you needed a change of scenery. Yeah. And you found it all right. Right here. Only the most expensive hotel in Savannah would do, right, Mom? Just a little shopping therapy?"

Now it was her mother whose mouth went tight and angry. "Charli, let's not make a scene. Why don't we find a quiet place, so we can talk?

Girls—" now she turned to her friends "—will you excuse us?"

"Excellent idea," Charli muttered.

She followed her mother away from the exhibit, to the hotel's main restaurant. At this point in the day—midafternoon—the dining room was deserted. They were seated at a table, their iced tea served, before her mother spoke to her again.

When she did, the words came out calm and careful, in a way that Charli knew meant Violet was steaming.

"I left a message. I could have sworn I told you where I'd be staying, but perhaps I didn't. In any case, I apologize for making you worry. But what I don't appreciate is you immediately assuming I'm bingeing."

"Aren't you? Isn't this you, Mom?" Charli swept her hand around the elegantly appointed dining room. "And I can see from the shopping bags you've been burning up that credit card. Or is it more than one card?"

A muscle twitched in her mother's cheek. Charli could see her draw in a breath. "I'm not staying here, Charli. We came to see the gingerbread exhibit. I'm staying—with Brenda—at Pauline's. Whom I would have introduced you to if you hadn't been slinging such an almighty hissy fit."

"Pauline's?" For the first time, doubt crept into Charli's certainty. "You're—"

"Pauline lives in Savannah. She's on our online support group. We've been making this Christmas trip a tradition now for about three years. It's a fun, inexpensive way to enjoy the holidays. We do all the free stuff. And yes, a little shopping—with a budget of a hundred dollars."

"But…but why didn't you answer your phone? Or return my messages? I must have called you fifty times." Charli wanted to believe her mother, but her dad had bought into her lies before, too, to his sorrow.

"Oh, Charli." Her mother's anger faded into sheepishness. "I forgot my charger. I—I guess I thought I'd left you Pauline's number, and so I didn't worry that you'd worry. You must have been out of your mind."

"I was. At first, I thought you'd realized I knew about you asking Lige for a loan to get you out of debt, and you'd turn up eventually, but then you didn't come home, and I couldn't find you—"

"Wait. Wait. What's this about Lige, and me needing to get out of debt?" Her mother's confusion was either real or of Oscar-winning caliber. "I'm not in debt."

"But he told me…" Charli put her hand to her face. "Oh, no. I can't believe I was so stupid. So gullible."

"What? What did he tell you? That I talked to him about a small-business loan? Well, I did. I want to start my own business—wedding cakes. I could do it. You know how I love to bake and decorate. It didn't occur to me until Beattie Trilby told me I could get big bucks for the cake I made for the Christmas bazaar, but it got me to wondering. I've never had a job, Charli. And I could start out small, see how it went. I was just in the bank, and there was Lige, and I asked. But…you thought—"

"No. No. Lige told me. And I believed it." Charli wanted to cry. Lige had played her. No. She couldn't blame Lige completely. She'd been ready to believe the worst.

Charli's mother extended a slim hand to grip Charli's fingers. "Honey, you look all done in. What on earth is the matter?"

"You…you haven't heard? You haven't seen the news?" Charli shook her head in disbelief. Had her mother been under a rock the entire time she'd been in Savannah? She had to have been. Her mother would have called her if she'd heard half the accusations the state and national news media were slinging at Charli.

"About what? What does this have to do with Lige? I haven't watched television—we've been too busy, and Pauline hasn't even turned it on."

How to explain the mess Charli had found herself in if her mother hadn't seen the wall-to-wall coverage of Charli's horrible mistake? She was almost glad her mother hadn't been watching the television. The last straw had been when Charli had heard Lige's thirty-second sound bite on CNN disavowing any knowledge of Charli treating the migrants.

After that, she had turned the television off and avoided newspapers. She had her own hands full with the medical board's inquiry and finding her mother.

Her mother. Who hadn't needed tracking down at all.

Charli began a stumbling explanation of all that had transpired, stopping and starting, having to go back and tell bits and pieces of it so that she could fill in gaps. But all the while, her mother sat, patient, still, intent on Charli's every word.

It was only after Charli had told her about the money and the notebooks and the donation, about Lige and the migrants and Julianne's little granddaughter, that her mother spoke.

"Sweetie. You've been through such torment. And I've been here, having a rollicking good time. I am so sorry. So sorry that in the midst of all this, you were worried about me. I am so sorry that you doubted me."

"I'm the one who's sorry, Mom. I guess I've got to learn to trust you."

"Trust doesn't come easy to you, does it? And I deserve some of that doubt. Still, Charli, you have to let people grow. And change. We're not always going to be the way you left us."

"Did you know, Mom? About Dad? And Lige? Or was Lige lying about that, too?"

Her mother stared down at the table. "I didn't know your father still had the money. Honestly, I figured he'd spent it all trying to get me out of debt years ago. But I knew that Lige had made some sort of arrangement Chuck wasn't very happy about. He didn't tell me the details, just enough. When he finally told me—the bare bones—I made up my mind I'd never put him in that situation again. That's when I got serious about the counseling and the support groups. It changed my life. It changed your father's. We... we had some very happy years. Very happy."

Charli dropped her head in shame. If she'd

just come clean to her mother from the get-go, if she hadn't been so certain that her mother was too fragile to face the truth, none of this would have happened.

"What about you, Charli? What are you going to do? Is there any way I can help you?"

"I don't know. I think I've blown it. I may lose my license. And I've lost Neil, too. I really screwed up, Mom."

"You're acknowledging it. That's a start. Are you working with the medical board? I mean, it sounds like, even though you dragged your feet about it, you ultimately did the right thing. And you saved that little girl. Whatever you have to face, I'll be there for you. I'll do whatever I can, whatever you need."

"How can you be so willing to support me, when I've made a complete royal screwup?" Charli couldn't wrap her head around how her mother was not the one in trouble, but was instead supporting *her*.

"Because there have been times when I screwed up. Royally. And if your father hadn't been willing to help me, I wouldn't be here."

"What do I do, Mom?"

Her mom's hands strayed to the strand of pearls at her neck, pearls Charli's father had given her for their twentieth wedding anniversary. "I say, don't hold back. Go ahead. Shout it from the rooftops. Give the whole story to Neil, let him print it in the paper. The world should know what a slimy piece of work Lige Whitaker is. Even if it makes your father look bad. It can't hurt him. Not anymore. And people will understand why you did what you did."

Charli didn't want to think about the paper. Correction, she didn't want to think about Neil. But she couldn't help it. Maybe it would be better if she did leave Brevis. Brevis to her would always mean the men she'd lost—her father, through death, and Neil, through her own stupid stubbornness and fear.

She couldn't think what the right words were to say to her mother. She found herself staring at her hands as though they could give her the magic answer. Lamely, she said, "People understand about addiction, Mom. But they're not going to understand—or forgive—what I've done."

"Maybe. I'm sure there will be consequences you have to face, Charli. I hope they're not permanent. But if they are, I have no doubt you'll find your wings again. And don't give up hope. Anything's possible." Rueful laughter shook her mother's slight frame. "After all, I would have never thought I could routinely get up in front of a crowd of strangers and say, 'Hi, I'm Violet Prescott, and I'm a compulsive shopper.'"

Their waiter swooped in, refilled their glasses and, when he found no takers on anything else, swept off to another table.

"I don't think it would do any good to try to talk to Neil," Charli started.

Her mother wagged a finger. "No. No cowardice. You never were a coward, Charlotte, and I won't let you start now. Begin with the hardest part, and everything will be easier from then on. It's Neil that's the worst of this, isn't it? Oh, the rest of it's no picnic, I know, but it's Neil you look as though you're ready to weep over." Before Charli could protest, her mother added, "So…promise me. No more secrets. No more skeletons rattling around in the Prescott closets, okay?"

Charli's stomach knotted at the prospect of seeing Neil. He'd been so cold and unforgiving the last time they'd talked. And the article he'd written—the last one she'd read—had skewered her inaction, squarely placing the blame of Bethie's illness and several other community members' sickness on Charli.

That's fair enough, she thought. *It was my fault.* She met her mother's eyes, saw a strong woman who had risen from the ashes of her life.

If she could face her mistakes and rise above her past, Charli could, as well. "I promise, Mom."

Charli's cell phone buzzed, immediately testing her new resolve. She glanced down and saw that it was the state medical board.

Here was her future. It had to be faced.

NEIL HUNG UP the phone, a sick feeling in the pit of his stomach. He sat at his desk at the paper, his email program open, seeing the dozen unanswered emails he'd sent to the one contact he'd developed at the state medical board.

No reply. Not even an automated response.

The guy had been helpful at first. He'd been delighted to get all of Neil's early reports, told Neil that he'd been doing the right thing forwarding an account of what had transpired at the migrant settlement.

Back then, when Bethie had first gotten sick and Neil was certain that the migrant workers had given it to her, he'd been glad someone in authority had agreed with him.

Even so, he'd never thought they'd take Charli's license—not until his medical board contact had speculated that Charli might be used as an example for the many, many doctors who flouted the reporting rules.

Then, Neil had felt a twinge of doubt—a

twinge that had morphed into a full spasm now that he knew that it wasn't the workers' illness but Lige's contaminated well that had spread the bacteria to the general population.

Neil had wanted to be sure the review board had all the facts—not just the ones Neil had put in his first tell-all article, the one that skewered Charli. He'd sent emails and links and even overnighted a copy of the *Bugle* with its follow-up article. But his contact had gone radio silent.

"No luck?" Dawn asked, breaking him out of his reverie.

He hadn't even heard her come around the divider, but apparently she'd been making plenty of noise in preparing to leave for the day. She had her purse on her shoulder, her nylon lunch bag in hand.

"No. I called the board, hoping to get some sort of official word at least, spent half my time either on hold or punching buttons on automated menus."

"But you did get somebody?"

"Yeah. A public-information type." He consulted his reporter's notebook. "She said, and I quote, 'We cannot comment on an ongoing investigation, and no statement will be made until the investigation is complete and the board has met.'"

"So when will the board meet? Did they at least say they'd gotten all the information?"

"Sometime next month. And I asked. The woman said they'd received lots of public input on the case and they were... What were her words?" He flipped up the notebook again. "Oh, yeah. They're 'reviewing all relevant material.'"

"I'm sorry, Neil."

"Why are you sorry? I was the one who went all editorial on Charli."

"You reported the facts. As you knew them."

"Right. And we all know that facts can't exist in a vacuum. I was angry. And I felt betrayed. And...I crossed the line. You know I did."

Dawn pursed her lips, pausing before she nodded her head. "It wasn't your usual impartial balanced reporting, that's for sure. And I was surprised when you put it on the wire and helped out the big papers and CNN. It was like...you were on a crusade."

"I was a self-righteous, arrogant jerk." He reached over and clicked the send/receive icon on his email. It refreshed and showed no new emails.

"And what about Charli?" Dawn's question was hesitant. "Have you heard from her?"

"No. But is that surprising? I threw her to

the wolves. I've probably cost Charli her medical license."

"You didn't do anything. Charli made her own bed."

Neil shook his head. He'd had this same argument with Dawn the day before. How could he explain the deep guilt he felt at what he'd done? Sure, he'd stuck to the facts, but he'd made sure those facts were hard to miss. He'd used every trick in his writer's arsenal to put a bull's-eye on Charli.

"Yeah, Dawn, she didn't report the outbreak according to state regulations. But that guy at the medical board told me lots of doctors don't bother to report small outbreaks and that the DPH was steamed about the regulations being flouted. That's why he thought the state might make an example out of Charli. Because she'd generated so much media coverage. And she generated so much media coverage because I made sure that first article was as sensational as possible. I could have waited. I *should* have waited."

Dawn shrugged her shoulders. "I don't know what to tell you. You've learned your lesson, crossing over from reporting to the dark side of editorializing. You won't make the same mistake again."

"No." But that promise was shutting the barn door after the horse was gone. It didn't bring Charli back to him, so he could at least…

What? Apologize for taking away her livelihood and the career she'd indebted herself to have?

Dawn shifted the lunch bag to her other hand and began to fish in her purse for her keys. "It's half past five. You can't do anything else tonight. Go home, Neil. Get some sleep. And try not to kick yourself, okay?"

He heard the front door jangle behind Dawn, but he sat there, alone in the office. Spreading out the current issue of the paper, he read the six-column headline: DPH Links Contaminated Well to Outbreak.

The subhead, in smaller typeface, was his personal apology to Charli: Local Doctor Not at Fault in *E. coli* Spread.

But, like his contact at the medical board, Charli had remained missing in action. She hadn't replied to his voice mails. She hadn't been at home. He couldn't find her anywhere. She must have taken her mom and fled town, away from the reporters and the satellite vans and the polished on-the-scene TV reporters armed with microphones and supersize cans of hairspray and bronzer.

TV reporters. He'd helped *TV reporters*.

One headline did cheer him—in a sidebar, he'd written a short story about Bethie's progress. The little girl was off dialysis and mending well.

If only a doctor could heal his broken heart the same as those Atlanta doctors had healed Bethie.

Wait. One doctor could. Only he'd hung Charli out to dry, cost Charli her license…and blown any chance with her.

He folded the paper and pushed back his chair. Maybe Dawn was right. Maybe he should just go home.

At home, though, his Christmas lights mocked him. They looked too cheery in the darkening evening light. Especially the Santa on the roof who, to Neil at least, had a leer instead of the benevolent grin he was supposed to have.

He noticed that Rudolph's nose had burned out, again, and walked over to the decoration to check it out. Sure enough, the bulb was blown. Maybe it was defective wiring, but this was the third bulb in as many days.

Maybe it had a short from its tumble off the roof.

Neil remembered that night, when Charli

had first taken in his lights. He recalled another night, too, the night under the mistletoe when they'd kissed. He'd been willing to give her the benefit of the doubt then...so what had changed? What had made it so easy for him to forget the heart of the woman he'd come to know?

As he unscrewed Rudolph's nose bulb, the sound of tires crunching on gravel caught his ears. He looked up, saw Charli's car pulling up into her drive.

Charli.

Here. In Brevis.

Neil stared as she got out of the car, slowly, as though she'd been driving all day. She came around the end of the carport and stood there.

Staring back.

For a long moment, they just locked eyes. Her chin went up, the way it did when she was determined to tough something out. She gave him the smallest and coolest of smiles. Then she turned on her heel and went inside.

The sound of the door slamming shut made him jerk.

Neil would have to face her. He at least needed to make some sort of amends. But if a six-column mea culpa on page 1A didn't do the trick, what would?

Well, buddy, you are the one who started the media circus and made her such a handy whipping boy for the state medical board.

His feet seemed cemented to the ground, staked as well as Ruldoph was. He couldn't seem to pick them up and make the distance across the lawn.

Charli's door opened.

Neil watched as she headed for the gap in the hedge, her back straight, her head high, her expression resolute.

She didn't appear to have the same hesitation he'd had. But then again, maybe she just wanted to cuss him out for writing first and thinking later.

"Charli—" he started, then stopped. What had he wanted to say? He'd been desperate to give her his side of the story, to apologize, to try to make things right. And now all of those words were gone.

"You should have these," she said, and for the first time, Neil realized she held a stack of notebooks. Charli shoved them at him, and he took them in pure reflex.

"What are they?" he asked.

"My father's journals. They're kind of jumbled up, with patient notes—patients he saw on the side. I've checked, and there are no official patient files on any of these people at the office."

"Why do you want me to have them?"

Charli frowned as if in pain. "I'm not making excuses. Please know that. But you need the whole story. About the money. And why I donated it."

"You said it was your father's. But I thought he was broke."

"He was. Officially. I found the money that I donated to the clinic in his safe deposit box. I didn't know how he'd come to have it, and I could find no legal, aboveboard way he could have acquired it. And then I found the notebooks, and apparently my dad must have got it from covering up a TB outbreak. Like father, like daughter, huh?" Her words were bitter and tinged with regret.

Neil couldn't process it very well. "Who?" he asked. "Who paid him the money?"

Charli shrugged. "I have no proof. When Lige first threatened to fire me and turn my mom in for tax evasion, it sure sounded to me like he was the one who'd bribed my dad. But I doubt he'd confirm it on the record. And Dad's notebooks don't tell that part. Anyway, it doesn't matter. What matters is that my dad took a bribe—or a lot of bribes—and I didn't want to spend it or have anything to do with it, so instead of doing what I should have done and going to the authorities, I donated it to the clinic."

Neil looked from Charli to the stack of notebooks in his hands. "And it was Lige?"

"Neil, it doesn't matter what I think. I have no proof. Lige will come out of all this as clean as a whistle."

"No, he hasn't. Haven't you heard? They found the migrants."

Now it was Charli who was surprised. "Where? How? Are they sick?"

"Just across the Alabama state line. They're okay—none of 'em got HUS. But Lige ran them off so they couldn't turn him in."

"Hmm. Sounds like something he'd do," Charli said. "The DPH didn't tell me that when I was meeting with them."

"That's where you've been?"

"Well, yeah, for yesterday and today, at least. I've been in Atlanta at their headquarters. And with the medical board. Before that, I was in Savannah, looking for my mom."

"I thought she was with you. You didn't take her with you?"

"No, she was…" Charli closed her eyes, and Neil saw exhaustion in her face. She opened them again and spoke. "It's a long story. Suffice it to say I jumped to some very wrong conclusions. But I've been doing that a lot lately, haven't I?"

Before he could tell her that she wasn't the only one who'd done that, Charli went on in a hurried voice, "There it is, what I came to give you. I just wanted to be sure you had it, so that you'd have time to read it and to ask me any questions before I, well, before I leave."

Neil swallowed hard. "You're leaving again?"

"Yeah, well. Student loans don't wait. I've got to find some way to earn a living."

"So they did take your license? I'm sorry, Charli. I sent them my newspaper article, and what all the DPH had said about the contaminated well, and I kept trying to get them word that the DPH had cleared you."

"No." She shook her head. "What do you mean?"

"They said—well, somebody said that the state medical board was going to make an example out of you, since you had all this media coverage—and that's all my fault, and I'm sorry. I was wrong."

"Neil, I don't know what you've heard..." Charli spoke slowly, as though she were trying to make connections that weren't coming together easily. "But the medical board and I came to an agreement today."

"Tell me you didn't give up. Tell me you didn't surrender your license. We can fight this! Other doctors haven't been prompt in reporting, and the DPH said you saved Bethie."

"Whoa. Neil. They let me keep my license. I agreed to a pretty harsh consent order that will stay with my record, and I'm going to be teaching a continuing ed course for the DPH on the importance of prompt reporting. Kind of like community service for doctors. But I have my license."

Relief pulsed through Neil, and it was like a huge weight had lifted off his chest. "So they did read everything I sent. I talked to them today, though, and they said the investigation was still ongoing, that the board hadn't met—"

"It's not official yet. But I signed the paperwork, so it will be. Next month."

"Then…why are you leaving Brevis?"

Now Charli did look befuddled. "Because. I don't have a job."

"But you do. Here. You have your dad's office."

"I need a hospital that will extend me privileges, Neil. And I don't think Lige will be doing that for me any time soon."

"Didn't you get my voice mails?" For the first time, hope coursed through him. If she didn't know about Lige...

Charli gave a laugh that came out bitter and harsh. "Let's just say I wasn't responding to any reporters' calls."

"But I'm not just any reporter."

She winced. "No, Neil, you're not. You're anything but. I let you down. I let Brevis down. Maybe it's better that I leave. Because honestly..."

"Honestly what?" Would she say that he'd killed off any chance at a future with her? If she stayed in Brevis, he had that chance—at least, he hoped so.

But Charli didn't explain her cryptic comment. She started to turn away from him, but he stopped her with a touch of his hand to her shoulder.

"You don't have to leave," he told her.

Charli sighed. "It's okay. Like my mom said, I have to face the consequences of my decisions. I made some really crappy ones, Neil. And I know I let you down. I know I'm not the person you thought I was—the person I should have been."

"Neither was I. I jumped the gun big-time. I let my anger get the best of me, and I broke a lot of the personal rules I'd made when it came to reporting."

She bit her lip. "Folks here definitely won't want me after they find out about my dad. Plus, I don't have a prayer as long as Lige is here."

"About Lige… I left you a voice mail or three about him. The other members of the hospital authority revolted, and when the migrant workers turned up and started talking, the board forced Lige to resign. Once I reported that the DPH cleared you, the new chairman lifted your suspension."

"Wow. Lige is gone?"

"Well, not gone, and he still has the bank, but he's a bit too busy now with immigration violations and keeping his onion farm going to be bothered with you."

"You mean I don't have to find another job?" Joy lit her face. "I don't have to leave?"

He pulled her into his arms, and gazed down at her. Life without her, just for the past few days, had been flat and empty, and not even Christmas lights could brighten it up.

"God, I hope not. I hope you'll stay in Brevis for the next hundred years. Right here with me. I hope I don't ever make you want to leave again."

She leaned her cheek against his shoulder

and hugged him back, hard. "No, you make me want to stay," Charli said firmly.

As if on cue, his timer clicked, and a version of "Winter Wonderland" blasted out of his speakers. Charli shook her head and asked over the music, "Guess the Christmas decorations are part of the package?" But she didn't seem to mind. Instead, she laughed and reached up and kissed him.

* * * * *

REQUEST YOUR FREE BOOKS!

2 FREE INSPIRATIONAL NOVELS
PLUS 2
FREE
MYSTERY GIFTS

Love Inspired

REQUEST YOUR FREE BOOKS!

2 FREE INSPIRATIONAL NOVELS
PLUS 2
FREE
MYSTERY GIFTS

Love Inspired

HISTORICAL
INSPIRATIONAL HISTORICAL ROMANCE

YES! Please send me 2 FREE Love Inspired® Historical novels and my 2 FREE mystery gifts (gifts are worth about $10). After receiving them, if I don't wish to receive any more books, I can return the shipping statement marked "cancel." If I don't cancel, I will receive 4 brand-new novels every month and be billed just $4.74 per book in the U.S. or $5.24 per book in Canada. That's a savings of at least 21% off the cover price. It's quite a bargain! Shipping and handling is just 50¢ per book in the U.S. and 75¢ per book in Canada.* I understand that accepting the 2 free books and gifts places me under no obligation to buy anything. I can always return a shipment and cancel at any time. Even if I never buy another book, the two free books and gifts are mine to keep forever.

102/302 IDN F5CY

Name	(PLEASE PRINT)	

Address		Apt. #

City	State/Prov.	Zip/Postal Code

Signature (if under 18, a parent or guardian must sign)

Mail to the Harlequin® Reader Service:
IN U.S.A.: P.O. Box 1867, Buffalo, NY 14240-1867
IN CANADA: P.O. Box 609, Fort Erie, Ontario L2A 5X3

Want to try two free books from another series?
Call 1-800-873-8635 or visit www.ReaderService.com.

* Terms and prices subject to change without notice. Prices do not include applicable taxes. Sales tax applicable in N.Y. Canadian residents will be charged applicable taxes. Offer not valid in Quebec. This offer is limited to one order per household. Not valid for current subscribers to Love Inspired Historical books. All orders subject to credit approval. Credit or debit balances in a customer's account(s) may be offset by any other outstanding balance owed by or to the customer. Please allow 4 to 6 weeks for delivery. Offer available while quantities last.

Your Privacy—The Harlequin® Reader Service is committed to protecting your privacy. Our Privacy Policy is available online at www.ReaderService.com or upon request from the Harlequin Reader Service.

We make a portion of our mailing list available to reputable third parties that offer products we believe may interest you. If you prefer that we not exchange your name with third parties, or if you wish to clarify or modify your communication preferences, please visit us at www.ReaderService.com/consumerchoice or write to us at Harlequin Reader Service Preference Service, P.O. Box 9062, Buffalo, NY 14269. Include your complete name and address.

LIHDIR13R

REQUEST YOUR FREE BOOKS!

2 FREE CHRISTIAN NOVELS
PLUS 2
FREE
MYSTERY GIFTS

HEARTSONG PRESENTS

YES! Please send me 2 Free Heartsong Presents novels and my 2 FREE mystery gifts (gifts are worth about $10). After receiving them, if I don't wish to receive any more books I can return the shipping statement marked "cancel." If I don't cancel, I will receive 4 brand-new novels every month and be billed just $4.24 per book in the U.S. and $5.24 per book in Canada. That's a savings of at least 20% off the cover price. It's quite a bargain! Shipping and handling is just 50¢ per book in the U.S. and 75¢ per book in Canada.* I understand that accepting the 2 free books and gifts places me under no obligation to buy anything. I can always return a shipment and cancel at any time. Even if I never buy another book, the two free books and gifts are mine to keep forever.

159/359 HDN FVYK

Name _____ (PLEASE PRINT)

Address _____ Apt. #

City _____ State _____ Zip

Signature (if under 18, a parent or guardian must sign)

Mail to the **Harlequin®** Reader Service:
IN U.S.A.: P.O. Box 1867, Buffalo, NY 14240-1867

* Terms and prices subject to change without notice. Prices do not include applicable taxes. Sales tax applicable in N.Y. This offer is limited to one order per household. Not valid for current subscribers to Heartsong Presents books. All orders subject to credit approval. Credit or debit balances in a customer's account(s) may be offset by any other outstanding balance owed by or to the customer. Please allow 4 to 6 weeks for delivery. Offer available while quantities last. Offer valid only in the U.S.

Your Privacy—The Harlequin® Reader Service is committed to protecting your privacy. Our Privacy Policy is available online at www.ReaderService.com or upon request from the Harlequin Reader Service.
We make a portion of our mailing list available to reputable third parties that offer products we believe may interest you. If you prefer that we not exchange your name with third parties, or if you wish to clarify or modify your communication preferences, please visit us at www.ReaderService.com/consumerchoice or write to us at Harlequin Reader Service Preference Service, P.O. Box 9062, Buffalo, NY 14269. Include your complete name and address.

HSPDIR13R

ReaderService.com

Manage your account online!

- Review your order history
- Manage your payments
- Update your address

*We've designed
the Harlequin® Reader Service
website just for you.*

Enjoy all the features!

- Reader excerpts from any series
- Respond to mailings and
  special monthly offers
- Discover new series available to you
- Browse the Bonus Bucks catalog
- Share your feedback

Visit us at:
ReaderService.com